The Dave Brewster Series

# THE SECOND PREDAXIAN WAR

## KARL J. MORGAN

**The Dave Brewster Series
The Second Predaxian War**

Copyright © 2013 by Karl J. Morgan



The Second Predaxian War may be purchased or ordered through booksellers or at www.karljmorgan.com.

ISBN: 0-9860270-1-4
ISBN: 978-0-9860270-1-7
Library of Congress Control Number: 2012919263

*Cover and text design:* Ronald Calica
Website: www.ronaldcalica.blogspot.com
Linkedin account: www.linkedin.com/in/ohnoitsronald/

*Sacred Life Publishers*™
*www.sacredlife.com*
Printed in United States of America

# CONTENTS

# CHAPTER 1

Michamanades Nolobitamore was in serious trouble and knew it. He was struggling to regain consciousness. He could feel hundreds of other minds reaching out to him, but not in the way another maklan would communicate. Those minds seemed to be blocking his brain from both consciousness and his own ability to sense others near him. Michamanades felt totally alone and helpless. He could not sense any of his team that had been defending Nom-Kat-La from the invading Alliance fleet. They had been assigned to help the human crew on the star cruiser Courage defend themselves from the mind control of the Predaxian maklans.

His mind was full of the buzzing thoughts from those trying to control him. He was finally able to force himself awake and use all of his energy to push those intruding minds away from him. In a natural defensive move, he flew up to the ceiling of the dark room he found himself in. His body glowed bright blue to illuminate his surroundings, but he only found solid stone walls and a small ventilation vent that was heavily armored. A heavy metal door was in the center of one of the walls. He scurried over to the vent to get fresh air. A small outcrop of lichen was growing around the vent. He extended a tendril and tasted it. Being very hungry, he ravenously chomped on the growth. Michamanades could feel his strength returning and tried to sense other minds in the area. He knew the walls must be very thick because he could only feel the slightest hint of three human minds somewhere near him. "How did this happen?" he thought. He knew he would have to remember what had happened that day on the Courage.

A view screen lowered from its concealed chamber and sprang to life on the wall opposite the door. Michamanades saw the face of a Predaxian maklan staring at him. The maklan was bright red with small black eyes. "Greeting fellow maklan," the creature said, "I am Emperor Nokalez Zendo of Predax, and you are my prisoner."

Michamanades, shocked that he could understand the Predaxian, said, "How are you able to communicate with me?"

The Emperor laughed, "We captured some of your compatriots when we destroyed their star cruiser. We were able to convince them to expand the language capabilities of our translator devices. It is very difficult to take over planets full of inhabitants when we cannot understand their thoughts, as you can imagine, my friend."

"Emperor Zendo," he replied, "My name is Michamanades Nolobitamore of No-Makla, a humble scientist by trade. I appreciate your rank and power, but you are no friend of mine. Your race is a disgrace to all the maklan descendents of Ai-Makla."

"What is it with you maklans?" the Emperor shouted, "You know nothing about Predax and our struggles over the countless generations since we all fled Ai-Makla. Our ancestors stranded us in one of the most violent, warlike areas of the galaxy. There were dozens of civilizations in this quadrant who waged war on each other and us for most of our history. We finally brought order to the madness by quieting the minds of their leaders. We brought peace!"

"And slavery, Emperor," Michamanades replied. "If you are so peaceful, why did you invade Nom-Kat-La?"

"Keep your sanctimonious drivel to yourself maklan!" the Emperor said. "The horrible creatures on that gas ball are an offense to any sane Being. You and your planet of peace-loving maklans have done nothing to improve the galaxy. It's time all maklans join together again and control the galaxy. We will discuss this later maklan. In the meantime, please enjoy the hospitality of my prison planet." The screen went black and slid back into the ceiling.

Michamanades was starting to remember the battle over Nom-Kat-La. He had been on the bridge of the Courage with two other maklans. Their job was to keep the Predaxians from gaining control of any human minds on the bridge. Captain London led her ship into a skirmish in orbit over the planet. Two Predaxian transport ships were rapidly shuttling troops and weapons to the forces below. They were protected by four star cruisers and several hundred fighters. Nom-Kat-La was not a typical gas giant planet that the Galliceans loved. It had a heavy atmosphere and a large solid surface. That made the planet an ideal launching pad for defending or attacking the Greater Gallia frontier. If the Predaxians could take the planet, they would have a strong fortress to support their takeover of the region. Courage was one of ten ships that had jumped from Io to attack the transport ships. The remaining ships either landed troops on the planet or tried to stabilize the frontier by blocking further incursions.

The Predaxian attack fleet was from the Palus star system. These Beings were very similar to their cousins, the Galliceans. They had been one of the largest and most advanced civilizations in that area and only lost dominance when the Predaxian maklans took over their leaders' minds. The Palians had become unwitting partners in expanding Predaxian control. They believed they were fighting for their own honor while the Predaxian maklans pulled their strings.

The Courage was ordered to fire upon the larger transport ship. They faced withering fire from the defending cruisers. The Kalidean cruiser Opus flew with her, trying to draw enemy fire. Kalidean defense shields were the best in the known galaxy, and the Opus extended her shields around Courage. Opus fired its blasters at the transport ship and explosions rocked the ship as it began to break apart. Escape pods from the transport ship littered the sky.

Courage aimed her weapons on the main thrusters of the transport ship and fired. The thrusters exploded in a huge ball of fire and the ship twisted and started to fall toward the atmosphere. Opus pulled off its attack and headed for the other transport ship. As it moved off, its shields came off Courage. The Palian cruisers all fired on Courage and explosions rocked the crippled ship. Opus turned and rushed to help Courage which was already breaking up. Captain London told her crew to abandon ship. Escape pods shot out of the failing ship. A dozen Kalidean troops jumped onto the bridge and began taking crew members back with them. Lauren London and the remaining crew donned their pressure suits on the order to abandon ship and waited their turn to be jumped to the Opus. Michamanades remembered her saying, "Mitch, we'll be okay. As long as there is life, there is hope, old friend." As she smiled at the maklan, a Palian fighter crashed into the bridge, causing a violent explosion. Michamanades felt he was floating in space, barely clinging to consciousness. Around him was the wreckage of the Courage. He saw several humans in pressure suits floating around him. Many of them were clearly dead, as their suits and bodies were smashed. He frantically tried to reach out to Lauren's mind but could not. He could sense life, but did not know where the sensation came from. Then he blacked out.

# *Chapter 2*

Admiral Dave Brewster arrived at Nom-Kat-La aboard the cruiser Defiant which had been repaired after the battle over Neptune. The Nom-Kat-La offensive had lasted nearly seven days until finally the Predaxian fleet was forced back into their territory. Thirty space ships and thousands of lives had been lost by the two sides. Dozens of Gallicean, Kalidean, human and maklan soldiers were missing and presumed captured or killed. Twenty Gallicean, ten Earth and fifteen Kalidean star cruisers orbited the planet now. It had been fifteen days since hostilities had ceased, but the Predaxians and Palians had made no attempt to contact the Galliceans. The entire quadrant was on alert and a second invasion seemed imminent. Jacomofledes Benomafolays the maklan jumped with Dave over to the newly commissioned fleet battle cruiser Amsterdam, which was the flagship for Fleet Admiral Arrin Adamsen. He was escorted to the Fleet Admiral's ready room where the captains of the human fleet in the area were convened to meet.

Dave walked around the table to greet each captain, most of whom he had met before. Each had been assigned a maklan to protect their minds from the influence of any Predaxians that might be in the area. He finished with the Fleet Admiral. "Admiral Adamsen, it is a pleasure to see you again," he said shaking the admiral's hand.

"Dave, it good to see you too, even though I wish we were in a better circumstance," Arrin responded. "Let's get down to business team," he said to the group.

Commodore Willis Washington began the meeting, saying, "The battle at Nom-Kat-La did not go too well for our forces.

Our defenses were not adequate to stop enemy fire. We lost three cruisers: the Courage, Freedom, and Honor. Eight hundred troops are dead, five hundred wounded and twenty missing in action, including Captains London and Whitaker. The only positive things I can say are that the Alliance forces have been repelled, and the Galliceans and Kalideans have agreed to retrofit our ships to improve our defensive shields and weapons."

"Thank you Willis," Arrin said. "I want you all to know that Willis lost one son in the battle. Wally Washington was the navigator on the Courage and is missing and presumed dead. The attack on that ship was horrific, and we are lucky that half of the crew was rescued by the Kalidean ship Opus. We honor your sacrifice, friend."

Captain Cadiz Carlyle of the Reliant said, "Willis, I knew Wally Washington and Lauren London very well. They were both on my crew until Lauren was promoted and asked that Wally join her on the Courage. I thought of both of them as dear friends. We share your loss, my friend."

"Jake, would you like to update the group on Predaxian mind control activity in the region?" Arrin asked.

"Yes Admiral," Jake began as he glowed bright blue on the center of the long table. "I have communicated with the other maklans in the area since Courage arrived this morning. We have found no remaining signs of Predaxian minds on Nom-Kat-La or on any of the ships in orbit. We do continue to sense a large amount of activity near the frontier, and we have to assume that several ships are near there. We have also calculated that two hundred maklans were either killed or captured during the battle. Ten thousand maklans are due to jump to Nom-Kat-La in the next few days. With that number here, we should be able to sense activity further into their space. That may enable us to know how many ships and soldiers from their races are nearby. We are also hoping to be able to sense any prisoners-of-war. If we find some, it is possible we could jump in and rescue them."

"Excellent news Jake," Arrin replied. "I hope you are successful. Please keep our group informed." He turned to Dave and said, "Admiral Brewster, what do you have to report?"

"As Jake mentioned, the maklans have been extremely helpful during this difficult time. We honor the sacrifice of their brave soldiers who were lost," Dave replied. "The High Council of No-Makla has offered to send as many as one billion maklans to help defend the Gallicean frontier. On the home front, Earth and all of the major colonies have diverted resources to build more star cruisers. There are currently twenty ships under construction. That is not a simple task though and will take a few months to complete. I spoke with Mencius of Kalidus, and he is sending engineers with the upgraded weapons and defensive equipment to help our builders. We certainly don't want to send low quality ships to fight these invaders. The cost in blood and treasure is too high."

"I completely agree," Arrin replied. "I have already told High Commissioner Fa-a-Di that our ships will play a back-up role only in any new combat until our ships are upgraded. Our soldiers were like fish in a barrel for those Predaxians. We won't be that stupid the next time." Arrin stood, "Okay, unless anyone has any questions or comments, this meeting is over. Dave, please stay, I need to speak with you and Jake. The rest of you can jump back to your ships with your maklan guards." The captains stood, glowed white and disappeared.

"Dave," Arrin began, "I'll never get used to that way of jumping. It's a heck of a lot easier on a man, but it almost seems like witchcraft, if you know what I mean. No offense to you Jake."

"None taken Arrin," Jake said. "Our species are so different that what seems ordinary to us may seem impossible to you. As you know, Arinofalez Zionaster developed this technology one million of your earth years ago. Imagine your predecessors from that far back looking at what you do."

"Point taken friend," Arrin replied. "I don't even think humans were around that far back. Anyway, I have a new job for you two and your ships. I know that everyone wants to help defend Greater Gallia from the Alliance, but there are other related needs that can't be ignored. Right now, the Galliceans are the key to protecting their own frontier. Kalidus has committed ships to support them. That takes some of the heat off of us. As Jake mentioned earlier, No-Makla has also made a major contribution to the defense, but I need them to do a little bit more."

"Arrin," Dave began, "just tell us what we need to do."

Arrin rose and went to a cabinet and removed a bottle of bourbon and a second of Gallicean whisky and three glasses. He poured bourbon for Dave and himself, and a full glass of Gallicean spirits for Jake. "Jake, Fa-a-Di tells me maklans love Gallicean hooch, so he sent me a case to share with our maklans. I think he is sending a few hundred cases to Nom-Kat-La. Let's have a drink to our success!" The three took long drinks. Arrin sat again next to Dave Brewster. "Dave, High Commissioner Darak and I think you need to start finding new worlds for humanity. You are the guy who will be known as Founder of a Thousand Worlds, right?"

Dave was stunned. After a moment, he replied, "That's what I heard Admiral. But isn't this crisis big enough to put that on hold? Also, we are just getting started on Far Sky and New Dawn. Those planets need a lot of attention, Arrin."

Arrin put his hand on Dave's shoulder. "Dave, the key to achieving incredible results is delegation. You can't do it all on your own, even if you live to be a thousand years old. You have a core team. That's Jake here, your wife the ambassador, Commodore Watson and his wife the colonel in the Temporal Command. I'll give you Captain Jon Lake and a few more, four colony ships, and ten cruisers. We hope to provide a personal maklan each crew member for protection."

"I am certain that High Commissioner Arroflenides Pakalanalan will agree to that," Jake replied. "But I am confused as well."

"Let me lay it out for you then," Arrin said as he rose and began pacing around the room. "I was told that Ai-Makla sent their maklans to five hundred worlds before the nova destroyed their home system. Jake, we know the maklans who landed on Predax did not turn out very well."

"That is an understatement," Jake agreed. "But we have no evidence that any other maklans devolved into warlike creatures."

"That is exactly my point!" Arrin shouted. "There are four hundred and ninety-eight maklan worlds we have no contact with. I spoke personally with Commissioner Pakalanalan on this matter. If several of those other maklan worlds can be found and help us explore more of the galaxy, all of our civilizations would advance a million years ahead. Also, if the Predaxian maklans want to cause trouble, maybe some of those other maklan cultures will help us." Arrin refilled his glass and drank deeply. "Even if we don't find a single maklan civilization, perhaps we'll find others that want to be partners in commerce or defense. For example, we know that the Alliance sphere of influence borders on Greater Gallia. We have no idea what other cultures lie on other parts of that sphere. Perhaps there are other civilizations being abused by Predax that we can help. If our sphere of influence could surround Predax, their threat would be reduced dramatically."

"Arrin," Dave said after he took a long drink, "that plan is brilliant. I hadn't thought of that at all. What do you think, Jake?"

"I agree completely, Dave," the maklan glowed. "If No-Makla could reestablish ties to other maklan worlds, it would be as though we were honoring the sacrifice of our ancestors when they set out blindly for new worlds to make their own. It would be a tremendous honor to help you Dave."

Dave touched his glass to the others and said, "We are in full agreement, Admiral. We can leave immediately."

"Fantastic," Arrin replied, "I am happy you like the plan and are ready to explore. I do have one confession though. It was not my plan." Dave looked confused. "This plan was created by Ambassador Darlene Brewster."

# CHAPTER 3

Dave and his core team moved their belongings from the colony ship Ticonderoga to the newly commissioned fleet battle cruiser Texas. His plan was to go ahead of the rest of his fleet and jump to star systems likely to contain planets suitable for human or maklan life. The star cruiser Nightsky would accompany his ship. The Nightsky had also been recently completed and was given the name of the pirate ship that Jon Lake had used to raid other Earth colonies before Admiral Brewster had been able to turn the situation around. The Far Sky colony was growing well and the terraforming operations were almost completed. Fulfilling his promise, Dave appointed Jon Lake captain of the Nightsky.

The plan involved using an existing permanent portal to open a wormhole to the desired system. The Texas would jump through the portal and scan the new solar system for positive and negative signs. Nightsky would remain near the permanent portal to guard against debris or alien ships jumping through the opening. Once it was deemed safe, the Nightsky and a colony ship would jump and deploy a portal near one of the most desirable planets and establish a permanent connection to the Far Sky portal. After the colony ship jumped back, Nightsky would join Texas in their search activities. The two ships would survey all of the planets and determine whether there were any candidate planets for colonization or other civilizations to befriend. If a civilization rejected them, they would remove the permanent portal and jump back to where they started. Otherwise, the rest of the fleet would jump to the new system and begin the work of colonization or treaty negotiation.

The first system selected was eight light-years from Far Sky. The location was as far as they could find from the Predaxian frontier. This early in the exploration they did not dare risk being too close to the enemy. None of the Earth colonies in the vicinity had ever detected communications or other signs of advanced societies coming from that system. The engineers manning the portal had taken several days to find a suitable location in the target star system to open a temporary portal. This kind of portal was very dangerous as passing asteroids or comets might slip through the opening and crash through near Far Sky, potentially destroying the portal and killing thousands on the planet. The crew of Texas spent the time loading supplies and offering shore leave to crew members. When the coordinates for the portal were finalized, it took another two days to get all of the crew back on board and ready to jump.

Dave, Darlene, Charlie and Aria stood on the bridge when the order to head to the portal was given. Captain Jon Lake was with them and offered to take a photo of the bridge crew. He transferred the shot to the ship's view screen. Dave said, "Wow, I remember this picture. How about you, Charlie?"

"This is the picture we saw when you made your first jump to the thirty-second and met Mencius the Kalidean and Arrin and Lanz, right?" Charlie Watson replied.

"Freaky, isn't it?" Dave said. He turned to Jon Lake, "Jon, you'd better jump back to Nightsky now. I don't think your crew wants you to jump with us."

"Aye-aye, Admiral, good luck and we'll join you when you are ready" Jon said as his maklan glowed bright white and the two disappeared from the bridge.

"Captain Cartwright, you have the comm. Let's make the jump at your command," Dave said to Carl Cartwright, captain of the Texas.

The captain turned to his crew and said, "Helmsman, ahead five percent."

"Aye-aye, Captain," Jack Johnson replied, "Ahead five percent!" The Texas moved slowly toward the portal several miles ahead of them. On the view screen, the bridge crew could see the portal starting to energize. Hazard lights around the rim of the huge circle began to flash to warn unwitting ships a space portal was being opened. After a few moments, the interior of the portal was bathed in light and energy. Gradually, a small perfectly black dot appeared in the middle and started to grow. Texas continued to accelerate as the black circle grew until it completely filled the portal opening, which at one thousand, five hundred yards across was large enough for any ship, even a Gallicean battle cruiser to fly through.

"Captain Cartwright," crackled the voice of Head Engineer Peter Paulsen of the Far Sky Portal Command, "our portal is fully energized and is ready for your ship to enter."

"Peter," Carl replied, "Thank you for your report. We are on course to intercept the portal in twenty seconds. Please advise me if the status degrades."

"Aye-aye, Captain," Peter replied. "Carl, have a safe jump. Far Sky Portal Command out."

The amount of energy needed to open an eight light-year wormhole was immense. Everyone on Texas could feel electricity tingling in their bodies as they approached the event horizon. Jake was glowing bright white from the energy hitting him from the portal. As the front of the ship touched the portal, the ship creaked and groaned as it was stretched between the void inside the wormhole and the normal space outside. The sound of metal on metal grinding grew louder and louder as the rest of Texas moved through the event horizon. The sound was becoming deafening on the bridge when it suddenly stopped completely. They were inside the wormhole, somewhere outside of the space-time of the galaxy. Warning buzzers sounded and lights flashed on all of the panels, but no one could hear the sounds. Dave looked at his wife, Darlene and smiled. Traveling through a wormhole was an experience that could not be explained, only experienced. Jack Johnson waved at Dave and Carl to get their attention. When they had entered the portal, their view screen showed nothing but blackness. Now, a small white dot appeared in front of the ship. It was growing rapidly. This was the opposite end of the portal. Within a minute, the dot had grown as large as the portal opening had been over Far Sky. As Texas touched the circle of white, the groaning and creaking sounds returned. The crew could now hear the alarm buzzers. Dave felt his body being stretched as the bridge passed through the whiteness and back into normal space. After a few moments, the creaking stopped and the alarms quieted. Texas was now eight light-years away from Far Sky, in a new star system that humans had never visited.

"Defensive shields at maximum," Carl shouted to Commander Donna Daniels, his Chief Weapons officer. "Bring all weapon systems online."

"Aye-aye, Captain," Donna replied as she tapped commands onto her control panel. A circle of red lights were illuminated around the view screen to show that their defensives were now activated.

"Lia," Dave said to Lieutenant Lia Lawson, Charlie's daughter and Chief Communications Officer on the Texas, "get your people scanning for any signals from the planets. Send a general hail and greeting in all languages."

"Aye-aye, Admiral," she smiled back.

"Great job on the jump Carl," Dave said. "My core team will leave you in command of your ship now. Please send us any information your probes and greetings receive. I expect it will be a few hours before anything meaningful happens. You can also report our progress to the rest of the fleet and Fleet Admiral Adamsen."

"Aye-aye, Admiral," Carl replied. As the four humans and four maklans left the bridge, Captain Cartwright continued issuing orders to the crew to prepare probes and begin scanning the nearest planet which they were approaching. "Jack, please put us in a high orbit over that planet. I don't want anything down there to be able to find us. Donna, get a group of maklans to do a flyover as soon as we get into orbit. They can see a lot more than we can without being seen themselves."

# CHAPTER 4

Michamanades Nolobitamore was forcing himself not to sleep. It had seemed like weeks since he slept last, but he knew the Predaxian maklans would love to have him unconscious again so they could try to take over his mind. While awake, he could push their thoughts away, at least as far as the stone walls of the cell he was locked in. He could still feel the three human consciousnesses, but not enough to recognize any of them. Somehow he had to build his strength enough to touch those minds, locate them and jump to where they were located. He hoped that Lauren London was one of them. He had been in charge of protecting her mind from the Predaxians and he hoped she had survived the battle. If she was alive in this place, they would control her and make her do their bidding. She would gladly lead a fleet of Palian battle cruisers across the frontier to attack No-Makla. They would brainwash her into believing he was her worst enemy. His twelve legs shuddered at the thought.

The outcropping of moss and lichen around the vent had been his only form of nourishment. The Predaxians dared not open the door to bring him food. They knew that he could jump through space to freedom if he could sense outside his cell. He flew up to the vent and ate some of the plant matter. It seemed very juicy today, and he assumed there was a lot of moisture in the air that day. He had become very dehydrated and was happy to replenish his bodily fluids. That extra liquid would also encourage more plant growth which would increase his food supply. It was a good day, he thought. Perhaps he will soon be able to push the Predaxian minds further away so he can see outside the cell and make his escape. As he ate, the view screen lowered again and came to life. The Warden of the Localus Prison World came into view. He was a Palian and looked much like a Gallicean, except with feathers and a bad attitude. His home world of Palus was Earthlike with large forests covering most of the planet. Only twenty percent of the planet was water covered. The Palians had evolved from flying dinosaurs from their ancient past. Unlike Earth, where mammals eventually evolved to control the planet, on Palus it was the birds who reigned.

"Hello again, my little insect friend," Warden Kogala hissed, "I see you are still alive."

"Thank you for your concern, Warden," Michamanades thought. "It's too bad that my dear friend Emperor Zendo did not decide to talk to me today."

"You have to understand bug," Kogala continued, "Nokalez Zendo is a friend and ally of Palus, but he had duties in his own territory. You are a prisoner of the Palian Federation, and I can assure you that our leader, Field Marshall Fongula Nokka has no interest in you."

Michamanades laughed, "You really think that your federation is not run by Predax?"

"Of course not," Kogala snorted. "We joined forces with our neighbors to fight our common enemy, the filthy bare-skinned Galliceans. What hideous beasts they are, flying around gas planets whose noxious atmospheres would kill any normal creature."

"I wish you had the courage to come to my cell for even one minute, Kogala," the maklan responded. "I would clear their influence from your mind and then you would see the truth."

"We are not stupid like a bug," the warden shouted. "We have been warned by our high command that you can take over our minds and make us believe anything. I heard you could make me believe I was a monkey man like your compatriots in my prison. With your tiny brain, I doubt that sincerely. I may even take you up on that offer one day, friend. But none of this is why I'm speaking to you today. Our doctors have been very worried that you are not sleeping. That has to be very hard on your body, bug man."

Michamandes laughed, saying, "If you weren't so well controlled already, you'd know there are at least one thousand Predaxians here on your prison world whose only job is to control my mind.  If they left for even a minute, I would leave and bring a hundred war ships to retrieve the other prisoners. I might even bring enough maklans like me to free your sorry brains from Predaxian control."

"You are a fool," Kogala continued. "I hope you are grateful that we've increased the liquids in your diet bug."

"What do you mean, bird?" he replied.

"Every creature needs rest, even flying insects like you," Kogala laughed. "There is little water on this world that we can spare for prisoners, but we did find something that seems like water that might help you sleep, my friend."

"You poisoned me?" Michamanades squeaked.

"Never, little friend," Kogala said. The maklan could see the image becoming fuzzy and darkening. "Think of it as a little medicine to help you get some rest. We have a surprise for you if and when you awaken, little bug. I'll talk to you then." The screen went black and returned to its slot in the ceiling.

Michamanades felt his legs buckling as he lost his grip on the ceiling and fell to the floor, unconscious.

# CHAPTER 5

Michamanades woke with a start. He flew straight up toward the ceiling in his cell and scurried into a corner and became invisible. The room was completely dark. He could hear liquid dripping down from the vent in the ceiling. He would not fall for that again. He wondered how long he had been unconscious, and was surprised not to feel the minds of the Predaxians pushing in on him. Perhaps Warden Kogala had been truthful when he said there was no poison, only something to help him sleep. He did feel remarkably well rested. Michamanades tried to sense outside his cell, but could not sense anything but the walls and vent. As his mind cleared from the effects of the sedative, he began to sense other living creatures in the room with him. He thought a moment about the risk of exposing his position, but knew it was better to know who was there than to hide forever. He glowed bright blue and could see he was not in the same place as before. There was no door in this cell, only an armored vent on the ceiling and a small drain on the floor near a puddle that had formed from the dripping liquid from the vent. The room was also twice the size of the previous cell. He noticed movement and saw two human bodies on the floor in the opposite corner.

He flew to the humans who were unconscious. He immediately recognized them as Captain Lauren London and Commander Wally Washington. He touched them with his tendrils and sensed their minds were not controlled by any Predaxians. Both had been severely beaten. Michamanades tried to heal their wounds with his mind. He could feel their bodies respond. "Lauren, can you hear me?" he thought to the Captain. She did not respond. "Lauren!" his mind screamed to her, but she remained unconscious and he could not reach her.

"Don't waste your time, little friend," said a voice from across the room. Michamanades flew up to the ceiling and disappeared. "Cute trick pal, but your magic doesn't matter here." Out of the dark corner of the room, a single Predaxian maklan walked toward the center of the room. "I'm no threat to you pal," the Predaxian said, "I'm just as much a prisoner as you, except you and your friends have been here a few hours, and I have been here ten solar cycles."

Michamanades felt no threat from the creature and its mind was not reaching out for control. He flew down from the ceiling and landed a few feet in front of the other, blocking his path to the humans. "Okay, let's say that's true for a moment," Michamanades thought to the Predaxian. "Who are you and how do we get out of this place?"

"Well, I can't help you with your second question since I've been here a long time and obviously haven't found a way out yet. The first question is fair enough I suppose. I am Panoplez Zendo, the son of our great Emperor."

"Son!" Michamanades exclaimed. "You want me to believe the Emperor locked his own son up in prison? What did you do to deserve that fate, Panoplez?"

"Well, Mitch, it's a long story, but since we are all locked down here forever, I guess you have time to listen," he replied.

"How do you know the humans call me Mitch?" Michamanades demanded. "You are not a prisoner at all. What do you want from us?"

"When my father's soldiers jumped you three in, they told me. They told me that Lauren and Wally here had been very helpful in updating the Predaxian systems so we could communicate with the humans, Galliceans, Kalideans and maklans like you," Panoplez said. "You should know that many Predaxians don't really care for the Emperor, myself included. Those soldiers had to do their job, but like me, they'd like to depose my father and stop all of this intergalactic fighting. One of the guys is my cousin. Fortunately, I get to see him every few months when they jump supplies in here and check to see if I'm still alive."

"But we're still on Localus, right?" Mitch asked.

Panoplez laughed, "No way pal. My father doesn't trust those bird-brained Palians to watch over me. He is terrified I might use mind control to build my own army to depose him." He thought for a moment. "He's probably right about that too. No, we are far from Palian space. This place is called Thuk. It is located in Predaxian space as far away from Greater Gallia as you can get. Nokalez Zendo doesn't want there to be any chance any of us can ever be found. I know why he feels that way about me, but I have no idea why you three are here. Predaxians have searched for other civilizations within a thousand light-years of this place and have found nothing. Thuk is a dead planet circling a white dwarf sun in the most lifeless portion of the galaxy."

"That's pretty depressing," Mitch replied.

"That's the truth pal. It gets worse. Thuk is a huge chunk of iron, probably ten thousand miles in diameter. My father had the military jump the biggest nuclear device they had into the core of Thuk and detonated it. That created an empty sphere one hundred miles in diameter. They installed equipment to provide air, water and some food, and then filled the rest of the void with the heaviest metals they could steal from other civilizations. Except, they left this one cell. My father built this entire complex for me. How generous of him, right?"

"That's awful, Panoplez," Mitch replied, truly saddened by this tale.

"It's okay Mitch. Call me Pan, it's simpler," he replied. "Hey pal, I think your friends are starting to wake up."

Michamanades rushed to the two people who had begun to stir. "Lauren, can you hear me, it's Mitch!" he thought. He could sense her mind was not under control from Panoplez Zendo.

Lauren London opened her eyes and saw Mitch next to her. "Mitch, are you okay?" she whispered as she attempted to sit upright.

"I think so Lauren," he replied. "We have been captured by the Predaxian maklans.  Wally is here and he is coming around now too."

Lauren looked around the room. Her eyes grew wide when she saw the Predaxian ten feet in front of her. "Mitch, isn't that one of them right there?"

"Yes, but Pan is a prisoner too," Mitch replied. "He represents those Predaxians who want an end to the tyranny and slavery, or at least that's what he told me."

"I hope you are right, Mitch," she said. Lauren turned her attention to Pan. "Okay, Predaxian rebel, how do we get out of here?"

Once Wally and Lauren had recovered and ate some of the food that had been jumped into the cell with them, Panoplez Zendo recanted the story he had told to Michamanades. He told them he had been Crown Prince of Predax until his father sent him here.  Fifteen years ago, he began to realize the Predaxian mind control activities were no longer for protection and had become weapons of tyranny. He had personally led invasions of planets where many thousands had died. The invading soldiers were controlled by Predaxians far from the field of battle. Many were from peaceful societies that had been turned into savages by their Predaxian controllers.

Pan told them how the Palians and Galliceans had been great allies many decades ago, before Palus was absorbed into the Predaxian Alliance. The mind control had been so thorough the Palians completely forgot their centuries of peace with Greater Gallia and became their mortal enemies. As a young man, Pan had led a Palian star cruiser into Gallicean space during the First Predaxian War with Gallia fifty years ago. The battle in the space over Nok-lak-a was brutal with dozens of ships destroyed and dead bodies and broken equipment filling the skies. The ground battle between the Palians and Galliceans was exceptionally vicious. Pan had felt many soldiers under his control being killed and blown to pieces. He had been relieved when the retreat was finally ordered.

When he returned to Predax, he told his father he could not do that anymore and was given administrative functions on the home world. Pan excelled at managing government ministries and was given ever greater responsibility. Many senior bureaucrats were given governorships on Alliance planets, and Pan took over their roles on Predax. He enjoyed developing his staff and helping them fill the voids when large numbers were sent to the colonies.

As more planets came under Predaxian control, Pan found that more were returning home to get away from the fighting and mind control roles, as he had. Twenty years after the war with Greater Gallia, he started a foundation to help Predaxians who suffered from trauma after combat. Pan found many Predaxians were becoming disenchanted with expanding the Alliance and controlling more Beings who simply wanted to live their lives in peace.  Pan was reminded why he came back to Predax and left the fighting to others. He had always been proud of his father, but was now beginning to see the old ways only brought dishonor to his planet. Predax had changed from being the target of other civilizations in the quadrant to a leach living off those once great cultures, forcing billions of Beings to do their bidding.

With his position as Crown Prince, Pan was able to secretly build a large network of Predaxians who wanted change. He hoped he would somehow be able to convince the Emperor to take a new course. Emperor Nokalez Zendo had become so thirsty for power he hatched a plan to invade Greater Gallia a second time.  Alliance power had grown tremendously since the first war. His plan relied on Predaxian spies to infiltrate the highest levels of Gallicean power and get their forces to move from the frontier. Once Nom-Kat-La was taken, it would open routes to hundreds of other Gallicean planets in the quadrant. The strategic importance of that planet had been ignored during the first war when the generals made the decision to attack Nok-lak-a. That defeat was a wound that would never heal.

As weapons factories geared up for the next invasion, Panoplez went to his father to stop the madness. He pleaded to cancel the invasion and to give greater freedom to the other civilizations within the Alliance. He told his father the Beings under their control were virtual slaves being sent into a battle they did not agree with. Pan told him there were millions of Predaxians who agreed with him and wanted nothing more than peace. Pan remembered how calm his father had been that day.  He smiled at his son and told him his spies had infiltrated Pan's foundation and his circle of friends. Thousands of Pan's followers were arrested and sent to prison planets throughout Alliance space.

The Emperor stripped Pan of his crown and authority and remanded him to Thuk to think about what he had done.

27

Texas had been in orbit over the new planet for ten hours. A meeting had been called in Admiral Brewster's ready room. Dave's core team and the ship's commanders were in attendance. Each commander was to make their report to Dave and Carl.

Donna Daniels began with her report on security. "All weapon systems and defenses remain on high alert. We have not discovered any threats yet, but we need to get complete reports from the planetary probes before we can be certain."

"Thank you Donna," Captain Cartwright replied. "Keep your eyes open for us." He turned to his communications officer, saying, "Lia, what can you report?"

"Captain, we have been sending general hails toward all planets since we arrived. We have not received any replies. We are scanning all signals from the planets looking for anything that might be considered intelligent communication. As of now, I'd have to say that our findings are inconclusive."

"Inconclusive?" Dave asked. "That's not good. Lia, what does that mean exactly?"

"Admiral, we are definitely seeing some anomalies in the noise from the planet below, but it is too faint for us to know exactly what might be going on down there," Lia replied. "We have sent five teams of maklans to fly over the planet and see what they can find out. We expect them back on board within a few hours. I've also sent the information we have to the science department for them to analyze."

"Jeff, I guess it's your turn," Carl said to Jeff Jackson, Chief Science Officer.

"Carl, I agree with Lia that the odd signals we are receiving from the planet are not natural in origin. It almost seems like a beacon of some kind. Perhaps it is so old that its power is failing. That may be why the signal is so weak. I have asked two of the maklan teams to check the area where the signal is coming from very carefully," Jeff said. "The probes we have sent to the planet below have returned. This planet is very earthlike and a good candidate for colonization, depending on what we find about the beacon. Sixty percent of the surface is covered by oceans. The land varies from frozen tundra at the poles to rain forests near the equator. The diameter is just under eight thousand miles, and we've seen some evidence of plate tectonics. The atmosphere is eighteen percent oxygen, eighty percent nitrogen and two percent other gases. It looks ideal in my opinion."

"Any news from the other planets Jeff," Dave asked.

"None of our probes have returned, however, we can conclude that the two planets closer to the sun are both too hot and small to support liquid water or an atmosphere. The next planet out seems similar to this one, but we won't know until the probes return. There are three gas giants and two frozen tiny planets further out. I'll report more when the probes return. Within two days we will have all the information we are going to get."

"That's great news Jeff!" Dave said. "God willing, we have a new colony beneath us right now. "What's the condition of the star in this system?"

"Spectral analysis shows it to be six billion years old. The size is similar to that of the sun in the Earth system, so we expect it to be around a long time. Macadalaka Vanokaraka, the chief maklan scientist on board is working on the exact calculations. She suggests it will take a day to complete."

"Jake, do you have anything to report?" Dave asked his maklan friend.

"Yes Dave," he thought, "that signal Lia and Jeff reported seems very familiar to me. There is something quite maklan about it. Assuming our teams don't find any signs of a living civilization, I think we should take a shuttle craft down to the place the signal is coming from."

"That sounds like an excellent idea," Dave began. "Captain, we'll stay here in orbit for two more days until all the probe data can be analyzed. If we all think it is safe, we'll call for Nightsky and Ticonderoga to jump here with the permanent portal. Does anyone have any other questions?"

Jake extended a tendril to Dave and thought, "Dave, I need to talk to you, Carl and the rest of the core team after the meeting."

"Captain, thank you for the meeting. I'm going to keep meeting with you and my core team on a couple of points. The rest of you can return to your stations," Dave said. The ship's crew filed out of the room, leaving Dave, Carl, Charlie, Aria, Darlene and Jake. "Okay Jake, what's up?"

"As I said earlier, the weak signal seems maklan to me," Jake began, "I've told you we have lived in the Earth solar system for one billion Earth years, with the last five hundred million on Neptune."

Carl said, "Yes, I have been briefed on that."

"From the history of Earth, you know the historical records are written by the winners. Over time, history books have a way of reinterpreting the past to show the current rulers in a better light," Jake continued. "The same thing has happened many times during mankind's brief time. Maklans have been around for a billion years. We were well developed when we jumped to that system."

"We agree maklan history has probably changed over time," Dave said. "What is your point and what does this signal have to do with it?"

"When I first felt the signal, it felt like a warning," Jake replied. "I could not understand any words, but I felt like it was telling me to stop and go back where I came from. That's why we need to visit that site. I might be completely wrong, and I hope our maklan crew can decipher the signal quickly."

Carl interrupted, "Jake, if it's a warning, what do we do? The signal is very weak, and maybe the threat has been gone for five hundred million years?"

"You're right Carl," Jake responded. "Perhaps there is no danger. Or there could be another Predax-like race of maklans near here."

"Maybe the signal was put to warn others about No-Makla before your people became peaceful," Darlene interjected.

"Exactly, that's why I talked about history," Jake replied. "We need to visit that site."

"I agree Jake," Dave said. "Let's wait until the morning when the maklans have returned from the planet and all the probe data is fully analyzed. If it is safe, we'll shuttle down then, okay?"

Dave heard a tone in his earpiece. He listened for a moment and said, "Sorry team, I've got a priority one message coming in. Please excuse me." The others left the room. Dave touched a contact on his control panel and the grinning beak of Fa-a-Di appeared on the screen.

"Brother Dave, it is good to see you again!" the Gallicean said. "I hope I am not intruding on important business, my friend."

"Brother, your call could never be an intrusion," Dave said, happy to see his friend again. He had seen Fa-a-Di last when they flew over Neptune two months ago. Fa-a-Di had been called back to resume his duties as High Commissioner after the Predaxian invasion. After he and Field Marshall Je-e-Bo defeated the Alliance invasion of Nom-Kat-La, he returned to Gallia to insure all Predaxian agents were captured or killed.

"Dave, I have news from the Predaxian frontier," Fa-a-Di said as he pulled a glass and bottle of whisky from his desk. He poured a glass and sipped it gingerly. "Dave, thank you for this Scotch whisky from your home world, but I have to admit that it is pretty weak stuff."

"We could never match fine Gallicean whisky, General," Dave smiled back. "Every time I taste it, I think my head will explode!"

Fa-a-Di laughed. "We Galliceans are a hardy folk Dave. We like strong drink and flying through Dar-Fa to keep us sharp. Let me tell you about the frontier though. We were very fortunate to have human and Kalidean ships fighting along with us. Without them, I think Predax might have taken Nom-Kat-La."

"Thank you brother. I know our ships were not a match for the Predaxians, but with your help, our defenses and weaponry are now much improved. Too many brave soldiers died or were captured in that battle. I was fortunate to spend time with Captain Lauren London of the Courage. I was saddened to learn that her ship had been destroyed in orbit," Dave replied.

"That is very true, Dave," Fa-a-Di said. "My brother-in-law fought on two ships that day. The Kong-Fa was smashed in the first assault. While his crew escaped, he jumped to the Konk-Fa and took command. That ship proceeded to knock out four enemy cruisers before the Alliance began to retreat. That boy will be a great Fleet Admiral."

"It was a great victory, but none of this is new information, brother," Dave replied.

Fa-a-Di leaned in so close to the screen that his beak almost touched it. He whispered, "We never should have won that battle Dave. The Alliance had an overwhelming advantage in their fleet. Nom-Kat-La should now be part of the Alliance, and the hundred million Galliceans living there should have been killed or enslaved."

"I don't understand, brother," Dave said.

"Brother, almost half of their fleet deserted just before they entered Greater Gallia space," Fa-a-Di replied, as he drained his whisky glass and refilled it. "We didn't know it at the time because they had thousands of minds blocking our sensors so we couldn't see beyond the border. Just a few days ago, the leader of the deserting ships contacted Je-e-Bo and told him the story."

"Can you be certain it's true, brother?" Dave asked.

"Very certain brother," Fa-a-Di said. "Two days ago, thirty Predaxian star cruisers were spotted two hundred light-years from Nom-Kat-La where the Predaxian frontier borders on Kalidean space. Those ships were given clearance to orbit Tantalus, a Kalidean colony in that quadrant. No-Makla sent ten thousand maklans to Tantalus to make certain that the Predaxians couldn't control any minds. Novolus, Governor of Tantalus met with them and learned a large portion of Predaxian society is turning against the mind control and tyranny of the past. Apparently, the former Crown Prince of Predax, Panoplez Zendo, the son of Emperor Nokalez Zendo was the leader of the movement. He made the mistake of directly confronting his father. He was imprisoned somewhere in Predaxian space."

"That is great news, brother," Dave said. "If Predax could change, it would be a benefit to the entire galaxy."

"We'll see, brother," Fa-a-Di answered. "I think we will need time to wait and see what develops. The rebels have asked for our help in finding Panoplez. I don't know what we can do since the prison planet could be anywhere. I just wanted to share the good news with my brother Dave. We'll talk again soon. Gallia out." The view screen went black.

On the following morning, the maklans informed Dave that the location of the signal had been pinpointed. The analysis of the probes showed no sentient life on the planet below. Dave summoned his core team to the shuttle bay to travel to the planet's surface. Each human in the party would be accompanied by a maklan for protection. At precisely 0900 local time the shuttle craft San Antonio left the belly of Texas and dropped into the atmosphere. Commander Avery Adamsen, son of Fleet Admiral Arrin Adamsen, was piloting the shuttle. All the sensor arrays had been set to look for potential danger, such as toxic gas levels, transmission signals and signs of sentient life.

As the San Antonio dropped through the cloud layer, they could see a large ocean below them and a coastline on the horizon. The craft moved very quickly and was soon passing over dry land. A large forest reached in three directions to the horizon. Avery slowed the craft as a small opening appeared in the trees. Jake told the group that the signal was coming from that opening. Avery flew over the opening at low speed several times to look for any signs of an installation, but they only saw a small hill rising in the center of the opening. At Dave's signal, Avery landed the craft at the edge of the clearing.

"Admiral," Avery said, "I'm reading the atmosphere as fully breathable. We can disembark on your command."

"Thanks for the ride Avery," Dave replied. "I think you should stay here with the ship in case we have to make a quick exit. Please keep the engines warm and the defense shields on high once we leave the ship."

"Aye-aye, Admiral," he responded as he opened the hatch and lowered the ramp onto the soft grass. "Good luck out there!"

The maklans exited first and flew around the opening to check for any danger. "Dave," Jake thought, "it's clear. You can come out and join us."

The core team took emergency breathers and blasters from the compartment and clipped them to their belts. Dave led the way down the ramp and onto the new world, followed closely by Darlene, Charlie, and Aria. The clearing was beautiful. It was about one mile in diameter. The trees in the forest around it were very large, most over three hundred feet tall. The clearing was carpeted in what looked to be grass, but it had not overgrown. It seemed to grow only to five inches tall. There was no one to clip it, so they assumed it was naturally short. The hill was carpeted with grass. At the peak, the hill was one hundred feet tall, with a gradual incline from the forest floor.

"Dave," Jake said, "the signal seemed to be strongest at the peak of the hill.  I'm going to land there and see if I can hear it better."

"We'll head that way too Jake," Dave replied, "It might take us a few minutes to get there." The humans started up the hill.

Within a couple minutes, Aria said, "We need to take a look at this, Dave. When I examined the ground at the base of the hill, it looked like ordinary soil. On the hill, it seems like some kind of artificial growing media."

Dave bent down and pushed the grass aside, and the ground was formed into a mesh and was jet black. "Well, I guess we have our proof that this is not natural," he said. "Avery, please come in."

"Aye-aye Admiral," Avery responded immediately.

"Avery, please ask Commander Jackson to send a team down here to analyze the growing medium on this hill. It is definitely not natural," Dave said. "Okay team, let's keep going up. Jake will be up there waiting." It took another ten minutes before the humans reached the top of the hill and joined the maklan group. "Jake, what has your team learned so far?"

"Dave, the signal is much stronger here, but not any clearer. This is definitely some kind of beacon array. My team has been sensing around for a hidden opening. There has to be a way to get inside this thing," Jake replied.

"Avery, take the shuttle up in the air above tree height," Dave said. "We're looking for an opening that might lead into this hill. The maklans have not been able to sense an opening in the clearing. Perhaps the opening is somewhere in the forest nearby."

"Aye-aye Dave," Avery replied. "Give me a few minutes and I'll get back to you." At the bottom of the hill, the San Antonio slowly rose above the grass and up to four hundred feet and began to fly slow circles around the clearing. Within a few minutes, the landing party could no longer see the ship as the surrounding forest blocked their view. Ten minutes later, Avery's voice came over the intercom, "Dave, I think I found it. The forest is very deep there so I can't land anywhere but the clearing. I'm headed back to your position. If your team wants to follow me, you should be able to see me through the tree tops."

"Great job," Dave said as the San Antonio reappeared in the sky above them. The core team headed in the direction of the shuttle and moved into the forest, always keeping an eye on the ship above. The forest became increasingly dense as they moved away from the clearing. Streaks of sunlight illuminated portions of the land which was littered with leaf debris, stones and fallen trees.  After fifteen minutes, they began to hear signs of animal life.  Creatures similar to birds flew among the tree tops. Insects scurried along the ground. "Everyone, please draw your blasters, but keep them on stun," Dave said. "We have no idea what we might find out here." As he said that, a large deer-like animal emerged from the darkness and ran across their path before disappearing into the dark forest again. "Did you see that?" he shouted.

"Dave, it was amazing!" Charlie replied. "That thing must have been ten feet tall at the shoulder. And the rack of horns was enormous."

A pack of twenty wolf-like creatures emerged from the same area and ran across their path. The beasts were the size of tigers showing large saber-like teeth. They had been chasing the other animal. All but one followed it back into the darkness. One had seen the humans and stopped in its tracks, twenty feet in front of Dave.  All four raised their blasters, but before they could shoot, the animal had jumped the twenty feet to attack Dave. As the beast reached him, Jake intercepted it and knocked it to the ground. They rolled around in the undergrowth. No one could shoot as the two were tightly intertwined. After a few seconds, Jake glowed red, and the animal was blown back ten feet and landed on its back yelping. It rose gingerly and disappeared back into the forest, following its comrades.

"Jake, are you okay?" Dave shouted as he rushed to his friend.

Jake brushed the litter from his body, saying, "I'm fine Dave. That thing caught me by surprise for a moment. I guess we should have expected such things on a planet like this."

"Thanks for saving my life again, Jake," Dave replied.

"Only doing what anyone would do if they could, Dave," Jake said. "I've asked my team to be on the lookout for other surprises out in the forest. By the way, the opening is just ahead about fifty feet."

The party continued ahead and came upon a small building with a large metal door on the far side. The door was ten feet high and seemed very thick. There was no apparent lock or handle. In the center was an indentation in the shape of a maklan. "Jake, I think that's proof enough this is a maklan installation. What do you think, Max?" Darlene asked.

Macadalaka Vanokaraka, the chief maklan scientist on Texas, was assigned to guard Aria on the shuttle crew. She thought, "Very true Darlene. This shape is a bit different from maklans from No-Makla or Predax. All maklan species have continued to evolve over the last billion Earth years. This must be another race, or perhaps our own from long ago."

"How do we get inside, Max?" Charlie asked. "There's no lock or handle that I can see."

"I have an idea Charlie," Max replied. She flew up slowly and positioned her body into the orientation shown on the door and landed softly on its surface. Nothing happened. She glowed bright red, but still nothing changed. She glowed bright blue, and the sound of mechanisms deep inside the planet started to react. Max jumped away from the door and it slowly slid aside revealing an opening. Lights came to life and they could see a long sloping corridor into the ground in the direction of the clearing. "I suppose this is our invitation to go inside," she said.

"Dave, I think this might be a bit risky for your team. We have no idea what we will find down there," Jake said.

"Jake, you have the coordinates of the clearing and the Texas, so you can jump us out in a second if needed, right?" Dave asked.

"Yes Dave, but I'm still concerned. We don't know which maklans built this facility. They could have been much worse that the Predaxian maklans for all we know," Jake argued.

"I'll compromise with you," Dave began. "You and Max will go inside with me. The rest of your team can lead the others back to the clearing, where Avery will fly them back to the Texas. Avery will come back with two more shuttles and a couple hundred troops to control the area."

"Dave, are you sure it's safe?" Darlene said as she held his hand.

"Ambassador," he replied to his wife, "compared to an out-of-work accountant in the twenty-first, probably not. But we chose this life and now this is our job. When you were negotiating with the Galliceans, I was worried. It's going to be fine. We'll jump back to the Texas at any sign of trouble. With two maklans around me, it will be simple."

"Darlene," Jake thought, "I'll take care of Dave. You have my word on that."

The larger group headed back to the clearing with the San Antonio leading the way from above. When they had disappeared into the dark forest, Dave and the two maklans stepped through the door and into the long corridor. There was another maklan-shaped indentation inside the door. Jake matched his body to the design and the door slid closed behind them. None of them wanted any of those giant wolves following them here.

# CHAPTER 8

Emperor Nokalez Zendo had been in a terrible mood for weeks since the failure of his fleet at Nom-Kat-La. He nearly went insane when he learned thirty of his own warships had deserted as the battle was about to begin. During his reign, Predax had increased the size of the Alliance sphere from five hundred to two thousand worlds. There were tens of millions of Predaxian maklans living on the colonies insuring that the local leaders would maintain order and allegiance to Predax. Now, many of his most loyal troops had dared to quit just before Predax was to win its greatest victory. Nokalez had dismissed the entire military leadership and replaced them with generals whom he felt shared his vision for Predax. He named his brother, Altamar Zendo to be the head of the Chiefs of Staff. Most days since the defeat, Nokalez met with his brother for hours trying to develop a plan to bring the deserters to justice. The planning was not going well.

"Brother, we have been talking for too long," the Emperor began. "We need to take action now and make those insolent bastards pay for what they have done!"

"I agree, Your Majesty," Altamar whimpered, "but it will not be easy. We took sixty-five ships to the frontier. The thirty traitor ships left us. We lost ten ships during the battle over Nom-Kat-La. Another fifteen ships were heavily damaged and are undergoing repair over Palus. If we could get another twenty ships from other regions of the frontier, our force would only match them. The battle would likely be a stand-off. When the people of Predax see we are involved in what seems to be a civil war, more will turn to the side of the traitors. Brother, we need more time to develop an overwhelming advantage so we can

45

crush the deserters." Altamar slumped down on a seat facing the Emperor.

"How long will that take, dear brother," Nokalez sighed.

"Field Marshall Fongula Nokka of Palus told me earlier today he expects to have five ships available within seven days. The remaining ten will take several weeks," Altamar replied.

"Weeks!" Nokalez screamed, "That is totally unacceptable. I should have known better than to put our invasion in the hands of those bird-brained fools. Do we have other colonies that can help?"

"Our governors of the other colonies are doing what they can," Altamar replied. "Many of their ships are guarding their own frontiers, and we risk invasion from several other planets if we weaken their defenses. The twenty ships I mentioned are probably the best we can do."

"Brother Altamar," Nokalez sighed, "these are dark days for Predax. You remember when we were young two hundred solar cycles ago." Altamar nodded. "When I learned I would take over from our father, I was overwhelmed. We were so full of hope and ambition for the greatness of Predax. Now look where we stand. If the Kalideans and Galliceans were to invade today, there would be little we could do to stop them. I fear that day may be coming sooner than we think. If those traitors team up with them, they could keep us from controlling the invaders' minds, and we would be truly helpless. I feel like a failure to our family and planet."

Altamar scurried over to a cabinet and withdrew two glasses and a bottle of liquor. He poured for his brother and himself. The two drank a toast to Predax and sat quietly for a moment. "Your

Majesty, we do have one thing in our favor. The Galliceans and Kalideans are very peace-loving. I think the odds that they will attack are very small. They would rather sign another cease-fire or peace treaty. That might give us the time to resolve our internal issues," Altamar said.

"You are correct as usual, brother," Nokalez replied. "Perhaps the Palians should initiate the contact with Greater Gallia. That way we are left outside the process. If Palus should invade them again, it would be their aggression, not ours."

"Brother, the presence of the maklans from No-Makla on the enemy fleet shows they are fully aware of our actions in this matter," Altamar said. "We have had dozens of agents captured or killed on Gallia and other planets across the frontier. I don't think we could fool them again."

"Maybe not, but I have the beginning of a plan, brother," Nokalez started, "Perhaps after Palus attacked, we could appear to join forces with Greater Gallia. We could even bring some warships from another colony, like Bastria. Those slugs never liked the Palians. If the Galliceans saw the Bastrians and Predaxians fighting with them against Palus, they would have to believe our intentions were honorable, wouldn't they?"

"That is an interesting idea, brother," Altamar said. "The likely outcome would be losing Palus as part of the Alliance. Then the gas monsters of Gallia would be on our direct frontier."

"Perhaps brother, but I feel that there is a plan in there some-where that could lead us back to Nom-Kat-La and victory. Perhaps you should put your generals on this issue and see what they come up with. We pay them dearly for their counsel, and it's about time they came through. It might also help us root out any other potential dissenters in our ranks before a civil war begins," the Emperor replied.

"Perhaps there is a way to put the blame on the deserters and my dear nephew," Altamar said.

"That is a very good idea!" the Emperor smiled. "With Pan buried inside Thuk, there would be no one to deny it. Brother, you have improved my mood greatly. Please take these ideas to your team and take a week or two to come up with some possible actions. I think I might go hunting on Parax for a few days to clear my mind and relax."

Max, Jake and Dave continued slowly down the long corridor. The sounds of the forest were gone now, replaced by the hum of equipment buried in the ground around them. Dave could see the end of the corridor a few hundred feet ahead. That area was bathed in bright blue light. There were no lighting fixtures to provide the light in the corridor, instead the light seemed to emit from the walls, ceiling and floor equally.

"Max," Jake noted, "this construction seems very different from No-Makla. It's very sterile and cold."

"I noticed that too, Jake," she replied. "It's been a long time since the Great Rebirth, so the differences are understandable."

Dave said, "It's almost looks like human construction to me, except the strange lighting. Perhaps the maklans who built this used another race for the construction crew?"

"I suppose that's possible," Max replied. "I just hope they are not like the maklans of Predax. Another highly evolved and dangerous civilization of maklans would be very bad for all of us."

They reached the end of the corridor and found a heavy metal door in their path. There was no maklan impression on the door or other apparent mechanism to open it. As they looked about, they saw and felt a beam of blue light pass over them. After a moment, the shape of a maklan and a human hand formed into the metal of the door. Dave reached out with his right hand and touched the hand impression on the door. The door slid soundlessly into a pocket in the wall.

The three stepped into the room as lighting came to life. In the center of the huge circular room was a massive machine that appeared to be the beacon generator. Its base disappeared into a deep well in the room reaching hundreds of feet into the planet, and the antenna rose to the top of the domed ceiling three hundred feet over their heads. Rows of computer stations formed concentric circles from the center well. Other equipment lined the walls of the room. Near them was a seating area in a large niche in the wall. Several plaques were mounted on the walls near the seats. They walked over to the niche and examined the plaques. The writing was a language they did not know. Dave tested the couch, and then sat down to take in all the sights in this place.

"Wow," Dave began, "this place is really amazing. There's no doubt this is a beacon of some kind."

As he spoke, a small glass globe descended from the ceiling until it was ten feet over his head. A beam of light shot from the globe and formed into a holographic image of a maklan similar to the outlines they had seen in the door impressions. It appeared to be standing in the center of the seating area. "Welcome, my human and maklan friends!" the holograph said. "My name is Ton Kalafledes, and I was the administrator for this place we call Beacon Station 801." Max and Jake sat on the seats next to Dave.

"Dave, did you hear that?" Jake said. "It is touching my mind exactly like another No-Makla maklan."

"Jake," Dave replied, "I heard perfect English."

Ton Kalafledes spoke again, "According to the system clock, Beacon Station 801 became operational four hundred million solar cycles before this date. Its nuclear core was rated to last three hundred and fifty million cycles. I am pleased that the system continues to operate beyond its rated life. The systems here have been programmed to answer most common questions."

Dave said, "Ton, my name is Dave Brewster. What is the purpose of this station?"

The holograph looked at Dave and replied, "Welcome Dave. I am glad that the humans of Earth have ventured so far from home. This station was designed to warn invaders they were approaching Tak-Makla and should not proceed further. It also was to welcome friendly explorers, and invite them to Tak-Makla to visit and become our friends and allies."

"Ton, my name is Macadalaka Vanokaraka, a scientist from No-Makla. Does this station have continuing contact with Tak-Makla?" Max asked.

"Welcome Macadalaka! It is my great pleasure to welcome a fellow maklan to this world. I certainly want to invite you and your friends to come to Tak-Makla and meet the maklans there. Unfortunately, this system lost contact with Tak-Makla fifty million solar cycles ago, when our power fell below twenty percent. I am registering our power level at seven percent now. Within another million cycles, the system will lose all power," the holograph replied.

"Ton, I am Jake Benomafaleys, also from No-Makla," Jake said, "Do you know why no one from Tak-Makla has come to reenergize the station or reestablish communications? It seems very odd to me."

"Sorry, Jake," Ton replied, "I have no information on that. The maklans of Tak-Makla have apparently decided there is no further need for this station. I would suggest you travel there and ask them directly."

"Ton, is this planet part of Tak-Makla's sphere of influence?" Dave asked.

"Dave, to my knowledge, the maklans of Tak-Makla only occupy planets within the one star system. I have been programmed to offer the planets of this system to any peaceful civilization that wishes to expand. We have been monitoring the situation on the planets and can report there is no sentient life in this system. Flora and fauna species are varied and abundant. We would hope that a civilization moving here would respect that life and learn to accommodate them in their plans," the holograph replied.

"Ton," Max asked, "where is Tak-Makla?  As fellow maklans, we are very interested in reconnecting with them. The maklans of No-Makla also inhabit only one system, which we share with the humans. It would seem we have much in common."

"Max, Tak-Makla is approximately thirty light years from Station 801. I have placed the coordinates for the home world into the memory banks of the star ship circling the station," Ton replied. "I know they will be eager to meet you as well. Go in peace friends. The lighting inside the station will remain on until you exit the corridor and reenter the forest." The image disappeared and the glass globe retracted back into the ceiling.

The trio left the room and returned slowly to the surface. They were very quiet, lost in thoughts about this place and the opportunity to meet another maklan civilization. They wondered why such an advanced civilization had abandoned this station so long ago. Could they have been attacked or died out from some other cause? Perhaps they had become barbaric themselves and were expanding into adjacent space. There was only one way to find out.

Dave, Darlene, Charlie and Aria sat quietly in Dave's ready room having breakfast. The Nightsky and Ticonderoga were due to jump from Far Sky soon to begin the process of installing a permanent portal in orbit. Dave had asked Captain Jon Lake to meet with the core team as soon as he arrived. Since they had returned from the planet yesterday, planning for a new colony had been feverish. Jake and Max had made their report to the High Council on No-Makla. Excitement about meeting another peaceful maklan civilization spread quickly across that planet.

"Charlie, I sure wish we had better coffee on the Texas," Dave sighed.

"This is certainly nothing like our neighborhood Starbucks, right?" Charlie answered. He waved at the window showing the curve of the planet far below them. "You do have to admit the view is better here though."

"You two never stop about the coffee," Darlene said. "Here we are, light-years and centuries from those days, and this is all you guys have to say!"

"Sweetheart," Dave replied, "I'm not complaining. I admit I am looking forward to taking a vacation in the twenty-first as soon as I can. But if I'm sacrificing my old life to establish a thousand new colonies, you'd think we'd have a better coffee system. The coffee on Ticonderoga was much better than this."

"Dave," Aria said, "I've already requisitioned several new systems for Texas. I know you guys too well, and the best coffee system is coming your way soon."

"You are a life saver," Charlie replied as he kissed his wife on the cheek.

A tone sounded on the control panel and Dave touched the contact. The image of Lia Lawson appeared on the view screen at the end of the table. "Admiral, Nightsky has jumped into this system and will be in orbit within the hour. Captain Lake sends his regards and will take a shuttle over to Texas as soon as they arrive."

"Thank you Lia," Dave replied.

"Dave, Captain Lake has requested a private meeting with you while he is on board," Lia said.

"That's fine, Lia, please confirm with him and put it on my calendar," he replied.

"Aye-aye, Admiral. I also have Fleet Admiral Adamsen calling for you and your team. Shall I put it through now?" she said.

"Please do," he said. Lia's image was replaced by Arrin Adamsen's normal stern expression. "Admiral, it is good to see you again."

"Dave, I'm glad you have your team together. I've seen the preliminary reports on the Station 801 system and it looks great. May I assume you are recommending this system for colonization?" Arrin asked.

"Yes Arrin," Dave replied. "There are two ideal planets in this system for human habitation. It looks like neither will require extensive terraforming.  We need to map the planets and find the best locations for the first outposts. Charlie, why don't you fill in the details for the Admiral?"

"Arrin, the resources available on these planets are very abundant. Fresh water and vegetation are everywhere. There is a large variety of fauna and sea life," Charlie began. "Most of the plant and animal life is quite different from what we've seen on other planets. I've been in contact with Chief Engineer Lagerfeld and he is already interested in establishing universities to study and catalog life here. Except for the lack of sentient species, the diversity of life rivals Earth."

"That's great Charlie," Arrin replied. "Has anyone come up with names for these colonies? We can't get our marketing teams working on the ad campaign for settlers unless we have catchy names."

Darlene said, "Arrin, we were trying to find names that speak to the abundance of these planets. Unlike places like Far Sky and New Dawn, these worlds are pretty much ready for immediate habitation. We want to capture people's imaginations about all the landscapes and wildlife. The names I prefer so far are New Frontier and Summer Garden. What do you think?"

Arrin laughed, smiled and replied, "Ambassador, you know I'm an old soldier. I'd probably name them after battlegrounds like Gettysburg or The Ardennes. Of course, I realize that no one would move to a place with those names. Whatever your team decides is fine with me. Send your final suggestions to the High Commissioner and I'm sure he will approve them. My interest is more about recruiting troops to provide security and setting up police and military academies. But let me ask one favor. Please set aside at least part of that forest near the beacon as a hunting reserve. The animals you mentioned in your report were simply amazing."

"Absolutely Admiral," Darlene replied. "I've sent a few maklans down there today to get video of some of the wildlife, as well as landscapes and other scenery for the brochures."

"Thank you Darlene," Arrin said. "I hate to break up your meal, but I do need a few private minutes with Dave and Captain Cartwright. Lia has already asked him to come to Dave's ready room." The others said goodbye to Arrin and filed out of the room as Carl stepped in.

"Arrin, we are alone now, please go ahead," Dave said.

"Gentlemen, I don't know what you've heard of the civil war brewing on Predax," Arrin began.

"Admiral, I have been somewhat briefed by High Commissioner Fa-a-Di," Dave replied.

"You have very good friends Dave," Arrin said. "The rebels have been asking for support to depose Emperor Zendo and replace him with his son. So far, the Galliceans are willing to help, but Kalidus has continued to recommend caution. I have spoken today with Governor Novolus of the Kalidean colony Tantalus. He has allowed the rebels to establish a consulate on his planet. The new consul, Zakamar Vondee has been working tirelessly to convince us that Predax is very weak. She claims much of their fleet was damaged or destroyed over Nom-Kat-La. She believes her small fleet could fight Predax to a stalemate. Even ten or twenty more ships from our side could bring about the end of Predaxian control over hundreds of civilizations."

"How can we trust the rebels, Admiral?" Carl asked. "Couldn't this be a trick to get us into another battle we might lose?"

"That is exactly the problem Carl," Arrin answered. "None of our civilizations have known peace with Predax. While they haven't attacked Kalidean planets yet, they have attacked Greater Gallia twice and did force the attack on No-Makla. While we all wish we could defeat them now and end the constant fighting, we have no real evidence. I'm told that fifty million maklans are headed to Tantalus and Nom-Kat-La now to help push back the mind control from Alliance space. We hope to be able to pierce their interference and see how many ships they have in our regions. If we find few ships, we might lend a few ships. That's where you two come in. Dave, I still need you and your team to go to Tak-Makla and negotiate a treaty with them. But I want Texas to move to Tantalus as soon as possible. We don't have many fleet battle cruisers and I want all of them in this fight if it happens."

"No problem Arrin," Dave replied. "Nightsky is due to arrive here any minute and my core team can transfer there when she arrives."

"Arrin," Carl interrupted, "We'll need a day or two to prepare. Once Ticonderoga installs the permanent portal, we should be able to do a direct jump to Tantalus. Will that be satisfactory?"

"You two make my life easy," Arrin smiled. "It sounds perfect. Carl, please advise me when your ship arrives over Tantalus. Dave, I am as excited as you about Tak-Makla. I cannot imagine a culture that could build the beacon array on Station 801 four hundred million years ago. That will be a thrill."

Dave grinned, "Arrin, we are all excited about what we might find. After Jake and Max made their report to No-Makla, that entire planet is buzzing with anticipation too."

"Dave, one last thing I almost forgot," Arrin said. "Since I'm sending you off again before you could develop your new colonies, I have recruited a new governor for your two planets. I think you've heard of Governor Lyra Lawson."

Dave laughed, "That's great!  She has been an amazing help as we have been developing Far Sky and New Dawn. How did you convince her to give up Day's End?"

"It wasn't easy Dave," Arrin replied. "Not only did I have to give her both planets, but I had to make another concession. I'm sorry about this Carl, but I had to make Lia her Secretary of State."

Carl smiled broadly, "Admiral, Lia is the best communications officer in the fleet. But if this is what's needed, you know I always follow orders. That is a great opportunity for Lia, and I would never stand in her way."

"You see," Arrin laughed, "you two do make my life easy. I'm off to have dinner with Lanz Lagerfeld. I'll give him your best regards as well. Earth out."

Captain Jon Lake of the Nightsky sat across the table from Dave Brewster in the admiral's ready room on the Texas. Dave sipped his coffee and sat back. "Jon, here we are for the private meeting. What's on your mind, Captain?" he asked.

"Dave, I know I haven't been on top of my game recently," Jon replied. "The Predaxian invasion was too much for me."

"I don't understand Jon. Neither of us was involved in that action," Dave said.

"Well, that's true. But Lauren was," Jon sighed, looking down.

"Are you talking about Captain London?" Dave asked. Jon nodded but kept his head down. "It was a terrible battle and her ship was destroyed. It pains me every day to think about it, Jon. Please tell me what you're keeping inside."

"Dave, Lauren and I had a relationship," he began, looking up and making eye contact with the admiral. "She and her crew were very helpful in getting us started on fixing Far Sky. She ended up spending most of her time on the planet helping me organize things. After a while, we started dating. During that first six months, we became very close. I was about to ask Lauren to marry me when her ship was called back to Earth. That was the last time I ever saw her."

"Jon, I had no idea," Dave replied. "I am so sorry. I can't imagine what you've been going through since the battle at Nom-Kat-La."

"The worst part is not knowing, Dave. Her body was never found.  While the odds aren't good, I believe the Predaxians captured her.  God only knows what those monsters are doing to her now.  Somehow, I've got to do something, but I just have no idea what can be done," Jon said as he dropped his head into his hands.

"We know that we can't invade and go looking all over Alliance space for her. At least not yet," Dave replied.

Jon raised his head and said, "What do you mean not yet?"

"We believe there is a civil war brewing inside the Alliance. Many Predaxians are tired of fighting and controlling other worlds against their will. Right now, we don't know how strong Predax is. We are waiting for enough maklans to arrive at the border area and try to push back their mind control so we can count their ships and potentially find any prisoners of war," Dave replied.

"Dave, if that happens, you have to let me go try to find her," Jon pleaded. "Let me take Nightsky and join the rebels. They'll help me find her."

"Calm down, Jon," Dave said. "This information is still very new and we don't know how accurate it is. The rebels may be loyal agents trying to draw us into a trap. It's going to take a bit of time. If and when we have actionable information on the whereabouts of any prisoners, Fleet Admiral Adamsen will send our best ships to get them. That I guarantee, Jon."

"I hope that happens soon, Admiral. Every day is torture for me not knowing where she is and being unable to do anything," Jon replied.

The door to the ready room opened and Charlie, Aria and Darlene entered. Each stopped by Jon and shook his hand, then sat down. Dave said, "Okay team, we have new orders. Fleet Admiral Arrin is calling the Texas to the Kalidean colony of Tantalus. Governor Lyra Lawson is taking over the establishment of the new colonies in this system. She is due to arrive in two days with the next colony ship and a cruiser. In the meantime, our team will relocate to the Nightsky. Jon, please make certain we have accommodations. We will need at least one conference room like this for meetings. Once we pass command of this system to the governor, we will proceed to Tak-Makla to make contact and establish diplomatic relations with them. Darlene, you will obviously lead that effort. I have already asked Jake to make certain an ambassador from No-Makla will travel with us as well. Are there any questions?"

Aria said, "Dave, I'll make sure that the new coffee system for Texas is diverted to Nightsky. We've got to take care of the boss!"

"I'll make certain all the arrangements are made on Nightsky, Admiral," Jon replied. "Will we be jumping to that system or flying straight?"

"According to the computer system on Station 801, Tak-Makla is thirty light years from here. We don't want them to think we are invading, so I think we will avoid jumping," Dave said.

"I concur, Admiral," Aria commented. "A heavily armed star cruiser suddenly popping into orbit is not a very friendly entrance. We will also find out how far out they can detect us. A few friendly conversations before we show up can't hurt."

"Admiral, at maximum speed, it should take Nightsky seven days to reach the target," Jon said. "After this meeting, I'll have my crew make certain we have provisions for at least four weeks. That should be sufficient."

"Thank you Jon," Dave replied. He turned to Charlie and said, "Charlie, I want you to know that Lyra has asked for Lia to be her secretary of state. Are you okay with all of this, old friend?"

Charlie smiled, saying, "Thanks for your concern, Dave. I am thrilled that Lia can help her mother on this project. I'll have the science team pull together detailed reports on the planets to give to the governor on her arrival. For a second there I thought you were going to ask me to stay here and help them. You know that you cannot get rid of me that easily, pal. We do have another problem though."

"Oh boy, let's hear it. I hope it's nothing serious," Dave replied.

"I don't think it's serious," Charlie laughed. "I'm sure you and Darlene remember that dinner we had at the Eiffel Tower before you two decided to come here."

"Who could forget that, Charlie? That day changed my entire life," Darlene responded.

"I'm sure you all remember the team that is supposed to fix human DNA and enable people to live to be a thousand years old," Charlie continued. "Aria has tried to convince Matt and Rob to come here. Unfortunately, she hasn't had any success. I think I need to go there myself to get the job done."

"I've already scheduled the temporal jump, Admiral," Aria said. "You and Charlie are scheduled for 0900 tomorrow. You'll arrive in San Diego one month after you left the last time."

"Me?" Dave said. "What value do I add to this?"

"Think of it as an early vacation, Dave," Charlie replied. "It was my idea. Darlene, Aria and Jon can take care of everything here. You've been looking forward to jumping back for a long time. I can use your help convincing my boys to come. I stay up most nights worrying about how I would feel knowing they died a thousand years ago and never fulfilled this amazing feat because I failed to try hard enough."

"Well, it sounds like everything is all set up," Dave said. "It will be great to see the twenty-first again. Aria, when will we jump back?"

"You are scheduled to return at 0900 hours the day after tomorrow. That will provide plenty of time before Nightsky is set to leave for Tak-Makla," she replied. "Don't worry we won't leave here without both of you."

"Well, Charlie, it looks like we'll be having our Starbucks coffee real soon. Frankly, I'm excited about this," Dave said.

"Me too, Dave. It's been a long time since I've seen my boys and I do miss them a lot. I've asked Muncie and Rence to meet us there and help out too. There's nothing like a man from the thirty-second to convince someone it really can happen," Charlie said.

# CHAPTER 12

"I think I'm losing my mind, Mitch," Lauren said to her maklan friend. "It seems like we've been stuck here for ever. I'm glad that Pan and Wally were able to get the lights working again."

"It is difficult for all of us, Captain. I still remember the last thing you told me on the bridge of the Courage. While there is life, there is always hope. We have to give our friends time to find us," Mitch replied.

Panoplez Zendo walked over and joined the two. "I fully agree," he began. "Even though my father said he eliminated all the Predaxians who followed me, I know it was a lie. There were too many to kill without starting a civil war. My fiancé told me she would take over the movement if anything happened to me. She's a lot smarter than me, so I know she's out there making trouble for dear old Dad."

"Tell me about her, Pan," Lauren asked.

Pan sat down on the floor and thought for a moment. "Her name is Zakamar Vondee. We met while attending college. I was always amazed by her intelligence. She convinced me that Predax was in decline. My whole life I was taught we owed our survival to our mind control abilities. The other civilizations in our area were brutal monsters who wanted nothing more than to destroy us. That was true at the time of the Great Rebirth, but tens of thousands of generations have passed since then. All the other civilizations had advanced and become simple traders and explorers. Predax had become dependent on the planets we ruled through mind control. We were addicted to power. After all those generations, we had switched places with the other

Beings in our region. While they had become peaceful, we had become the barbarians. Without her, I never would have realized how evil our society had become. I would have continued my father's plans to subjugate more innocents."

"She sounds like an amazing woman, Pan," Wally said as he joined the group. "Do you think she is out there trying to find you?"

"I hope not, Wally," he replied. "I hope she is gathering the resistance and making plans to depose my father. That is the real fight. After that happens, there will be plenty of time to find us."

A siren sounded and the lights began to flash. Pan said, "Don't worry, that means our jailors are about to pay us a visit. Stay together on this side of the room. They will read our position and jump to the other end with fresh supplies." A blast of white light filled the opposite end of the room. As it faded, a single, heavily armed Predaxian maklan appeared in the room with two pallets of supplies. Pan laughed, "Hey, Dokalak, they sent you alone?"

The other Predaxian leaned against the containers. "Cousin, you won't believe what's going on in space. Thuk might be the only safe spot in Alliance territory," Dok replied.

Pan walked to the other Predaxian and hugged him. "Dok, you've got to tell me all the details. But where are the other guards?  Don't they know I could take you with six legs tied behind me?"

"Pan, is it safe to talk in front of your cellmates?" Dok said.

"Dok, come on now.  There are five thousand miles of iron over our heads. We're not going anywhere. We've haven't been asked to do any interviews recently," Pan laughed. "By the way, these are my friends, Jake, Lauren and Wally."

"How are you all?" Dok said. "Sorry, that was a stupid question. I tend to ask lots of odd questions. You are in prison and I am your keeper. Of course you aren't having a great time. Cousin, there is civil war brewing in the Alliance. The invasion of Nom-Kat-La was a disaster. Half of the Alliance ships deserted just as they were supposed to enter Gallicean space. The rest of the ships took a terrible beating. The rumor I heard was the deserters are trying to get the Galliceans or Kalideans to join them now.  People are panicking all over Predax."

"Gee cousin, I'm sorry to hear that," Pan laughed. "Does anyone know who is behind the uprising?"

"There are more rumors about that. Most people believe you escaped from prison and are leading the rebel fleet. My uncle keeps reassuring the populace you are safely hidden, but fear makes people think strange things. My personal opinion is that girlfriend of mine you stole is running this," Dok replied.

"Zakamar running a rebel army?" Pan laughed. "Don't be silly. What makes you think she is capable of such a thing?"

"Pan, you know darned well Zak is smarter than you and me combined, except when it comes to her choice in men," Dok laughed. "If she is running it, I think your father is in real trouble. My dad has been working day and night with the emperor to find a solution to the insurrection."

"I still don't know why they sent you here alone," Pan said. "Even if I was gentle as a lamb, they don't know what the other three could do."

"Cousin, almost all troops have been called back to Predax in case of a rebel attack," Dok replied. "There are only three of us on the ship, the pilot, the loadmaster and me. Normally the ship would have a crew of thirty. If there is any problem down here, they have orders to leave me behind. I guess they assume you won't kill your own cousin."

"That makes sense, Dok," Pan said. "Don't worry, we'll let you finish your job and go back. Without supplies, we won't live long.  It looks like you brought double rations too."

"Exactly. They don't want us coming here too often in case a rebel ship spots us and realizes how odd it is for a supply ship to be here in the dead quadrant," Dok said. "The pilot has orders to jump me out in a minute, dead or alive. I hope I get to see you again Pan. Believe me, I want you out of this rock as soon as possible."

"If you mean that cousin, you need to do me a favor," Pan said. "You need to get a message to Zak and let her know where I am."

"I don't know Pan. That would likely land me here with you. I love you, cousin and I'll think about it," Dok said as the white flash returned. After it faded, they could see that Dok was gone.

"Your cousin seems like a nice guy, Pan," Lauren said. "I don't understand how the nephew of the Emperor of Predax would end up a prison guard though."

"Dok is the greatest," Pan replied. "He and I have been close friends our entire lives. He has never had much ambition. His father is Altamar Zendo, my father's youngest brother.  Before I came here, Altamar was Minister of Internal Affairs, which is code for head of the secret police. Dok has nine other siblings who have mostly entered the Bureau of Mind Control. They are probably living on other Alliance planets making sure the locals do what my father says. Dok could never decide whether he wanted to be a poet or a bum. I guess his father finally convinced him to join the military to get him off Predax. It seems clear to me they send him here because they know how close we are."

Jake asked, "Do you think he will get word to Zakamar?"

"No, I don't, Jake," Pan replied. "He's too afraid of his father and uncle to risk such a thing. He loves to gossip though. I'm hoping he'll tell someone he knows where I am. If I'm lucky, at least one person he talks to will be part of the resistance. Then they'll kidnap him and make him tell them where we are."

"That seems pretty unlikely," Lauren said.

"That's true Lauren, but what other hope do we have?" Pan replied.

# CHAPTER 13

Dave Brewster was very comfortable sitting in the overstuffed chair. The sounds and smells of the Starbucks coffee shop were very familiar and inviting. It had been almost a year since he had been here, although only one month had passed on the twenty-first century calendar. A small table was a few feet in front of him. A beautiful woman was seated at the table looking at her laptop screen. Every few seconds she would type a few keys and continue looking. Women didn't wear short dresses in the thirty-second, and Dave was a bit sad about that. The woman turned her head and smiled at Dave, who quickly averted his eyes.

"Here you go Dave!" Charlie said as he sat on the chair next to the admiral. "One venti latte just the way you like it, and I didn't forget the chocolate croissant."

"Thank you Charlie. It seems like a million years since we've been here. This place is so homey that coming here alone was worth the jump," Dave replied.

Bea entered the store and walked over to Dave and Charlie. "Hi guys!" she said. "I haven't seen you two in a while. I'm just starting my shift and wanted to say hello."

"Hi Bea," Charlie replied. "It's good to see you too. We've been out of town for a few weeks, but came here as soon as we got back. I'm sure we'll see you again in the next few days."

"Great, I look forward to that," she said as she turned and walked toward the counter to take her place.

"Dave, you were right about Bea. She is beautiful and does look a lot like Darlene," Charlie said. "You are a lucky guy, old friend."

"Thanks Charlie," Dave replied. "I have a strange feeling about that girl.  Something about her seems almost too familiar. Do you know what I mean?"

"Dave, I've told you before there are no coincidences. Maybe we need to talk to Rence and Muncie about her when they get here," Charlie said. "Honestly, I know nothing about her. I just know when that sixth sense kicks in, there is more to know."

Charlie's son, Robert walked into the store and stepped up to the counter. He did not see his father at the back of the store. Bea walked around the counter and hugged Robert, kissing him lightly on the cheek. Rob ordered a coffee and stood near the barista station waiting for his order. Charlie saw all the activity and went to say hello.  He tapped Rob on the shoulder. Rob was startled to see his father, and hugged him tightly. Rob took his coffee and the two came back to where Dave was seated.

"Dave, this is my youngest, Rob," Charlie beamed. "Rob, this is Dave Brewster. I guess you could say we are coworkers."

"Good morning, Mr. Brewster," Rob said formally, "It's good to meet you. My dad doesn't talk much about the people he works with."

"It's nice to meet you too Rob, but please call me Dave," Dave replied. "Would you like to join us? We just got our coffees and were going to chat for a while."

"No thanks, Dave, I'm in a rush to get to work. Thanks for the offer," Rob said.

"Work?" Charlie started. "When did you move here?"

"Don't you ever listen to your voice mail, Dad?" Rob said. "I called you two weeks ago and left a message that I took a job here in San Diego."

"Sorry son, Dave and I have been out of town for a month, and my cell phone didn't have service where we were," Charlie answered. "That's great news. You'll have to tell me more about it later."

"I'm staying with Matt until I can find my own place. I'll call him and maybe we can all have dinner at your place tonight or tomorrow?" Matt said. "If you've been out of town, I'm sure you are anxious to see the grandkids again."

"That is absolutely true, Rob. It's a great idea. After you two decide, just call Kally or me and we'll make certain that every-thing is ready.  I love you, son," Charlie replied.

"I love you too, Dad," Rob said. "I really have to get going or my bosses are going to bite my head off. See you guys soon." Rob turned and headed to the door. As he approached it, Rence and Muncie opened the door and stepped in. Rob shook each of their hands and spoke to them for a moment before stepping out the door and disappearing around the corner of the building.

As Dave sat, he said, "Charlie, that's good that Rob knows Rence and Muncie. Are you sure he doesn't suspect anything unusual?"

Charlie sat heavily and looked startled. "Dave, until two weeks ago, Rob was living in Dallas, Texas. I never introduced him to them. I have no idea how they met. Matt doesn't live in this part of town, so this wouldn't be Rob's neighborhood Starbucks."

Rence and Muncie picked up their coffees and walked to the back of the store to join Dave and Charlie. Dave was a bit disappointed when Muncie took the chair opposite him and blocked his view of the leggy blonde.

"Okay," Charlie started, "I have a question for you two. How did you meet Rob? I told you about him but you never met him before as far as I know."

"Well, to tell you the truth, we hired both of your sons and have them working with us on our anthropological projects. You and Aria were having trouble convincing them to move, so we thought we'd help out," Muncie replied.

"I suppose I should thank you, but don't you think you could have told me?" Charlie asked. "How much do they know?"

"We've told them very little so far," Rence replied. "They are working gathering background material for a new series of books.  Our last book sold fifty thousand copies in the first month."

"In the thirty-second!" Charlie blurted.

"Okay, that's enough," Dave interrupted. "I don't think this is an appropriate venue for this kind of discussion. Why don't we just enjoy our coffee and we can talk more at Charlie's house."

"Dave, I understand and you are right," Muncie said. "Just so you know, besides you and Charlie, all the people here now are from the thirty-second. This is where we get together before each day to coordinate our plans. Locals come here all the time, but there are none here at the moment."

The beautiful blonde stood and came over to the where the men sat. She bent over and kissed Muncie on the cheek. "Admiral Brewster, my name is Lieutenant Alana Albright. Muncie is my fiancé. I've been assigned to help convince Matt and Rob to join us in the future. After that task is completed, I am scheduled to join Colonel Aria Watson on your team. I am looking forward to that greatly, sir."

Dave stood and shook her hand. "Alana, it is great to meet you. You are a beautiful woman and Muncie is a very lucky man," Dave said as he patted Muncie on the shoulder. "Okay, what's the story on Bea, the barista?"

"Bea is on special assignment to assist our team. Her specialties are biomedical engineering and languages," Alana said. "I'm told that she can speak Gallicean, Kalidean and Predaxian. She's the only person I know who doesn't have a translator planted in her ear all the time."

"Dave and I have some conflicting feelings about that girl," Charlie said. "What else can you tell us, Alana?"

Muncie replied, "I'm sorry Charlie. High Commissioner Darak Daniels has sealed her records. We have told you everything we know."

"That seems very odd indeed," Dave said. "I suppose we'll find out at the appropriate time."

Charlie's cell phone vibrated in his pocket. He pulled it out and answered. "Hello? Oh, hi Rob . . . Tonight at seven o'clock sounds great . . . look forward to it too, son . . . Goodbye," he said as he disconnected. "It sounds like we're all set for the big dinner tonight. I'll make sure Kally has everything set up."

Zakamar Vondee sat quietly at her desk in the new Free Predax Consulate in the heart of Palidus City on the Tantalus colony. She thought about Panoplez Zendo, her best friend and love of her life. He was out there somewhere needing her help. She had no idea how to find him in the vastness of empty space. Thousands of her spies were infiltrating every part of the government on Predax trying desperately to find any clue about his location. In the ten long years since he disappeared, they had found nothing. Two rebel cruisers orbited high above, while the remaining ships returned to Alliance space to disrupt inter-planetary commerce and find others to join them. Currently, the rebel fleet included thirty five cruisers. Her rebels would stop at nothing to bring down the despotic emperor.

A tone sounded on her desk and she touched the contact. The door slid open noiselessly and Lucius Valamar, her one Kalidean employee entered the room. "What is it, Lucius?" she asked.

"There is a group from No-Makla here to meet with you, Consul," he said in his thick colonial brogue.

"That's great news, Lucius. Please let them in and bring us some Predaxian brandy to celebrate," Zak replied.

The Kalidean left and twenty maklans entered the office. After a moment, Lucius returned with several bottles of brandy and a tray of glasses. He opened two bottles and poured brandy into all of the glasses, and left.

"Welcome fellow maklans," Zak said. "I am very grateful that you came to see me. Predax has been under the foot of Nokalez Zendo and his henchmen for too long."

"Consul Vondee, I am Ambassador Konomalocus Nolobitamore from No-Makla. I have been sent to Tantalus for two missions. First, I am leading a team of several million maklans who intend to push back the mind control from the frontier so that we can judge the strength of the Predaxian fleet. Under the assumption they are as weak as you contend, my team will assist any Gallicean, Kalidean or Earth star ships in the attack on the Emperor's forces," the ambassador said.

Zak glowed with joy. "Thank you Madam Ambassador," she smiled. "You will find that everything I said is true. I have some fine Predaxian brandy here. Shall we toast to our success?"

"That sounds like a wonderful idea, Consul Vondee," she replied. The group drank to the success of their plans.

"I have a question, Ambassador," Zak said. "I am alone here on this planet. I'm a bit confused why you have such a large entourage for this meeting."

"That's a fair question," Kono said. "We maklans from No-Makla can jump up to twenty light-years if we are in a group of ten or more. To be honest, we had no idea what to expect from this meeting. There are those who believe your forces are trying to lure us into a trap deep in Alliance territory. My team came along today just as a precaution."

"I understand, Ambassador," Zak replied. "After so many generations of aggression, it is difficult to believe there are Predaxians who are not power-hungry. You can tell I am not trying to exert control over your minds. You can see that my assistant is not being controlled either. Perhaps you can even monitor my crews in space and see the same thing. My dear friend Panoplez and I will not rest until Predax joins the civil societies of the galaxy."

"I want to believe you, Consul" Kono continued. "My own brother, Michamanades was captured during the battle over Nom-Kat-La. He is part of the reason I volunteered for this mission. If there is anything I can do to secure his rescue, I will do it."

"I know there are several prison planets in the frontier," Zak replied. "My ships are constantly looking for weaknesses in their defenses. Perhaps as a symbol of our sincerity, we could capture one or two and release all the prisoners? There are many Predaxians held on those planets as well.  Emperor Zendo likes to lock up those who do not agree with them, including his own son."

Kono took another drink of the brandy. "That is a very good idea indeed, Consul. Are their any such planets near the Gallicean frontier? A prison planet there would likely hold many prisoners of war from the recent invasion," she said.

Zak thought for a moment. She replied, "The planet Localus has long been known for its prison facilities. I have heard three star cruisers are stationed there. That's a big investment since the war. The empire only has thirty or forty ships they can spare from regional duty. The Alliance has many more enemies than Greater Gallia. If more ships are diverted to the Gallicean frontier, other civilizations would be encouraged to invade. My fear is that if we attack, all the prisoners would be executed before the space battle could be won."

"Perhaps there is another way, Consul," Kono said. "How far is Localus from the Gallicean frontier?"

"Localus is the frontier, Ambassador," Zak replied. "There are at least half a million Predaxians on that planet using their minds to block Greater Gallia from seeing inside Alliance space. I believe Localus is two light-years from Nom-Kat-La."

"Consul, you have made my day," Kono smiled. "Please call me Kono, friend. I have a plan that will require four of your ships to travel to Nom-Kat-La as soon as possible. If we are lucky, we will free those prisoners, destroy the imperial fleet there and hopefully begin the rescue of the Palian civilization."

"Kono, you can call me Zak," she replied. "I don't know what your plan is, but I can't wait to find out. If it is okay with you, I'll join my fleet at Nom-Kat-La. I wouldn't miss this for anything."

"Absolutely, Zak," Kono answered. "It will likely take a few days to put plans in place and get approval from our friends on Gallia, Earth and Kalidus. I look forward to seeing you there. If you don't mind, my team will jump back to our headquarters from here. We didn't want to startle you by jumping into your office. That would have been rude. It is a much quicker way to travel though."

"I don't mind at all, Kono," Zak said. "Thanks again for coming today." As Zak stopped talking, the maklans glowed bright white and disappeared. "Wow, I wish I could do that!" she sighed. She tapped a contact on her desk and said, "Lucius, please get Captain Narka on the Parax for me."

The image of Vandamar Narka appeared on Zak's view screen. "Good day, Zak," he said. "What's going on down there? We read some odd energy signatures in your office a moment ago."

"Van, I just met with a group of maklans from No-Makla. They have a plan to wreak havoc on our glorious emperor. It sounds like fun. Please prepare the Narka to leave orbit later today and send a shuttle for me. Then, arrange for three other ships to meet us at Nom-Kat-La as soon as possible."

"No problem, Zak," Van replied. "There are at least eight of our ships within a day's travel from Nom-Kat-La. What's the plan anyway?"

"Honestly Van, I have no idea yet. The goal is to liberate the Localus prison planet. Do you have any idea how many Predaxian political prisoners are held there?" she asked.

"My helmsman used to be a guard there," Van replied. "When he left to join the invasion force, he said there were at least fifty thousand Predaxians held there."

"Hopefully, we'll have fifty thousand more rebels joining us real soon Van," Zak smiled. "Signal me when the shuttle is going to arrive. Tantalus out."

Zak walked over to the brandy and poured another full glass. She raised it up and said, "Here's to you, Pan. Our plans are starting to come true. I swear I won't rest until your father is deposed, the slave planets are freed and you are back in my arms again, my love." She drank the brandy and walked back to her desk. It was going to be a great day on Tantalus.

# CHAPTER 15

Darlene Brewster was meeting with Jon Lake and Aria Watson in the core team conference room on the Nightsky. The final reports from the planetary probes were complete and they were reviewing the results. It had been six hours since Dave and Charlie had jumped back to the twenty-first. The view port was open and Station 801 filled the view. The terminator was moving across the planet slowly as night was turning into a new day.

"Darlene," Aria said, "the reports on the three gas giants look very promising. This may be an opportunity to build our relationship with the Galliceans even more. All three have a massive Dar-Fa. Charlie told me that the Galliceans love those since they bring large amounts of usable materials up from the surface, and they are a lot of fun to fly through. As well, the densities and atmospheric components seem almost identical to Gallia itself."

"That's great news, Aria. We'll try to contact Fa-a-Di or his brother-in-law when we're finished here and give them the good news," Darlene replied. "What about the other earthlike planet?"

"Planet 4 is much drier than this world, Darlene," Jon said. "We will probably have to terraform some parts of the surface to provide adequate crop land to support a full colony. The amount and quality of ores is through the roof. It might make sense to have Planet 3 be the bread basket for the system and focus Planet 4 on mining, at least at the beginning."

"I suppose that will be up to the Governor when she arrives," Darlene replied. "Is the permanent portal operational yet?"

"Sadly no, Darlene," Jon answered. "We have two crews working on it now. We are expecting the cruiser Excalibur within the hour. She is bringing Engineer Dovid Dickens and his team. They have been appointed to manage the Portal Command in this system. Do we have a planet name yet? I keep confusing myself using Planet 3 or Station 801."

Darlene smiled, saying, "Yes, we do actually. I received the report from Darak's office an hour ago. Planet 3 is now officially Golden Dawn. Planet 4 is New Frontier. Engineer Dickens will manage the Golden Dawn Portal Command. It sounds nice, right?"

Jon said, "The names sound great, Darlene. Dovid's team will be able to get the thing going in a couple hours after they arrive. I've been talking to him and he has dealt with the issues we have many times. He did ask if we had a thousand rolls of duct tape, though." All three laughed.

"Darlene, I've seen the first images for the brochure on Golden Dawn and they're amazing. There are thousands of miles of pristine beaches; forests even more majestic than the one near the beacon; mountain ranges twice the height of those on Earth. Our team has located at least five hundred sites for the first settlements," Aria reported. "I've been talking with Governor Lawson. She is convinced that she can get half a million people from Day's End to move here right away. Darak has promised to recruit another million from Earth."

Darlene laughed, "We're doing all the work and Lyra is going to get the credit again! This is great news. Let's contact one of our Gallicean friends and offer them three more planets." Darlene touched a contact on her panel, and said, "Mindy, please get either Commissioner Fa-a-Di or Governor De-o-Nu for me, please."

"Aye-aye, Ambassador," replied Mindy Marshall, the communications officer on Nightsky.

"Darlene," Aria said, "before they call in, I wanted you to know that the new coffee system was installed on board four hours ago. I know that Dave and Charlie will be thrilled."

"Thanks Aria," Darlene said. "Did you try it yet?"

"It is fantastic," Aria said. She touched the contact on the panel, saying, "Mindy, could you have someone bring us three cappuccinos from the new coffee system?"

"Aye-aye, Colonel. By the way, I've tried it too, and the coffee is wonderful," Mindy replied.

After a minute, Mindy entered the conference room with a tray and three coffees, which she placed in the middle of the table. "Ambassador, Fa-a-Di is not available, but De-o-Nu should be calling any minute. I hope you enjoy the drinks," she said as she turned and left the room.

As they sipped the coffee, a tone sounded on the control panel. Darlene touched the contact, and the smiling beak of Governor De-o-Nu appeared on the large screen. "My dear sister, Darlene, it is a pleasure to see you again. Aria, you look beautiful as always." De-o-Nu laughed out loud. "Is that the pirate Jon Lake? I'm sorry that our only previous meeting was less than cordial."

"Governor, I will never forget that day," Jon began. "I thought I was an able pirate, but your fleet got the better of me. I owe you everything for capturing me, friend. That day marked the end of desperation for Far Sky. As you can see, I have turned a new leaf and am now captain of this noble vessel."

"You are welcome, Captain," De-o-Nu said. "When my brother, Dave Brewster calls for help, all of Greater Gallia will rush to the call. What can I do for you today, my friends?"

"De-o-Nu, I am certain that you recall the great treaty we signed with your brother-in-law," Darlene said.

"Of course I do, sister. That treaty led me to be governor of two worlds, which is the best job of my life," the Gallicean replied.

"Perhaps now you can petition Fa-a-Di for a new job," Darlene smiled. "As you know, we have been sent to find more planets suitable for human colonies. Today, we orbit a planet that will be the new colony, Golden Dawn, which is eight light-years from Far Sky."

"Congratulations to you and all humanity on another great discovery by Dave Brewster, Founder of a Thousand Worlds!" De-o-Nu shouted. "All Greater Gallia wishes you continued success."

"Thank you, brother. But the story gets better. This system also contains three gas giants, which we are pleased to offer to you," Darlene said.

De-o-Nu pulled a whisky bottle from his desk and filled a glass. "This calls for a drink." He swallowed half the whisky, and refilled the glass. "I am speechless, sister. The generosity of mankind knows no bounds. Will you be able to send me all the information you have on those planets?" the governor asked.

"Of course, brother," Darlene replied. "There is more to tell you now though. We have spotted Dar-Fa on all three planets." De-o-Nu was smiling broadly. "Dave looked at the preliminary data yesterday, and he asked me to let you know that he thought he saw evidence of Ka-la-a, whatever that is."

De-o-Nu was laughing and wiping moisture from his eyes. "Darlene, this is another miracle. Clearly, God is with the humans and Galliceans. I shall call Fa-a-Di immediately after we conclude and give him the good news. For your information, Ka-la-a are natural islands that form from ice crystals and flotsam in the clouds of gas. The existence of those structures on Gallia is what led to the evolution of my species. When Dave and Charlie flew over Jupiter with Fa-a-Di and me, we found Ka-la-a. Then we flew through the Dar-Fa there and were amazed."

"There is still more, brother," Darlene continued. "On Golden Dawn, we found proof of another peaceful maklan civilization thirty light-years from here. We plan to leave here tomorrow and make contact with them. We found a sophisticated warning beacon here that has been operational for four hundred million years. You can imagine how advanced they must be."

"This is unbelievable Darlene," De-o-Nu gasped. "My flagship, the Kong-Fa has recently been repaired and is in orbit here. If I could jump there later today, could my ship join yours on this journey? My society owes the greatest of debts to No-Makla. I would be happy to take maklans from here to join your expedition."

"That's what I was hoping for, brother. Ambassador Carakala Pakalanalan, the sister of their High Commissioner is looking for a ride. I told her you would be calling her later today. She is planning a contingent of five hundred maklans. We have two hundred here on Nightsky. If you bring her and three hundred others, we will be ready to go. We are hoping to have the Golden Dawn Portal Command operational within a few hours.

Engineer Dickens will alert you when the portal is operational. You can arrange a jump from Io Star Port here. Is that an acceptable plan, brother?" Darlene finished.

"On one condition, sister," De-o-Nu grinned, "before we leave Golden Dawn, I would like to offer the three of you rides over one of the gas giants."

"Dave and Charlie never stop talking about that, Darlene," Aria said.

"Brother, we accept your generous offer," Darlene said.

"This is a great day for all of us. I will see you after we jump. I'll have my crew set up a platform over the gas giant closest to your location. Thanks to all of you. Greater Gallia is in your debt. Jupiter out," the governor said as the signal ended.

Rather than being alone in his own home, Dave Brewster decided he would stay in Charlie Watson's mansion while they visited the twenty-first. After he and Charlie had returned from the coffee shop, Dave sat quietly in his room. He had been waiting to make this journey for a long time, but now he found himself missing the thirty-second and his life there. He tried watching television, but the news was depressing with nonstop coverage of the recession and continuing international strife. He thought about the story of the Kalideans arriving on Earth and ending man's preoccupation with self-destruction. That would not happen for almost four hundred years. Each person is born into a particular era and finds the events of their time to be totally normal. Having lived far in the future for a year, Dave knew the normal of the twenty-first was still primitive and violent.

Dave heard a knock on his door and went to open it. Standing there was Bea, the cute barista from Starbucks. Dave let her in and she sat on the couch, where he joined her. "Bea, this is an unexpected surprise," Dave said.

"Admiral, there are some things I want to talk to you about," she replied. "The Chief Engineer would kick me out of Temporal Command if he knew I was talking to you, but I can't ignore the elephant in the room."

"Bea, first of all, please call me Dave. Second, I don't want you to get in trouble. I feel like I'm kept in the dark on many things, so I don't mind not knowing," Dave said. "Darlene keeps a lot of secrets from me, for example. As an ambassador, she is privy to many things going on at the High Council for Humanity that I know nothing about."

"I'm sorry, but my mind is made up. The only way I can help with this mission is by using my secret weapon, which is what I want to tell you," she answered as she put her hand on top of his. "Dave, I am your granddaughter."

Dave was too confused to speak. He had seen Bea at the same Starbucks for many months, even before he met Charlie Watson. Neither Bill nor Cybil were married. While he and Charlie both thought she looked like Darlene, he never would imagine that she was his grandchild. "I'm sorry Bea, but I just don't understand. How could you be my granddaughter?"

"When the High Commissioner assigned me to this team, she hoped I would be a resource of last resort. If Charlie, Aria and the rest failed to convince Rob and Matt to jump forward with them, I am to confess that I am the daughter of Rob Watson and Cybil Brewster," she said. "The High Commissioner thinks this might be the one thing that can convince them to move."

Tears felt a lump in his throat as he thought this girl could really be Cybil's daughter. He put his arms around her and hugged her tightly. He laughed, "Charlie and I both thought you looked a lot like Darlene. Is this really true, Bea?"

"Yes, Grandpa, it's true," she whispered as she wiped tears from her own eyes. "You can't tell anyone about this, especially not Charlie, Aria or Darlene. You have to promise Grandpa. I'm not going to tell anyone about this unless it's the only way to convince my dad and uncle to come with us."

"I promise, sweetheart," Dave said. "Can you tell me more about yourself? I already heard the bombshell, so you're not revealing anything secret now."

"Okay, Grandpa, I can tell you some more," Bea started. "My mom and dad met while getting their doctorates in biomedical engineering at MIT. The few folks from the twenty-first tended to hang out together there. It was difficult to blend in with the people from my time since they looked so different and had completely different backgrounds. They got married one month after they both graduated in 3192. They immediately joined the DNA team with my uncles and Jake the maklan. The High Council built a special scientific campus in San Diego for the team. I think they had five hundred scientists working there full time. Now for the important stuff! I was born on May 31, 3195 in San Diego."

"Wow, that's incredible," Dave replied. "My little baby girl is a mother. Tell me more."

"I have two younger sisters who are still in college, Gracie and Darlene. When I graduated with my doctorate in biomedical engineering, I joined the team. I was twenty-four at the time. When the project was finished, High Commissioner Lyra Lawson asked me to join this team," she continued.

"Lyra is High Commissioner?" Dave said. "That's fantastic. That woman can do anything. Keep going, Bea."

"Apparently, Chief Engineer Muncie Morgan had sent teams into the future to see if all of the people from the twenty-first had the expected impact on our time. The results were less than they hoped for. Of the twenty or so jumps, twelve were similar to what had been seen when Rence and Aria had jumped before you came to my time. In the other eight, the DNA project was never completed. In those futures, the phrase 'Dave, Founder of a Thousand Worlds' had been replaced by 'Dave, the Great Explorer.' When more historical records were searched, they found in each of those eight cases, Rob and Matt Watson stayed in the twenty-first," Bea finished.

"That's why you are here, Bea," Dave replied. "In those alternative futures, Rob and Cybil never meet, and you and your sisters are never born. But I still don't understand. Here you are, sitting right next to me. Doesn't that prove that they do come with us since you were really born?"

"Time doesn't work that way. Until they actually jump in time, the future is still fluid. If they stay here, then the futures that include me will disappear. Even if they do jump, there are many more things that have to happen in order for me to exist in the future. I have to admit it does give me an incentive to get them to jump!" she laughed. "Seriously Grandpa, it's okay. I know that the spirit within me will be alive, but that person just won't be Bea Watson in those futures. There are advantages to being me though. Even though I look like a person from the twenty-first, I am from the thirty-second. When your grandparents are Admiral Dave Brewster, Ambassador Darlene Brewster, Commodore Charlie Watson and General Aria Watson, you get a lot of respect. Not to mention my aunt Elaine, who represents North America on the High Council."

"Bea, I can see why your records are sealed," Dave said. "If anyone knew what you know, it could very well change the future even more. Your secrets are safe with me, don't worry. We will all do our utmost tonight to convince Matt and Rob to jump with us without revealing your secret."

"Thanks, Grandpa," Bea smiled. "I feel so much better having that off my chest. I have been worried to death about when or how I would tell my dad. I am afraid if I tell them, the future will be altered immediately. If he thinks he must now marry my mom, it might sour their relationship. I know the mission is not about me, but in a way, it is."

Dave put his arm around her shoulders, saying, "Bea, it is all about you in my mind. I don't want to lose the chance of having you in my life either." He kissed her on the cheek. "I'm pretty sure we can convince them to jump. Charlie had Darlene and me jump to the Eiffel Tower to break the news to her. It's hard to argue that it's crazy when you've already jumped once. Frankly, I'm surprised they would put you in this position. I don't think it was fair to tell you to jump here to save your own life. I'd probably scream at Lyra for doing this, but she would have no idea what I'm talking about in 3187."

# CHAPTER 17

Darlene, Aria and Jon sat anxiously on the shuttle craft as it passed into the upper atmosphere of Planet 5 toward the platform that had been placed there by the crew of the Kong-Fa. They were wearing their pressure suits, but had not donned their helmets yet. The claustrophobic feeling of being trapped in the suit in a poisonous atmosphere was not to be rushed. Planet 5 had a thin ring like Neptune. The atmosphere was broken into rapidly moving bands of clouds and gas. The large Dar-Fa swirled like a massive hurricane in the southern hemisphere. Darlene thought about Dave's tale of flying through the Dar-Fa on Jupiter. They could now see the platform directly ahead of their ship. A Gallicean shuttle had already docked and six Galliceans stood there waiting for them. When the shuttle landed, the three put on their helmets and pressurized their suits. They would not breathe fresh air until they returned. The shuttle pilot joined them and checked the fittings and settings on their suits. When he was convinced they were ready, he donned his own suit. When he was ready, he opened the door of the shuttle and extended the short ramp. They walked out into Planet 5's atmosphere and walked over to the Galliceans. The shuttle door closed behind them.

De-o-Nu laughed, "Welcome, my friends! It is a beautiful day on this wonderful planet." He shook hands with all of them and introduced the others from his crew. No-ka-De and Nan-de-Bo had been with De-o-Nu during the showdown over Neptune. They had jumped to the other two ships attacking the maklan cities and dispatched the Predaxian spies there. Both had then fought at the battle of Nom-Kat-La and had been injured when the Kong-Fa had been badly damaged. They were back with their beloved Governor and had been honored to take Aria and

Jon with them on this preliminary exploration of the new planet. "Darlene, my crew has reviewed the reports you sent to me. This planet does look like an exceptional place for our people. The High Commissioner has asked me to accept your generous offer. In two days, three cruisers and two colony ships are due to arrive here to begin more extensive studies of this and the other two gas giants." As the three shuttle craft crew helped the humans into the harnesses on the governor and his lieutenants, De-o-Nu continued, "The ambassador from No-Makla asked if she and her team could join us. They should be jumping here very soon. She also contacted Jake and has invited his team to come as well."

Darlene Brewster was now firmly locked into the harness on the governor's chest. "Of course, brother, that is a wonderful idea. We will all be stuck in our star ships for the next seven days, so a little fresh air and exercise is a good thing." While she was speaking, two bright flashes occurred near the platform. The five hundred maklans appeared and began flying around the group. Two maklans flew up to Darlene.

"Darlene," Jake said, "please let me introduce you to Ambassador Carakala Pakalanalan from No-Makla."

"Welcome to Planet 5 in the Golden Dawn system, Ambassador," Darlene said. "It is an honor to have you join us today and on this great journey to Tak-Makla."

"Ambassador Brewster," she began, "The honor is ours. We have lost contact with all other maklan worlds since shortly after the Great Rebirth. The only one we know is Predax, and that is not a good thing. The opportunity to meet this highly advanced maklan civilization is fantastic."

De-o-Nu was fidgeting. "It's great that you are both so honored, but we are here to explore this great planet and have some fun. I recommend you two diplomats just enjoy the day." The shuttle crew told De-o-Nu everyone was ready to go. He turned to his lieutenants, saying, "No-ka-De and Nan-de-Bo, you have been given the honor to make the first flyover of this world due to your heroism at Nom-Kat-La. I am entrusting the lives of two great humans and I want you to show them a great time."

Nan-de-Bo laughed, "Governor, we thank you for this thrill. The air is very fresh and wonderful today. Let's hope the sighting of Ka-la-a is correct. We are ready when you are." He looked down at Jon in his harness. "Don't worry, Captain Lake, I take my own children around in one of these and I've only dropped them a couple of times!" He shrieked with laughter as the group dived off the edge of the platform into the swirling gas.

Darlene could feel De-o-Nu being buffeting by the air current. It felt as though she were on a county fair roller coaster. Jake was flying next to her. She could see the external air pressure rising on her heads-up display as they dived deeper and deeper into the atmosphere. She could see Nan-de-Bo and Jon flying corkscrew turns around them. The cloud of maklans made incredible acrobatic maneuvers even as they dived downward. Far below, Darlene could see a massive cloud stretching to the horizon in all directions. The cloud was varying shades of blue and green, twisting and swirling into strange shapes. She remembered looking up at clouds as a little girl and imaging what creatures they looked like.

"Brother, what do you call that cloud below us?" Darlene asked as they rapidly approached the tops.

"Sister, we call that a good time! Hang on!" he replied as they hit the clouds. De-o-Nu was bouncing back and forth and

Darlene held onto the harness as tightly as she could. Dark rain drops splashed over them both and ice crystals were forming on her suit. Within a few seconds, they exited from the bottom of the cloud and the governor extended his wings and leveled off. The rain was still falling around them, but the air was very calm here. "Darlene, we are getting close to the pressure level where we would expect to see a Ka-la-a. I'm heading to the spot where Dave thought he saw one. The amount of rain and ice is a very good sign."

They flew onward. The rest of the group rejoined them and seemed to be enjoying the ride. No-ka-De said, "Governor, I think I can see the Ka-la-a ahead. Aria and I will check it out." Being somewhat smaller than De-o-Nu, No-ka-De could fly faster and they rushed ahead. The Ka-la-a appeared to be very large, with its edge stretching for miles. Soon, the Galliceans had all landed and folded their wings. The surface was covered with moss, similar to what Dave had encountered on Jupiter. The sheer size of the floating island was more than any Gallicean had ever seen. There were no large lumbering herbivores as there had been on Jupiter. Many different types of insects scurried about on the surface. There were small jellyfish-like animals eating the moss. It seemed that the insects fed off the dead herbivores and each other. No-ka-De picked up samples from the plant life while Nan-de-Bo collected sample animals. These would be checked by the scientists on the Kong-Fa to make sure they were not poisonous.

They walked along for some time, in awe of the size of this icy island floating on the heavier gases below. After twenty minutes or so, they came upon the bleached skeleton of a large bird-like creature. At first, De-o-Nu thought it might be Gallicean. Upon inspection, the creature was clearly native to this world and probably not sentient. Its brain cavity was quite small, although it had large jaws full of sharp teeth. "I think we need to leave the sample boxes here for now," De-o-Nu said, drawing the blaster from his holster. "If there are more creatures like this, we need to be ready to fight." The other two Galliceans drew their weapons as well.

"Governor," Ambassador Pakalanalan said, "there is no need to leave the boxes here. I'll have two of my team jump them directly to your lab now." At her word, two maklans flew over and touched the boxes. After a bright flash, they and the two boxes were gone. Within a minute, the two maklans returned.

"Thank you Cara," De-o-Nu replied. "Yet another example of Gallicean-maklan cooperation. Let us continue and be vigilant." They walked for another twenty minutes and came upon the rotting carcass of another large animal. It seemed similar to the tiny jellyfish that floated in the gas or their larger cousins who fed on the moss, except its canopy was thirty feet across and very thin. "What an odd beast this is." he said.

"It's incredible, Governor," Aria replied. "Do you think that beast floats around the planet?"

"Yes, Aria. We used to have creatures similar to this on some of the colony planets. I don't think any were this big though," he replied.

Jake glowed red and said, "Look up above us now!" The group looked up and saw a herd of the giant jellyfish floating several hundred feet above them. Their long tentacles stretched fifty or more feet below them as they tried to catch food floating in the streams of gas. There were hundreds of animals in the herd, all being carried along in the wind, their large, almost transparent canopies billowing like the sails on a ship. "I suggest we exercise caution here. Those tentacles are likely to be very poisonous."

"I concur, Jake," the governor replied. "This is indeed a miraculous planet, my friends. It will take our scientists years to assess the life on this planet and make recommendations to the High Council. If the other two planets are anything like this, we have been given another gift of incomparable value."

In the far distance, they could now see wings flapping against the current. De-o-Nu wondered if others from his crew were joining them. As the wings approached, they could see this was a pack of ten creatures like the skeleton they had seen. The birds were very large, with wings spanning twenty feet. They were bright red and their screaming filled the air. The beasts were closing in on herd of jellyfish that were almost straight overhead. The jellyfish started moving around frantically, while the birds flew among them, trying to separate one from the group. One bird swooped down on a jellyfish with its beak wide open. A second jellyfish came to the rescue by wrapping its tentacles around the attacking bird. The bird screamed in pain and abandoned its chase.

The remaining birds had managed to separate one jellyfish from the group and they attacked it viciously, tearing out big chunks of the canopy. After a minute, its canopy failed and it fell toward the Ka-la-a. It crashed to the ice two hundred feet away from them. All the birds landed next to their victim and began to feed on it. The bird that had been injured by the jellyfish came down to join the feast. After a couple bites, the other birds forced it to leave. It looked up and noticed the Gallicean group and began walking toward them. All three Galliceans pointed their blasters at the bird. It stopped twenty feet from them and looked at them quizzically, moving its head from side to side and blinking rapidly.

It stood as tall as it could and stretched its wings to their full fifteen feet and baring its teeth to show its dominance. Some of the other birds had noticed the activity and were watching; however they had no intention of leaving their meal to see these other creatures. As if on cue, De-o-Nu and his lieutenants extended their wings to their full forty to fifty feet. A cloud of maklans flew around the bird which was startled by both the lights and the giant size of these other birds. It folding its wings and dropped its head to the ground. Then it turned and slinked back to the rest of its pack.

"Well, I think we've had about enough of this," De-o-Nu said. "I still want to see the Dar-Fa on this planet. I will have our crews wear armor and weapons as we investigate this wild place. I have never seen such large predators on a gas giant before. It is said that we evolved from bird like creatures long ago. Perhaps these creatures will do the same some day." The group flew away from the Ka-la-a and the feeding frenzy as quickly as they could, while keeping a watchful eye behind them in case they were followed.

It took an hour of flying to reach the vicinity of the Dar-Fa, which loomed across the full horizon. Unlike the Red Spot on Jupiter, this Dar-Fa was dark blue. They were miles from the edge and the winds were pushing the group all about. On the governor's command, they flew upward toward the top of the atmosphere. It was simpler to penetrate the Dar-Fa from above. Darlene looked at her heads-up display. The oxygen level read thirty-five percent. The external air pressure was very low and the Galliceans had grown even larger in the thin air. She was thinking about how wild this system was, with the birds here and the giant wolves on Golden Dawn. Her lab assistant days were long over, she thought.

They dove into the top of the Dar-Fa. All the Galliceans went tumbling due to the high swirling winds. The humans hung onto their harnesses. The maklans were everywhere, with their small bodies blown about with abandon. After a minute, they broke into the eye of the Dar-Fa. Other than the color change, it was exactly like Dave had told her. The wall she could see was moving incredibly fast. Most of the edge was far over the horizon in all the other directions. While the air here was very calm, she could see the tops of countless tornadoes below them. "Aria," she said, "it's just like Dave and Charlie told us. Isn't this unbelievable?"

"Darlene, I could never have imagined that such a place existed," she replied. "I am so happy to be here with you and Jon."

"Don't forget Jake," the maklan said as he flew between them. "I remember these things from textbooks when I was in school. When our people first jumped to the Earth system, we explored all the planets, so there are detailed books and videos on them from almost a billion Earth years ago. Of course, when we found life on Jupiter, we left there to allow it to flourish naturally."

"Enough chit-chat," De-o-Nu said. "You can talk all the way from Golden Dawn to Tak-Makla. My comrades and I have picked a tornado to fly into. This will be the roughest part of the trip, so hold on tightly." The group dived into the open mouth of the tornado. The upwelling of air and material was like a sandblast. They were spinning and tumbling in the violent windstorm around them. The Galliceans had folded their wings tightly against their backs to keep them from being ripped off by the savage gusts. They fell for several minutes and the winds became stronger and the noise level was growing. Darlene saw that the external pressure was high enough to crush a human not in a pressure suit. When he had enough, De-o-Nu signaled the others and they dived into the wall of the tornado.

They were tumbling uncontrollably now. Darlene could feel her harness loosening and she struggled to hold on. The wind noise was overpowering and she moved violently about De-o-Nu's body. Now she could feel his arms around her, holding her tightly. She relaxed a little. The noise suddenly stopped completely and the wind calmed. They were now in the middle of the Dar-Fa. Around them were thousands of tornados swirling about. Heavy black rain drops and small hail pelted them. "I thought you were going to lose me for a minute, brother," she said.

"Sister, I panicked completely when I felt the harness starting to slip. A human free falling in a Dar-Fa would be a very bad thing. Since you are my sister, I would give my life to protect you," he replied. "Jake, you need to get over here and help me with Darlene's harness. I almost lost her back there."

Jake and two other maklan immediately landed on De-o-Nu and began working on the torn harness. "Brother, this harness is heavily damaged," Jake reported. "I think it would be best if I jump Darlene back to the platform from here. I'll have others check Aria and Jon's harnesses just to be safe."

"Jake, I'd like to stay here for a little while longer," Darlene said. "This is an amazing experience and I can't go just yet. Perhaps before we get to the edge again, you can jump me out. Is that a deal?"

"Okay, Darlene, I'll wait. I'm going to stay right here though and keep an eye on you," he replied.

The group flew onward in the black rain and hail. They swooped around some of the tornadoes, in awe of nature's majesty. De-o-Nu thought about his great ancestor, De-no-Ko, who discovered that the materials rising in the tornadoes could be used to build massive floating islands. He thought about the coming voyage to meet what would likely be the most advanced society in the galaxy. The cold rain on his back was refreshing. He longed to fly here the rest of his life. As they approached the edge of the Dar-Fa, Jake glowed bright white, and Darlene and Jake were gone.

# CHAPTER 18

Dave walked into the family room of Charlie's house. Rob Watson had just arrived with his brother Matt, Matt's wife, Elaine, and their two children, Sophie and Brian. Charlie was busy hugging his grandchildren when Dave joined the group.

"Hi Rob," Dave said, "It's good to see you again." He turned to Matt and continued, "You must be Matt, and this is your lovely wife, Elaine. My name is Dave Brewster. Your dad has told me all about you."

"It's good to meet you, Dave," Matt said. "Dad says you two work together. Are you helping him with his books?"

"In a way, I suppose I am," Dave answered. "I try to find new and interesting things for Charlie to write about. Wouldn't you agree, Charlie?"

"Working with Dave has been very educational," Charlie replied. "Even though I traveled a lot when I was in business, my pal Dave has certainly introduced me to lots of new things. Let's all sit down while we wait for the rest of the party."

As they sat, Matt said, "I thought this was just going to be a family dinner, Dad?"

"It is, son, but there are a few folks I feel are part of my family now, like Dave here," Charlie said as he walked to the door. "I'll have Kally bring us a few bottles of wine and some refreshments for the kids too. You all keep chatting while I'm gone." Charlie left the room.

"Dave, Dad told us the story about how you two met in the Starbucks. Don't you find that coincidence amazing?" Rob asked.

"Not long ago, I would have agreed with you, Rob. Now, like your Dad, I don't believe in coincidences," Dave said. "I like to think there is a course in time that pulls us all along. We may not expect the things that happen, but they were surely meant to be."

"You've been hanging around him too long, Dave," Rob laughed. "There are so many people and things on Earth. It only makes sense that random chance plays a big role."

"I know how you feel, Rob. I can only go by my own life experience. To me, things always seem to move along a trajectory. Maybe Charlie and I are nuts, but you can see how things have worked out very well for him. And I have no complaints," Dave answered.

Charlie reentered the room followed by Rence, Muncie, Alana, Bea and Kally. Kally went to the bar, opened bottles and poured red wine for all. He also prepared two Shirley Temples for the children, with extra maraschino cherries, just the way they liked them. Rence, Muncie, and Alana sat on a couch across the coffee table from Matt and Rob. Bea pulled up a side chair next to Dave and joined them.

Rob and Matt looked very concerned. They both worked for Rence and Muncie, but had no idea how Charlie knew them. Rob had met Bea at the coffee shop when he moved here, but had no idea why the barista was here. "Dad, what's going on here?" Rob asked.

"It's kind of a long story, Rob," he replied. Kally was passing out the drinks. "Give us a minute to relax and then we can get to the more serious business."

"Let's have a toast!" Charlie said as he stood up. "To our family. And that means everyone here." They all sipped the wine.

"I'm confused, Dad," Matt said. "You know Muncie and Rence?"

"Yes, son, they both have worked with me for quite a while," Charlie smiled. "I honestly had no idea they had hired you two. I've been out of town for a month with Dave and we didn't have cell coverage where we were."

"Dad, they have coverage almost everywhere now," Matt stated. "Where could you be where there was no reception, Mount Everest?"

Charlie turned to Dave and said, "Dave, do you want to tell them where you've been since we left here a month ago? I think now is the time to jump into it, so to speak."

Dave thought for a minute. He knew that if things did not go well, the short term memories of Charlie's family would be cleansed of the discussions, so there was little danger. He said, "Most recently, we have been in orbit over a new planet twenty-eight light-years from Earth. Oh, and the year was 3187."

"That's absurd, guys," Rob laughed. "My dad the author and his friend the accountant flying through space a thousand years in the future. You're kidding, right?"

"What Admiral Brewster said is factually correct," Muncie said.

"I'm a bit surprised by you two," Charlie said to his sons. "You've taken jobs from Muncie and Rence and never noticed how different they look? Didn't that raise any suspicions in your minds at all?"

"Dad, we're not racists," Rob said. "We don't judge people by the way they look. They just look like two brothers."

"Rob, we are not related at all," Muncie began. "In our time, society has blended and very few racial differences remain. I was born in Cedar Rapids, Iowa. Rence here comes from Pennsylvania. Alana, my fiancé, was born in Florida. We were all raised in the early 3100s. I met Rence at MIT when we were getting our doctorates in temporal engineering. I met Alana when she joined the Temporal Command a couple of years ago."

Bea had moved and was playing with Sophie and Brian on the floor. Charlie kept a box of toys and games in the room for just such an occasion.

"Okay, let's say we believe you, which we don't, what about Bea here?" Rob asked. "I just met her at the Starbucks a couple weeks ago. She doesn't look like you guys. Is she from this time?"

"Bea is from the future too," Dave said. "Unfortunately, her file is restricted by the High Commissioner. Suffice it to say she has some influential friends and family, and her part of this mission is secret for now." Dave winked at his granddaughter, who smiled back.

"The barista is a spy?" Elaine asked.

"No, I'm no spy," Bea said. "I think they picked me because I love coffee and kids. I suppose the High Commissioner knew that Muncie would need a baby-sitter on the team. Elaine, Sophie and Brian are so cute. Sophie looks just like you."

"I'm beginning to understand why Aria had such a hard time with these two," Charlie laughed. "They are a tough couple of nuts to crack."

"Aria never told me anything about the future, Dad," Matt said. "What are you talking about?"

"Oh, yes she did, Son. You have to imagine how advanced a society eleven centuries in the future would be. They have the technology to selectively erase memories in the event of temporal anomalies," Charlie replied.

Alana withdrew a small electronic device from her purse and set it on the coffee table. "The Commodore is correct. This device can be used to erase certain memories when someone sees or learns something unintended about the future. I have trained for two years to be able to use it well. At the end of the evening, Muncie will decide if we let you keep the memories of this discussion or not. I will carry out his decision."

"Dad, I've seen Aria a couple times in the last month. I still remember every detail of her stays. I even remember Dave's wife, Darlene was with her the last time," Matt said. "I remember all the great food Aria cooked for us. I just assumed she was a chef somewhere."

"Matt and Rob, everything you are hearing is the truth," Dave began. "When Darlene and Aria came the last time, their purpose was to recruit you two as well as my own son, Bill. He also believed they were crazy until his sister, Cybil jumped there with me. I know this all sounds ludicrous, but we are here on important business tonight. In the future, Rence here is on a team that will perfect human DNA. In 3187, most people live to be four or five hundred years old. Medicine and science have made miracles over the centuries since today. After the DNA team completes it work, disease will be virtually eliminated and people will live as long as a thousand years."

"That's impressive for a science fiction story, Dave," Rob said. "But why tell us this? What does it have to do with Matt, Elaine and me?"

"Rob, you and your brother, as well as both of my children are on that team," Dave said. "Without both of you, there is a strong likelihood that the project will fail. We need you to help us."

"Dave, we are both engineers, but not doctors," Matt said. "I don't think our qualifications could be better than people in the future. It doesn't make sense."

"Admiral Brewster is correct again," Muncie started. "Before we found Dave Brewster in our timeline, we felt that our medicine had advanced greatly. Once Dave became aware of his potential in the future, we started to find evidence of the DNA project. We took a great risk and went further into the future and learned about this team."

"You have to understand why I jumped to the future," Dave said. "Society in the future had stagnated. People became so intellectual that society lost its spark, that certain something entrepreneurs have to take a risk and find new solutions to problems people didn't even know they had. In my case, the Temporal Command found that Charlie and I could kick-start humanity to reach out into space and establish new worlds and meet new civilizations. It didn't make sense to me either when I was an unemployed accountant. Since I've been there, we have started to rebuild two abandoned colonies and have located two new worlds for mankind to explore and inhabit."

"You did that in a month?" Rob asked.

"Time travel has unique benefits, Rob," Dave continued. "Charlie and I have been living in the future for a year now. When we jumped back, we came here one month after we left. I had the same brain-freeze on this. When we are in a specific time, days go by one by one. Humans do not know how to deal with jumping in time. It upsets our internal clocks."

"I'm still expecting someone to come out of the closet and say we're on Candid Camera," Elaine said. "You can't seriously believe we would accept this. Matt, let's go before the kids get scared." She stood to leave. Kally moved to block the door. Alana began pressing keys on the device on the table.

"Elaine, let's hear them out," Rob said. "We haven't eaten yet and Charlie is my dad. I know it sounds crazy, but all of these people keep telling us the same story. It's just one evening after all. Tomorrow, we'll all be laughing about this, okay?" Elaine shrugged her shoulders and sat down again.

"Dave, shall I signal the Io Star Port now?" Rence asked.

"Yes, Rence," the admiral replied. He turned to Matt and Rob and said, "When my son Bill had a hard time believing us, we took a jump into the future with him. Seeing is believing, after all. There is a time portal in the next room. We will now jump to 3187 and the star port orbiting Jupiter's moon Io. Rence has arranged us to arrive there at dinner time. We'll be dining in the main dining hall with the scientists who work there. I recommend that Bea and Alana stay here with Sophie and Brian.

We'll go, eat and come back. We have planned the return jump to come back in thirty minutes Earth time, although we can stay there as long as you like. Okay?"

After a few moments of consideration, they walked to the portal room. Muncie went to the control panel and started pressing buttons. Other than the people and control panel, the room was completely empty. After a few moments, a small black dot appeared on the wall opposite the door. The dot grew quickly to a seven foot black circle. There was no sound from the portal, just shimmery perfect blackness.

"I'll go through with Elaine," Dave said. "Charlie can go through with Matt, and Rence can take Rob. This is a very unique experience. We will be temporarily leaving space-time and entering a wormhole. Inside, you won't be able to hear anything. We'll just step in and wait for a white circle to form in front of us. When that circle becomes stable, we'll step through and be there. I've done it plenty of times, so there is nothing to worry about."

"Admiral, Io reports ready," Muncie said. "You are cleared to enter."

"Thanks, Muncie," Dave replied. "Elaine, please hold my hand. Everything is going to be okay. If you all go with us now, you'll be back here before Sophie and Brian know you are gone. After you are back here, you three need to decide what you want. If you don't want that future, Alana will erase certain memories, especially this trip, and you can go back to your everyday lives. I guarantee that." She had taken his hand, and Dave could feel her trembling.

As they stepped toward the blackness, Elaine turned her head to look at her husband. "I love you, Matt," she said. She turned her head and stepped through the event horizon with Dave Brewster.  She could feel her body being stretched between the absolute blackness and the room she was leaving behind. She felt the warm air in the room on her leg that had not yet passed through the event horizon. Inside the wormhole, she felt nothing except Dave Brewster's hand in hers.  She looked at him and he smiled back. Dave squeezed her hand and pointed in front of them.  Elaine could see a small white speck in front of them. Within a few seconds, it had grown to a seven foot circle, gleaming into the blackness. Dave squeezed her hand again and they stepped into the whiteness. Again, she could feel herself stretched between the black and white. After a second, they were in another room with a short, blue man manning the control panel. His large unblinking black eyes were dazzling.

"Admiral Brewster, how good to meet you," the blue man said. "You must be Commodore's Watson's daughter-in-law," he said as he extended his hand to her. "My name is Conomus. I am a scientist here at the Io Star Port. As you will learn, I am from the Kalidean community of planets. Please move over there." As they stepped aside, Charlie and Matt appeared out of the circle.  They were quickly followed by Rence and Rob.

"We're all here. Let's eat!" Dave said as he led them out the door.

Dave and his group entered the main dining hall. The large room had a glass dividing wall across the center. They could see huge bird-like creatures on the other side of the glass. They appeared to be enjoying their food and conversations. Several tables were set against the wall. They saw humans and Kalideans sitting on this side talking to the bird-men on the other side. Dave led them through the buffet line, where they were given servings of pot roast, steamed vegetables and baked potatoes. Everything smelled so good and the jump had activated everyone's appetites. Dave had them sit at a large table against the glass wall.

"Dave, what is this place and what are those things on the other side of the glass? Are they dangerous?" Elaine asked.

"Not at all, Elaine," Dave replied. "Those are Galliceans. They originated on a gas giant planet called Gallia. The Greater Gallia community of worlds has thousands of planets."

Charlie jumped in, saying "Dave's wife negotiated a planet sharing treaty with them a year ago. We gave them Jupiter and Saturn to colonize. This station was greatly expanded so that we could all work together. Come to think of it, Dave, we need to start visiting their systems to see how many Earth-like planets they can offer to us."

"I can't believe I'm seeing this with my own eyes," Rob said. "This is so unbelievable, Dad. Are we going crazy, or is this real?"

"Oh, it's real all right," said a pretty young woman who approached the table with a man. She bent to kiss Dave on the cheek. "Hi, I'm Cybil Brewster, Dave's daughter. This is my baby brother Bill. My dad asked us to meet you folks and give you our perspective having moved to this time recently." Cybil and Bill walked around the group introducing themselves. She returned to Dave, and said, "Dad, Bill and I will get some dinner and be right back." They walked toward the buffet.

A large bird-man sat at the table across from them and put his hand against the glass. Dave put his hand against the glass near the Gallicean. Charlie quickly pulled three communicator earpieces and offered them to the twenty-firsters. They could hear loud squawking from the alien, but when they inserted the devices, it resolved into perfect English. "Admiral Brewster, it is an honor to have you and Commodore Watson with us tonight. I thought you were examining another planet for colonization."

"Doctor No-o-Ka, it is great to see you again," Dave said. "Please let me introduce you. These are Charlie's sons, Matt and Rob, and Matt's wife, Elaine."

"It is a distinct pleasure to meet you all," the doctor smiled. "Dave and Charlie are great friends of Greater Gallia, and I look forward to working with each of you as well." He focused on Dave, saying, "I had heard that Colonel Watson had trouble recruiting them to our time. I'm glad you are having more success. I have been briefed by High Commissioner Daniels. He told me how important these people are to your future history." No-o-Ka put his two hands on the glass in front of Rob and Matt, and said, "Welcome to our time. There is much work ahead and plenty of adventure. I hope you have long and healthy lives."

Rob and Matt put their hands on the glass. Rob said, "Thank you Doctor. I have to admit this is almost too much for me to comprehend. We only arrived a few minutes ago."

No-o-Ka laughed out loud and said, "Well, I suspect you never imagined to see someone like me! I believe the largest flying creatures in your time were eagles or albatrosses." No-o-Ka stretched out his wings to their full forty feet. "I'm a little larger than that!"

"Doctor, I was hoping to see the governor while we are here. Do you know where he is?" Dave asked.

"That's odd. I thought you would have known. Darlene contacted him and invited him to join your expedition to the new maklan world. The Kong-Fa jumped to Station 801 only one hour ago," No-o-Ka replied. "He took several Gallicean diplomats and three hundred maklans."

"That is wonderful news, friend," Dave said. "That is just like Darlene. Poor Dave is the last one to know anything. Thank you, No-o-Ka and I hope you enjoy your dinner."

"Farewell, my friends," he replied as he left the table and joined a large table of Galliceans in the center of their portion of the hall.

Cybil and Bill rejoined the group and told Rob, Elaine and Matt their story of choosing the thirty-second. It had been simple for Cybil. Her job was not fulfilling, but she needed the money to complete her graduate degree. When her parents told her about the future and what she could accomplish, she eagerly agreed. Bill was not so certain. Dave had to convince him they were not crazy and to at least try a jump and see what happened. Bill had been instrumental in deciphering the maklan language to avoid an intergalactic crisis over Neptune.

"Okay, I'll bite. What are maklans and what does Neptune have to do with anything?" Matt asked, clearly confused again.

 A crystalline spider floated through the room on its silky wings and landed on the table. "I can help there," it said. "My name is Pamalakara Benomafolays, but you can call me Pam if you like. I am a maklan."

"Hi Pam," Bill said. "I haven't seen you since the translation job.  What brings you here?"

"My brother Jake told me what Charlie and Dave were trying to do, so I offered to help," Pam said as she glowed light blue. "My species has been in the galaxy for billions of your years. One billion years ago, we learned that our sun was going to become a nova in two hundred thousand years, which would kill all life.  We took all that time to develop portals like the one you took to get here. Ultimately, all maklans relocated to one of five hundred star systems that seemed compatible with our needs. Ten million relocated to this star system. Over time, we lived on all but the two innermost planets. We abandoned Earth, Jupiter and Saturn when we discovered nascent life there. Our society believes we must not interfere with any planet's natural progression. We colonized Mars for half a billion years. Since it is a small planet, the atmosphere was slowly dissipating. After years of research, we moved to Neptune, which we call No-Makla. A small portion of our population settled on Nok-Makla, which you call Uranus.  How am I doing, Admiral?"

"Perfect, Pam, but it's your history so you should know it best," Dave replied.

"Not long ago, when Jupiter and Saturn were given to the Galliceans, they came to explore our worlds. They misinterpreted our communication as an attempt to attack them. At the time, many Gallicean leaders were under the mind control of another maklan species, the Predaxians. They turned that misinterpretation into an opportunity to destroy our planets and pull vital defenses off the Predaxian frontier. Fortunately for us, my brother Jake teamed up with Admiral Brewster and the great Gallicean general, Fa-a-Di to turn the battle and save our worlds."

"I can see your eyes glazing over," Cybil said. "I've been here almost a year, and I'm still learning this stuff. Just let it wash over you and accept it. You'll learn, don't worry, right Billy?"

"That's for sure, Sis," he said. "I've been here half a year and I'm just beginning to understand how things work. It took me a long time to figure out the toilets, so you can imagine how complicated everything is!" Everyone laughed.

"But is it worth it to leave everything you know behind?" Elaine asked.

"For me, absolutely," Bill replied. "I've done things here that really matter. I am now studying to be part of the team to fix human DNA. I know that's why you are all here too. It's amazing here and they treat those from the twenty-first very well. They know why we are here and that they need us. Back in the twenty-first, I was on a team of engineers trying to enable amputees to move prosthetic limbs with their minds. I was very happy knowing my work could help many unfortunate people. After two years, the company canceled the project. That was two years of my life down the drain. That doesn't happen here."

"I fully agree," Cybil joined in. "Not only am I going to be part of that DNA team, I have been able to study and travel." She turned to Dave, saying, "I was going to ask you something Dad. No-o-Ka has offered to fly me around Jupiter. I remember you and Charlie talking nonstop about your trip around Jupiter. Can I go?"

"Of course, sweetheart, I couldn't deny anyone that pleasure. Just hang on tight," Dave responded.

Rob had been staring at Cybil, watching her eyes light up as she spoke about the future. "Dad," he said, "do you think I can stay overnight and go flying with Cybil? If that's okay with you, Cybil?"

She smiled broadly at Rob, saying, "Sure, the more the merrier. I'll contact the doctor and arrange another flyer." She winked at him.

"It's okay with me too," Charlie said. "So, kids, what do you think about the future?"

"I'm in, Dad," Rob said. "This place is amazing. I was so certain that you two were crazy, but now, I'd be the crazy one to go back to 2012. What about you, Matt?"

"I need to discuss this with Elaine. This has big implications on our whole family. We have to think about her parents, my mom and our children," Matt said.

"That's completely fair, son," Charlie said. "You two should go sit at another table and talk about it. But before you go, let me make it a bit easier for you. The High Council has been very generous with those of us from the twenty-first century. The number of people authorized to jump through time is very small.

The risk of altering the flow of time and events is too great to have people popping around history. Since your contribution to these people is so great, you will get that same reward. Dave and I are allowed to jump back to our time once a year for vacation. I've been doing this longer than Dave, and what I have done is jump back to the time one week after I left. That way, while I'm getting my job done here, the people in the twenty-first hardly notice I was gone. Since time is not an issue, I could jump to the twenty-first and spend months in that time and then jump back just after I left, keeping my vacation."

Rence said, "We don't really allow that though. We prefer to have the return jump at least one day after the jump out. In that way, the risk of creating ripples or eddies in time is eliminated. We've also found that if people are in a different time for more than a week or two, they can forget what they were doing when they left. But Charlie is right, the Temporal Command will be generous with you. You can imagine the benefit to our society if your team helps us double human life spans."

"That's why I need to keep working," Dave said. "As people live longer, the population will keep rising. All those people need places to live and jobs to do. That's where I come in. Think of me as the ultimate real estate broker." Everyone laughed.

"Matt honey," Elaine said. "I don't need to have a private chat. If you can do all of those wonderful things here, that would be amazing. As a mother, if you can help our children live longer and healthier lives, I'd be crazy not to come here. We will need to visit our mothers for a couple weeks a year." She turned to Rence, saying, "Was there anything in your history about me? I don't need to extend lives or found worlds, but I'd like to know I have a place in the thirty-second."

"Elaine, I'm sorry but I never looked for you," Rence said. "That doesn't mean there was nothing. The DNA team was the only project I was sent to examine."

Dave smiled, and said, "Don't worry, Elaine. I have top secret information that you will be prominent in this time too. Unfortunately, I can't say anything else."

Elaine smiled. "Thank you, Dave. And thank you Charlie for giving us this incredible opportunity. When can we bring Sophie and Brian over?"

Rence said, "If you like, I can ask Bea and Alana to jump over with them right now."

"That would be perfect, Rence. They are going to love it here," Elaine smiled as she wiped a tear from her face.

Dave stood up, saying, "Charlie, it's been a great day. If you don't mind, I'm going to jump back to the Nightsky now. Stay here a while with your kids. Just be sure to get back to the ship before we leave for Tak-Makla." Dave hugged his kids and thanked them for their part tonight.

"Okay, boss," Charlie said. "I'll hang out with them here until the grandbabies arrive. I'd like to put them to bed before I jump back to the ship."

Rence said, "Dave, now that this job is complete, I'll have Alana jump to your ship with Charlie. She might as well start on her new assignment now. She seemed very excited to be working with you and Aria."

"Check with Muncie first," Dave cautioned. "I don't want to ruin any quality time or vacation they had planned before she starts this new life."

"Aye-aye, Admiral," Rence replied.

Dave hugged and kissed Cybil and Bill again, and walked slowly toward the door, and his jump home.

The Nightsky and Kong-Fa left orbit over Golden Dawn on schedule. Charlie Watson and Alana Albright jumped from Io one hour before the scheduled departure. As the ships left the star system, Captain Jon Lake instructed his helmsmen, Lieutenant Ali Bai to accelerate the ship to maximum. It would take six days to reach Tak-Makla at this speed. Commander Frake Landres, the ship's weapons officer reported that all systems were on line and the deflectors for space debris were at full force.

Jon reminisced about his days on the first ship named Nightsky. It had been a captured Kalidean research vessel that he had converted into a pirate cruiser. His home world of Far Sky had been abandoned by the High Council for Humanity, and his people had to resort to piracy to obtain critical medicines and other goods to stay alive. The day of their capture by Governor De-o-Nu and his fleet seemed very recent, but here he was now a captain of a new star cruiser flying wing to wing with De-o-Nu's flagship. Ali and Frake had been the best men on that crew. He was honored that they continued to work with him. Sitting to his right was Admiral Brewster, who was not looking well at all.

"Dave, I know those space jumps are hard on you," Jon said. "Perhaps you should rest some more in your cabin."

"Thanks, Jon, but I slept all night and that didn't help," he replied. "It will pass in a little while. I think I just need some coffee."

As if on cue, Lieutenant Lia Lawson and Darlene Brewster entered the bridge. Lia had a tray of coffees from the new coffee system. She handed a cafe latte to Dave with a quick smile. Darlene sat next to her husband.

"Lia, what are you doing here?" Dave asked, "I thought you'd be working with your mother on Golden Dawn."

"Admiral, I talked to her about this," Lia began. "Everyone in the known galaxy understands how important this trip is. The Beings on Tak-Makla are incredibly advanced. The opportunity to meet the maklans who built Station 801 is too great to be missed." She sat at her station next to Ali. "Besides, without any colonists for several months, Mom doesn't need a secretary of state yet."

"That's true," Dave replied. "I'm sure Jon agrees with me that you are the best communications officer in the fleet. We are grateful to have you with us." She smiled broadly at him and turned to her console. Dave took a long drink of the hot coffee and felt better. "Darlene, please remind me to thank Aria again for getting this new coffee system online. The quality is outstanding!"

"Yes, Dave, I'll remind you," she said. "By the way, I have to meet with De-o-Nu and Cara in a few minutes. We are roughing out the framework for treaties with Tak-Makla. Did you know that De-o-Nu has been promoted to Ambassador for this trip?"

"No, I did not. He is perfect for the job though," Dave responded, as he continued sipping on his coffee. "I have the feeling that De-o-Nu will be High Commissioner for Greater Gallia one day. The only mistake I know he made was to almost drop you in the Dar-Fa on Planet 5."

"Oh, Dave," she laughed, "it was just an accident. He is my brother after all."

"Mine too," Dave said. "I'm just glad I wasn't there to see that. I probably would have fainted or had a heart attack."

A tone sounded in Darlene's earpiece. "Dave, I just got word that De-o-Nu is ready for my call. I'll see you later." She rose and left the bridge.

Lia said, "Captain, I've receiving a distress call from the Kalidean ship Manila. They were on course to intercept us in twelve hours to deliver their ambassador for our journey. They report they are under attack."

"Lia, advise Kong-Fa of the situation. Ali, change course to intercept Manila as fast as we can," Jon shouted.

"Aye-aye, Captain," Ali barked. "The new course is laid in. At maximum speed, we should intercept in two hours."

"Captain, I have De-o-Nu for you," Lia said.

"Put him on screen, Lia," he replied.

"Captain, Ambassador De-o-Nu here," the Gallicean began. "My ship is faster than yours. We can intercept Manila in forty minutes. The maklans on my ship have jumped to yours for safety. We will advise when we reach the scene."

"Aye-aye, Ambassador," Jon said. "Win the day for us. Nightsky out." The screen went blank. The Kong-Fa raced ahead of Nightsky. Within two minutes, it was out of scanner range.

"Frake, please bring all defensive and weapon systems up to full strength," Jon shouted. "There may be more of those attackers out here."

"Aye-aye, Jon," Frake replied. "We are armed and ready at your command."

"Jon, I have Captain Theodus of the Manila. I'm putting him on screen." Lia said.

The captain appeared on the screen. There had been some damage to the bridge area. All the crew members were wearing pressure suits. "Captain Lake," Theodus said, "I've spoken with De-o-Nu and he advises that he is forty minutes out, and that your ship will take up to two hours to arrive. The attackers took us by surprise. Approximately ten star fighters of unknown origin suddenly appeared into our vicinity. Before we could take evasive action or raise our defenses, they had attacked without warning. We were hit by five laser volleys. Fortunately, our defenses are now up and they have not been able to penetrate them. We are following a zigzag course in your direction."

"Captain, were you able to fight back?" Dave asked.

"No, Admiral, our ship has no offensive weaponry," Theodus replied. "We are a scientific research vessel, except for the time your captain turned this ship into a pirate vessel."

"Are the assailants following you, Captain?" Jon questioned.

"Yes, so far they are with us. I am only at fifty percent speed now. I thought it more important to get a cruiser here than to let these attackers slink back to their base," Theodus replied. "I have been in contact with our nearest ships, but they are far away. We have another issue, gentlemen. Several of my people have been injured, including Ambassador Petrodus. Our sick bay is not adequate to help them. Could some of your maklans jump here and take them to your ship?"

"My team will arrive momentarily," Jake said as he landed on the arm of Dave's chair. He glowed bright white and disappeared. Jon and Dave could see Jake and several others appear on the bridge of the Manila. "Theodus, take us to your injured," Jake said.

The bridge view screen split to two images as De-o-Nu's face appeared on the right side. "I am entering sensor range of the Manila now," he said. "I can read the Manila and ten small craft approaching us. My weapons officer indicates the fighters came from Planet 4 of the star system closest to their current location."

"Aye-aye, Ambassador," Jon said. "We will arrive at Manila in one hour. De-o-Nu, you Galliceans need to share your engine technology with us. You get to have all the fun."

The Gallicean laughed. "Jon, you humans are so demanding. We get one toy and you can't be happy until you get the same one too! For your information, my plan is to disable as many of the small craft as possible. We need to find out who we are dealing with. I'm not aware of any civilizations in this area. Kong-Fa will be in weapons range in ten minutes. May God be with us. Kong-Fa out."

"Captain," Lia said, "Doctor Marron advises that twelve Kalideans have jumped to sick bay with our maklans. He is performing triage and has put all medical personnel on highest alert. He advises that none of the injuries appear to be life-threatening."

"Thank you Lia," Jon said, "finally, we have some good news. Please provide all the information we have to the Fleet Admiral's office."

# CHAPTER 21

Unbeknownst to Jon and Dave, twenty maklans, including Jake did not return to the Nightsky. After the injured were evacuated from Manila, they jumped to the bridge of the Kong-Fa. They shared their plan with De-o-Nu who could only laugh and smile at maklan ingenuity.

Kong-Fa roared into the battle zone at full speed, with its defenses at maximum. By the time the small fighters recognized what was happening; the Gallicean cruiser flew just below the Manila and directly in their path. Jake jumped to the cockpit of the first fighter. Without the pilot noticing, he sampled the atmosphere and communicated its contents with other maklans on the Kong-Fa. All the fighters fired their blasters at the Kong-Fa, but their weak energy was absorbed into the defenses of the large ship, strengthening it. The maklans told the crew the atmospheric contents so they could fill cells in their brig with the mixture. All the maklans jumped to the fighters that were rolling and spinning to avoid the massive Gallicean star cruiser. With two maklans in each cockpit, they disabled the engines of the fighters, and then jumped the dazed pilots to the holding cell.

De-o-Nu was happy the plan worked so well, but in his heart he wanted the thrill of battle coursing in his blood. All his crew could do now was use tractor beams to pull the dead fighters into their hangar bay. The Nightsky arrived as the last fighter disappeared inside the massive ship. The atmosphere needed by the attackers was almost identical to Earth, so the ten pilots were transferred to Nightsky. The combination of an Earth-like atmosphere with the Gallicean air supply was explosive, so all agreed transferring was the best course. De-o-Nu donned a pressure suit and jumped over to the Nightsky to see the prisoners with Dave and Jon. He had to crawl to get through the low opening of the brig door and remain on his knees. The eleven foot ceilings were painfully low for the twenty foot tall Gallicean.

"Dave," De-o-Nu said, "I feel more like a prisoner than these Beings. I have to be in this suit and walk about on my knees."

"I'm sorry, brother," Dave said. "While we can work together and share solar systems, our size difference does make for some issues. You are mighty big for a Gallicean though!"

"It's a curse, you know," he replied. "I have to stoop when I'm around my brother-in-law. He gets self-conscious that he is so much shorter than me. Where are my prisoners?"

At they spoke, a Kalidean entered the brig with an assistant. He was in a wheelchair. "Good day, I am Ambassador Petrodus," he said. "I am very grateful that your team was able to evacuate me. Please don't worry about the chair. I am told this is only temporary. I should be well when we arrive at Tak-Makla."

"Ambassador, I am De-o-Nu, and I am honored to be an ambassador for Greater Gallia on this mission. Please pardon me if I don't get up," he said. They all laughed.

"De-o-Nu, it is an honor to meet you," Petrodus said. "I have enjoyed working with your brother-in-law for many years. He speaks of you constantly."

"All good things, I'm certain," De-o-Nu said.

"Ambassador, I am Dave Brewster and this is our ship's captain, Jon Lake," Dave said as he extended his hand.

"Thanks to both of you for the ride to Tak-Makla," Petrodus responded, shaking everyone's hands. "I agree with De-o-Nu that we would like to meet our attackers."

Jon touched a panel on the wall. A large section of the wall became transparent, showing the interior of the holding cell. The ten pilots looked remarkably human. They had the same body shape, except the tallest was barely four feet. Their skin was very light brown, and their narrow blue eyes sat below a large forehead. They were wearing their flight suits, which were light blue with ribbons and insignia on the chests and shoulders. The transparency was one way, so the prisoners could not see who was watching them. Jon and the others could hear them talking and arguing, but their language was not known by the translation database. The shortest Being was three and one-half feet tall. It had long white hair and acted as the leader.

Jon said, "Gentlemen, we have been sending their conversation to the language team on Io since they arrived. We found some written documents on the fighters that we are sending now. We are intercepting communications from Planet 4 in the closest system using the same language. We are funneling that to Io as well. Conomus, the lead scientist on the team, has reported many similarities in this language to older Earth languages and even some maklan root words. Hopefully, we will get some understanding soon."

"Well, I would say that Conomus is the best man for the job," Petrodus said, "but since he is my son, that might prejudice my opinion."

"While I love the idea of visiting their home world and blasting away, I know we must focus on our trip to Tak-Makla," De-o-Nu said.

"Two of our star cruisers have jumped to Golden Dawn in the last hour," Petrodus replied. "They should arrive here in an hour. I recommend we turn the prisoners and captured ships over to them. They will also be able to repair the Manila and provide more aid to our wounded. Within thirty minutes of their arrival, we should be able to resume our course to Tak-Makla."

"That should only delay our trip by six hours, Admiral," Jon said to Dave. "It seems like a perfect solution. I will ask Lia to communicate with the two captains on the details of the transfer and all the information we have on the language translation efforts. I am very happy this potential tragedy has turned out so well."

"If we're finished, could some of your maklans jump me back to the Kong-Fa?" De-o-Nu cried. "My back and knees are killing me. I'm going to need to work out in our gym to get the knots out of my muscles."

As they left the room, the Beings inside the cell continued to argue among themselves. Commander Kleeg shook her long white hair in contempt for the failure of the glorious mission. "Where did you fools learn to shoot? Only half our team hit the target ship. If you had done your jobs, we would have disabled and captured it."

Ensign Fraal sighed, "Commander, clearly those aliens are much more advanced that we are. We didn't have a chance. Those glass spiders that appeared in our fighters and magically flew us to these ships frightened me half to death."

"That's because you are a coward, Fraal," Kleeg answered. "We never should have allowed males into our military. You don't have the killer instinct like we do. I remember the stories about those creatures. They attempted to invade our planet a million revolutions ago. Our most glorious emperor, Naark the First, was able to push them back into the hell of space they came from, freeing Nanda from their oppression."

Ensign Zoolk laughed, "Kleeg, you are a fool. Those stories from a million revolutions ago are just legends. Countless generations have come and gone since them. I remember my schoolbooks too. Those spiders would not pop in and out of places. They were also much larger and bright red. Imagine that, Nanda taken over by some little glassy spiders, what a joke!" Everyone except Kleeg laughed.

Kleeg was blushing with anger. She said, "Zoolk, you will pay for your insubordination. Those invaders from the past used mind control to get other races to attack us. When we get back to Nanda, I will personally hold you for court-martial. Don't think your aunt, the general will be able to protect you then."

Ensign Zoolk smiled, "Commander, maybe you are right. At this moment, I wish I was back on Nanda with my family. We are in the hands of highly advanced Beings who took us from our ships magically and locked us in this room. Our weapons couldn't help us then, and we have no weapons now. No one on Nanda will risk their lives or incarceration to attack again. These Beings may leave us here to starve to death. We have no control of our futures."

Kleeg slumped to the floor and put her hands over her eyes. After a moment, she looked up at Zoolk and said, "Well, if they are that advanced, I don't think they'll starve us. They could have blasted us out of space easily. We'll just have to wait and see. I hope they have good food and drink, though."

# CHAPTER 22

The Free Predax cruiser Parax settled into a high orbit over Nom-Kat-La. Captain Vandamar Narka sent a message to Zakamar Vondee in her quarters to let her know they had arrived. She rushed up to the bridge and sat in the command chair next to Vandamar. Through the view screen they could see the three other Free Predax cruisers Vandamar had ordered to join them. The sensor array told them there were twenty Gallicean battle cruisers, seven Kalidean and eight Earth star cruisers also in orbit. Both Predaxians smiled broadly at each other.

"Zak, this is like a dream come true," Van said. "When you convinced me to join your rebellion, I was certain that we would all be either killed or sent to a prison planet to be worked to death."

"Van, that could still happen," she replied. "But this time we will have the resources to inflict some major damage on the Emperor and his minions before they get to us. Please see if you can contact the maklan ambassador."

"Tak, my communications officer has already sent her a message. We have been in communication with Nom-Kat-La Central Command since we've been in their sensor range," he answered. "I'm certain we will be hearing from them soon."

A tone sounded on the communications officer's panel. He touched a contact and the image of Ambassador Konomalocus Nolobitamore appeared on the screen.

"Zak, I am very happy that you and your fleet have arrived," Kono said.

"Greetings Ambassador," Zak replied. "I must admit that Captain Narka had a difficult time keeping the number of our ships at four. Every ship in the Free Predax Forces demanded to be part of this action."

"That's wonderful," the ambassador said. "I think it is crucial to keep the rest of your fleet in Alliance territory. We hope their presence will keep more Predaxian assets away from this area. If you don't mind, I would like to jump to your bridge now, Captain. I will bring another maklan along with Earth and Kalidean captains. Many Galliceans wanted to join us, but the atmosphere and size of your ship won't work for them."

"You have my permission, Ambassador," Van said. "We have a ready room to the side of the bridge. We can all meet there if you like. At Consul Vondee's request, we have brought along several cases of Predaxian brandy for toasting and gifts for our visitors."

A bright flash of white light filled the bridge. After it subsided, Kono and her entourage were standing in front of Zak and Van. They stood and greeted their guests. Van led them to the large ready room off the bridge. As everyone took seats, Van opened several bottles of brandy, filled and offered them to his guests. He took his seat next to Zak. Across the table sat Kono, Captain Carl Cartwright, Captain Donimus Zakar and Kono's assistant, Belanomara Narakamara.

"Thank you for your hospitality," Kono began. "We would like to fill you in regarding the next steps in the operation. As I mentioned on Tantalus, we still have some reservations about the truth of your rebellion. For that reason, we would like your approval to house twenty maklans on each of your ships. They will monitor communications to and from your ships. If there are any problems, they will jump back to the other ships and we will determine what the next steps should be."

"Ambassador, we feel that is a waste of time, but if it cements our relationship, you have our approval," Zak said.

"Wonderful. Now my assistant will jump back to Nom-Kat-La and arrange the teams for your ships," Kono replied. The other maklan glowed bright white and was gone. "The maklans will have another purpose. If we all engage in battle, and any of your ships are badly damaged, they will be able to jump your crews to other ships. I can't imagine what horrors would await them if the emperor's forces captured them."

"Thank you, Ambassador," Van said. "I believe they would execute us immediately for treason without a trial. If your teams save even one life, I will be forever in your debt."

"I think we can be more casual for this meeting," the ambassador said. "Everyone can call me Kono, and the captains are Carl and Don."

"And we are Zak and Van," the consul replied.

"Perfect. My assistant has just notified me that the first team of maklans has already jumped onto this ship," Kono continued. "For those who do not know, we can communicate among ourselves telepathically. With that crew here, we can continue without worry. I will let Carl and Don provide the details of the operation."

"Thank you, Kono," Carl started. "There are now one million maklans on Nom-Kat-La. This operation, code-named Dar-Fa, will commence on the order of Field Marshal Je-e-Bo, who is on Nom-Kat-La.  When the order is given, five hundred thousand maklans will use their minds to push back the mental blockade from the frontier in this area, focusing on the prison planet of Localus.  We have thirty-five ships in orbit. With your four, we have thirty-nine. If the maklans are successful pushing back their blockade of our sensors, and if there are less than a dozen Predaxian war ships in the immediate vicinity, another three hundred thousand maklans will jump to Localus from Nom-Kat-La. Their goal will be to isolate the Palian guards to keep them from harming the prisoners. Once the guards are separated, they will find and quarantine the Predaxians on Localus so they can no longer control the minds of the Palians. Your turn, Don," Carl finished.

"Thank you.  If all of these steps are successful, we will launch all of our ships at top speed to intercept the war ships in orbit. There will be four hundred maklans on each ship. As we approach those ships, half of the maklans will jump to the Predaxian ships. They will attempt to break the mind control of the crew. We hope that the Palian crews will then decide not to fight. If they fail, we will attack. We should have more than three of our ships to each of theirs. Any casualties we take should be limited. As Predaxian ships are disabled, our maklans will jump as many Palians out as they can. Any Predaxians found will be left on board," Don explained.

Kono said, "When the battle subsides, we will release all of the prisoners and evacuate them and their Palian guards to the ships in the fleet. The Predaxian prisoners will be locked into the prison and held by a crew of one hundred thousand maklans until a solution can be found to house them safely. That's it, what do you think?"

"It sounds amazing," Van smiled. "I have another six ships in the vicinity. I will ask them to keep any other Predaxian vessels far from the area."

"Very good, Captain," Kono said. "That was one reason we have so many ships. If other Predaxians try to stop us, we will have overwhelming resources."

"When will we begin, Kono," Zak said.

"Zak, as you know, I believe your intentions are honest, but there are those who are still not convinced. The operation has already begun," Kono replied. "When my assistant advised me that the first team was on this ship, she also signaled that the maklan team had begun to push back the Predaxian mental blockade. I will now jump these captains to their ships and we will advise when we learn how the effort is working. Zak and Van, it was great to see you, and we all look forward to our success at Localus." Everyone stood and shook hands.

"Captain Cartwright and Captain Zakar," Van began, "it has been a pleasure to meet you both. My crew and I will see you again this day on the field of battle. May God have mercy on our souls."

The two captains put their hands on Kono, who glowed bright white, and then the three were gone.

"Zak," Van said. "These folks don't mess around. You are welcome to sit with me on the bridge. I'll signal the other ships and sound battle stations."

"It would be an honor to share the bridge with you, Van," she replied. "Today is the day of our destiny. We either defeat the emperor's force or die trying. God willing, Pan will be among those rescued today." The two hugged and exited the ready room.

# CHAPTER 23

The mental blockade was proving difficult to break. The team was seeing spots of clarity, but the overall picture was faint. Kono added an extra hundred thousand maklans to the team and slowly the sensors began to read activity near Localus. Only three Palian cruisers were in orbit. Two other ships were headed toward the system, but were still an hour away at top speed. Je-e-Bo advised Kono that her troops were authorized to jump immediately to Localus.

The maklan invaders were divided into three hundred teams of one thousand each. As more sensor information became available, they could see the structure of the prison and the location of guards and prisoners. The surface of Nom-Kat-La was bright with flashes of light as the teams jumped one by one to their assigned spots.

Warden Kogala was frantically trying to determine what was happening. The Predaxian governor on Localus, Valamar Zendo, advised him that their blockade was down but she did not know why. Kogala ordered his men to gather the prisoners together in case he received the order to execute them. That had been ten minutes ago and none of his guards had confirmed they were in position. Kogala had sent a request for enforcements to Palus High Command, but no signal had returned. Valamar rushed into his office.

"Warden," she began, "I'm afraid we have been invaded. Thousands of maklans are appearing all over the planet."

"Maklans," he shouted, "you mean like that little guy we turned over to you? I told you we should have killed him when we had the chance."

"Relax Kogala, that particular maklan is under our control," she replied. "We believe these have come from Nom-Kat-La, as our defensive mental shields are completely down in that direction. Have you given the order to execute the prisoners?"

"I am no fool, Governor Zendo," Kogala said. "I did so more than ten minutes ago. None of my guards have responded yet. I fear these maklans may have captured them. No doubt those filthy Galliceans are behind this. If your leaders weren't so incompetent and your military so traitorous, we would have won that planet months ago."

"Watch your words, Palian," she screamed. "My uncle the emperor will hear of your insolence."

A group of forty maklans and Fa-a-Di flashed into the room. Fa-a-Di laughed out loud and said, "It's a good day to die, bird-man," and fired the blaster in his left hand, striking the warden in the chest, causing him to fall to the ground. "Where is his Predaxian controller?" he asked.

The maklans had surrounded Valamar. The maklan commander shouted, "Stun this one too, General!" He shot the Predaxian with the same blaster and she crumpled to the floor. "Fa-a-Di, this maklan has very strong mental abilities. She was likely controlling the warden and several others here," the commander answered.

Fa-a-Di laughed again. "I am very happy to be with you today, my little friends. Can you tell me the status of the rest of our teams?" He rifled through the cabinets in the office and smiled broadly when he found some bottles of Predaxian brandy. "Do you think you'll be able to jump these back to our ship? I'd open one now and drink it if the atmosphere wouldn't kill me."

"General, all teams report success. The guards have been quarantined far from the Predaxians. We are gathering the prisoners into a meeting hall two hundred feet below us," the maklan replied.

Fa-a-Di touched a contact on his sleeve. "Je-e-Bo, you old dog, we have won the day. Localus is secure. You may send in the invasion fleet! Localus out," he said.

The maklans injected a drug into the Predaxian to keep her unconscious. Warden Kogala was coming to. "What is going on here?" he asked.

Fa-a-Di lifted the much smaller Palian off the ground and set him in his chair. "Warden Kogala, I am General Fa-a-Di of Greater Gallia and you are my prisoner. My friends and I have released Localus from Predaxian mental control. How do you feel?"

"Mental control, what do you mean?" he asked. "We have a peace treaty with Predax, but there are none in our region. I thought Greater Gallia was our ally. Why did you attack us?"

Fa-a-Di pointed to the Predaxian on the floor. "Dear Kogala, your entire civilization has been under Predaxian control for many years. Here was your master. We have found almost half a million of these beasts on this planet. Under their control, the Palian fleet has attacked Greater Gallia twice. We are getting a count of the number of political prisoners and prisoners of war you have here."

The maklan commander reported, "General, the prisoner of war count is eighteen humans, two hundred Galliceans and fifty Kalideans. There are also four thousand Palian and forty-five thousand Predaxians political prisoners."

"That's impossible," Kogala whimpered. "This prison is only for Palian felons, not other life-forms or political prisoners. I don't believe you."

Fa-a-Di laughed, "I'm not surprised my friend. Your mind has been under direct mental control. We are on our way to meet with the prisoners now. Please come with us and see for yourself. The Predaxians could not control every Palian mind on this planet.  You can hear the truth from your own guards." He turned to the commander and said, "You'd better find a secure location for that Predaxian. I think she is big trouble. Kogala, do you know this creature's name?"

"General, my brain tells me I've never seen her before. Somehow when I look at her, the name Valamar Zendo comes into my mind. It doesn't make any sense to me," Kogala replied.

"Ah, so she's related to their emperor. That explains why her mental power is so strong," Fa-a-Di replied. "Let's go see the prisoners." Ten maklans flashed out with the Predaxian. The rest followed the warden and general out of the room.

The fleet battle cruiser Texas led the fleet out of orbit and toward Localus. Fleet Admiral Arrin Adamsen transferred his flag to the Texas and he sat in the command chair next to Captain Cartwright on the bridge. Carl shouted orders to his staff as they closed quickly on the border with the Predaxian Alliance.

"All defensive and weapon systems are online and at your command, Captain," shouted Donna Daniels, the Chief Weapons Officer. "We are still reading three Alliance cruisers near target and two more heading this way. Long range scanners show five Alliance cruisers may be on the way, but they are at least a day out. "

"Thanks, Donna," Carl replied. "Sylvia, please advise the fleet and tell the maklans to prepare for their jumps. We should be in range in ten minutes."

"Aye-aye, Captain," Sylvia Smithson, the Chief Communications Officer said. "We have an incoming message from General Fa-a-Di, sir."

"Put it on our screen," Carl replied.

The image of the general filled the screen. He was standing in a group of Galliceans. "Captain Cartwright, we have rescued the prisoners. As you can see, I am in the section of the prison reserved for the Galliceans, so I have taken off that horrible pressure suit. Warden Kogala has been meeting with his guards and a large group of Palian political prisoners whom we have freed.  I can tell you he was shocked to find out he had been an unwitting dupe for the Predaxian horde. We have had to confine loyal Predaxians in cells deep within the planet. It seems their mind control powers cannot penetrate thousand miles of iron and rock."

"That is excellent news general," Carl replied. "What can you tell us about human prisoners of war?"

"We have released eighteen prisoners whom the maklans will jump to the recovery ships when they arrive," Fa-a-Di said. "I will be joining Captain Fa-Ne-Jo on the cruiser No-De-Ka when it arrives. Could you please forward a few messages for me, Carl?"

"Of course, Fa-a-Di, please continue. For your information, we are only five minutes from your position now."

"Please let their families know that Captain Lauren London, Commander Wally Washington, and Mitch Nolobitamore were here at one time, but have been moved elsewhere. Also let Consul Vondee know that Pan Zendo was never here, but the Predaxian political prisoners are desperate to join her rebellion," Fa-a-Di said. "I have questioned Warden Kogala about the moved prisoners. All he knows is that they were moved into Predaxian space on the direct order from the Emperor. It's been a great day here, but there is always bad news to report. Localus out."

"Captain, our maklans have jumped to the Alliance cruiser just ahead," Donna said. "They are reporting that a mutiny by the crew began before they jumped."

"I can't say I'm surprised," Carl replied. "If I ordered the crew of this ship to attack forty star cruisers, I suspect they'd take me out too."

"Tell the maklans to expose the Predaxians," Carl replied. "Once the Palians recognize they have been under Predaxian control, the fighting should stop. If possible, have the maklans jump the remaining Predaxians to that holding cell deep inside Localus."

"Aye-aye, Captain," Donna confirmed. "One of the Alliance cruisers is headed away from the planet, shall we pursue?"

"Negative. Contact the Free Predax ships and have them do it. Make certain they have plenty of maklans on board," Carl said. "Where is the third ship?"

The Alliance ship Zarka had managed to slip undetected behind the forward-rushing fleet from Nom-Kat-La. The Zarka was the flagship of Governor Valamar Zendo. She had convinced her uncle to provide enough agents to control the mind of each Palian on board. She was paranoid that Predax would lose control over the Palian system of planets, leaving the path open to a direct attack on the home world. Zarka energized her weapons and settled behind the invaders to pick her targets.

"Captain, the Gallicean cruiser ahead has minimal shielding on her aft," Dek the Zarka weapons officer shouted.

"Fire all weapons, Dek!" Captain Zen shouted.

Blasts rocked the Gallicean cruiser No-De-Ka. The ship twisted and shuddered under the barrage. Captain Fa-Ne-Jo signaled to abandon ship just as Fa-a-Di was jumped onto the bridge with his maklan team. Escape modules littered the sky over Localus. A second blast smashed into the bridge, opening a huge tear in the ship's hull. Without a second to spare, the maklans jumped the bridge crew onto the star cruiser No-Be-No which had changed course with ten other ships to attack the Alliance cruiser.

Fa-a-Di stumbled as he walked on the bridge of the No-Be-No. Blood dripped from wounds on his head and upper torso. He wiped blood from his eyes and relieved the captain of command, almost collapsing into the command chair. "Communications officer, open a channel to those bastards," he shouted.

"Com-link open, General," he replied.

"Palian and Predaxian fools, there can be no mercy for vile creatures like you," Fa-a-Di shouted. "Weapons officer, have all available ships fire at will."

All eleven cruisers fired at once. The first volley destroyed the Zarka's defensive shields. The second round of blasts smashed the ship like a bottle in a vacuum. The final barrage blew the ship into thousands of bit of metal. Bodies and debris floated in a cloud where the ship had been.

Fa-a-Di slumped down in the seat. He turned to the captain, saying, "Je-e-Ka, I must apologize for taking your place."

"General, there is no need for that," Je-e-Ka replied. "I have studied your life since I was a young girl. My grandfather, Je-e-Bo, told me many tales about your exploits during the First Predaxian War. It is an honor to have you command my humble ship."

"I don't understand why those Palians chose to die for their Predaxian overlords," Fa-a-Di said. "They could have run or surrendered. One ship facing forty is not survivable, even for the greatest general like your grandfather. What a waste of life!"

Kondimakaleys Manadeles, the lead maklan on Fa-a-Di's team interrupted, "General, if I may tell you, we discovered the ship had one maklan for each Palian. The two hundred Palians on board had no hope for survival unless their masters gave up."

"Now I have the blood of two hundred innocents on my hands," Fa-a-Di said with his head down. "The Predaxians are a murderous parasite on our galaxy. God willing, we will win the day and stop their heinous crimes."

"General, if I may interrupt you again," Kondi said. "You have suffered a number of internal and external injuries. You need to be taken to sick bay immediately."

"But what of the battle, Kondi?" he asked, the blood flowing more heavily from his head wounds.

"The battle for today is won, General," she replied, but he did not respond. Kondi floated up and landed on Fa-a-Di's chest. The general was unconscious. She glowed bright white and both jumped to sick bay.

# CHAPTER 25

Dave Brewster was reviewing the latest reports on the odd Beings that attacked Ambassador Petrodus's ship. There had been little progress over the last two days on deciphering their language. Three Kalidean star cruisers had arrived at the scene of the encounter to repair the Manila and assess the situation. After Manila had been repaired, one of the cruisers escorted her back to Kalidean space. Dave sipped his coffee as he flipped the pages. The remaining cruisers took high orbits over Planet 4 in the nearby system from which the fighters had come. Without landing on the planet or deciphering the language, there was little else they could do.

Charlie Watson entered the ready room with a bottle of Gallicean whisky and two glasses. He opened the bottle and sniffed the booze. His head snapped back. He poured two glasses and took a seat with Dave. "Hey Dave, this is on orders from Ambassador De-o-Nu. He wants us to contact him," Charlie said.

Dave pressed a contact on his control panel and said, "Lia, please get De-o-Nu for us and put it in here."

After a moment, the image of De-o-Nu appeared on their view screen. He had a glass of whisky in front of him as well. He looked very somber. "Brothers, I am happy you called. I have much news from the Alliance frontier, and not all is good."

Dave looked at Charlie and then back to the screen, saying, "Please tell us, brother."

"My brother-in-law has been badly injured during the attack on Localus," De-o-Nu said. He raised his glass toward the screen. "I have been told that he will recover, but I would like to offer a toast to the greatest general in Greater Gallia's history."

Dave and Charlie raised their glasses. "To Fa-a-Di, our brother and dear friend," Dave said. All three drank. "What happened, brother?"

"The battle for the planet had already been won. A single Alliance star cruiser chose to sneak behind the fleet and attack one of our ships. One ship attacking forty was a clear desire for death. Unfortunately the ship they chose to attack was the one that Fa-a-Di had moved his flag to," De-o-Nu said. He poured himself another glass. "There were twenty Gallicean cruisers in that battle. The likelihood they would pick that one ship was very small. On that day, the course of God's Will ran against my brother-in-law and that ship. One hundred other Galliceans died in the attack, along with forty maklans."

"This is truly a terrible tragedy. The doctors have said that Fa-a-Di will recover though," Charlie said.

"Yes, brother, but he has been evacuated to Gallia in order to get the very best medical attention. My wife is totally distraught. She is on one of my cruisers headed from Jupiter to the home world now. She will arrive there tomorrow," De-o-Nu said. "Brothers, I am a soldier. I should have been with him fighting for my civilization. I feel so helpless being this far away. I have petitioned the Chiefs of Staff to go to the front, but they have denied my request."

"We are very sorry about all of this, brother," Dave said. "Any one of us would have gladly taken Fa-a-Di's place if we could. What do we do now?"

"We sit back, drink a little whisky, cry a little, and then get on with our mission," De-o-Nu said. "Fa-a-Di always told me a soldier must follow orders. Although it pains me greatly, I will follow mine."

"We will pray for Fa-a-Di and all of the others who are fighting this battle in our place," Charlie said. "In a few days, we will arrive at Tak-Makla, and hopefully we will find something that can help us in the crusade against Predaxian tyranny."

"One maklan against another," De-o-Nu sighed. "It reminds me of the textbooks I read as a child about life on Gallia before we moved into space. One tribe would try to kill others just for the shape of their wings or their accents. That same insanity has now followed us into space."

"Our human past is littered with examples of the same thing, friend. Let us hope the maklans are an exception, brother," Dave said. "After all, their society is billions of years old, and was forced to separate into five hundred different societies long ago."

"I know Dave," De-o-Nu said. "It is just the tears in my wife's eyes and my many wonderful memories of the general have caused me to be very melancholy today." De-o-Nu forced a smile onto his face, "Tomorrow will be a better day. I'll drink to that," he said, drinking the last of his glass of whisky. "I do have more news.  Fa-a-Di sent a message while on Localus, after they had liberated the prisoners of war."

"Please continue, brother," Dave said.

"Apparently, Captain London, Commander Washington, and the maklan Mitch Nolobitamore had been prisoners on Localus," De-o-Nu said. "According to the warden, they were moved elsewhere deep in Predaxian space weeks ago. I know that Commodore Washington, Captain Lake and Jake would like to know this."

"We will let them know, De-o-Nu," Dave replied. "It's good to know they were alive not long ago. What was it that Lauren always used to say?"

"While there is life, there is always hope," Charlie answered. "I heard her say that several times."

"The captain is a smart woman," De-o-Nu said. "Let us hope fate allows us to find them alive and return them to their loved ones. As a soldier, I know we must be prepared to deal with death and injury any time we wear our uniform. We all hope when the battle ends we will be able to resume normal lives. It is my sincere hope that ending Predaxian tyranny will usher in many millennia of peace for us all. Brothers, I have to admit my mood is greatly improved after talking to you both. I've been drinking since I heard the news about Fa-a-Di, so I must assume our friendship made the difference. Thank you for that."

"It is our pleasure, brother," Charlie said.

"One more thing I almost forgot, my brothers," De-o-Nu said. "I sent one of my cruisers to help the Kalideans learn more about those crazy little humanoids that attacked us two days ago. This is amazing. The Kalideans are focusing on Planet 4 where the Beings live. My ship has sent probes and teams to the other worlds. We believe we have found evidence of ancient maklan ruins on three of them."

"This is unbelievable," Dave said. "I should tell Jake about this."

"Don't bother, Dave," De-o-Nu said. "When I told Ambassador Cara about this, she started jumping teams from our ships to those planets. She told me we will still be in their jump range for two more days."

"Great. When you said maklan, did you mean like our friends on No-Makla?" Charlie asked.

"That is the interesting part, brothers," De-o-Nu smiled broadly. "Planet 5 is a Mars-like planet. Those ruins appear to be designed for Predaxian maklans. Planet 3 is more Earth-like. Those structures are similar to what you found on Golden Dawn. Planet 6 is more like Nom-Kat-La, a large solid planet with a dense atmosphere. The ruins there seem to have been built by a new species unlike anything we have seen. Do you remember those creatures grazing on the Ka-la-a on Jupiter?"

"Of course, brother, they were as big as trucks," Dave said. "You don't mean the maklans were that big?"

"Yes, that's exactly what I mean, Dave," De-o-Nu said. "We have found fossils of exoskeletons where the body was five feet across, and the leg span was twenty feet. That's as big as me!"

"This is incredible news, brother," Dave replied. "If I discount the Tak-Makla and giant maklans, it still appears that Predax penetrated the galaxy more than we could have imagined. That is very dangerous."

"Let us hope that Predax hasn't already contaminated Tak-Makla. If they could turn such an advanced species into slave masters, all of our worlds are in desperate trouble. Fortunately, I don't believe that could be the case. With their technology, they would have already taken over our home worlds. I'll keep you updated on what we learn. Kong-Fa out!" De-o-Nu said as the screen went dark.

# CHAPTER 26

Emperor Nokalez Zendo was insane with anger. He learned about the invasion and capture of Localus within hours of the battle. He cut short his vacation on Parax and immediately returned to Predax where he had his brother and Chief of Staff, Altamar and his son Dokalak arrested and exiled to Thuk, the prison planet. Knowing all of his generals to be incompetent, he assumed the job of Chief of Staff himself. Despite the pleading of his senior generals, he ordered almost all war ships to divert to Palus to push back the invaders. For their insubordination, the Emperor executed the generals who were not family members. The rest were sent to prison colonies throughout Predaxian space.

Admiral Branak Zendo, the emperor's great nephew cautiously entered the throne room. Two days ago, he had been a Lieutenant on a cruiser protecting Predax, only six months out of the military academy. Now it was his job to manage the entire fleet. There had been constant complaining from the ship captains until they learned the fate of their former generals. "Your Majesty," he squeaked, "you wanted to see me?"

"My dear nephew Branak, how are you today?" the emperor asked.

"I am well, Great Uncle," he replied, keeping his eyes focused on the floor. "How can I help Your Majesty today?"

"Have our traitorous troops been incarcerated?" he asked.

"Yes sir," Branak said. "Except Altamar and Dokalak. Their vessel is to arrive at Thuk in four hours."

"Excellent!  With those fools out of our business, we can win the day at Localus, don't you think?" Nokalez smiled.

"Of course, Majesty," Branak said. "We will have one hundred star cruisers on their way by the end of the day. The entire fleet is due to arrive at Palus in five days."

"We can't get there more quickly?" Nokalez asked.

"No, Majesty. The ships are coming from all different coordinates, some from as far as a thousand light-years. They need to find portals and make a series of jumps, while sharing the portals with other cruisers," Branak said.

"Very well, I know it is complicated to move so many ships quickly. You are doing a fine job, nephew. I am very proud of you," Nokalez smiled. "Pour us some brandy, Branak."

Branak scurried over to the cabinet and filled two glasses. He realized that both had the same amount, so he carefully poured some of his back into the bottle. His great uncle, Altamar, had always trained him that the emperor must have the largest portion of everything. He walked quickly back to the emperor and handed him the full glass. The emperor pointed to a chair near the throne, and Branak gratefully sat down.

"To Predax and our victory," the emperor said as he raised his glass toward Branak, who carefully touched his glass to the other. They both drank. Branak almost choked, since he seldom drank alcohol. "There, there boy, take it easy."

"I am sorry, Majesty, I guess I'm not much of a drinker," he replied.

"The taste of battle will change that. Now tell me of the enemy," Nokalez said.

"They have thirty-eight surviving ships in orbit over Localus. Thirty five ships full of traitors will join them within the day," Branak replied. "I can also report there are rumors that General Fa-a-Di of Gallia was killed in the attack on Localus."

"Wonderful!" the emperor shouted. "That slug has been a stain on our civilization since our first encounter fifty years ago. If we can eliminate his friend, Je-e-Bo, we will have the advantage. It sounds like we have a strong advantage for the coming battle. Pick our best ship and I shall move my flag there."

"Emperor, do you think that is wise?" Branak asked. "You are far too important to lose in this battle. The empire will collapse without you at the helm."

Nokalez patted Branak on the head gently, saying, "My great nephew's concern is heart-warming. Thank you for that. However, I must put an end to the Gallicean threat once and for all. My other admirals and generals have proven themselves to be cowards and fools. With my leadership, we will win the day."

"Yes, Majesty," Branak replied, "in that case, I recommend the battle cruiser, Pondi. She is our newest ship with the best systems we have available. She also does not need aliens to man the systems. It was built for our species. I have served on her protecting the home world since I graduated."

"An excellent choice, Branak. Please advise Captain Borka that I will join him on this trip. When is Pondi due to depart for Palus?" Nokalez asked.

"In six hours, Majesty," he responded. "After our meeting, I will go there and make certain adequate preparations are made for you, Emperor."

"Thank you, Branak. I was saddened to hear that your mother was captured on Localus. She is a loyal Predaxian. I sincerely hope we will rescue her after our glorious victory. Now go off and do what you need to do. Your great uncle is tired and needs some rest. Please have Captain Borka send a shuttle for me when Pondi is ready," Nokalez said. Branak left as quickly as his legs would carry him. Nokalez refilled his brandy glass and swallowed the contents. He sat down and smiled broadly. Now was the time for his revenge on the filthy Galliceans. All of his ships would descend on them like locusts and kill them all. Then it would be time to move against the Kalideans and the humans.

Sirens sounded in the darkness of the cell buried in the center of the dead planet, Thuk. Lauren, Wally, Mitch and Pan were jostled awake by the sounds, and they crouched in the darkest corner of the room. A brilliant flash of light blinded them and they turned their heads away. Pan touched the sensor to activate the room's lighting.

In the far side of the room were five Predaxians and ten pallets. Three of the Predaxians were wearing battle gear and armed, while the other two were in shackles. After a moment, Pan's eyes grew accustomed to the light. He smiled and walked toward the group. "Uncle Altamar and cousin Dok, what a pleasure to have you come to visit," he said.

Commander Bandamar Nostra, the leader of the armed Predaxians, leveled his blaster at Pan. "Don't come any closer prisoner, or I will be forced to stun you!" he shouted.

Pan stopped in his tracks. "Relax pal," Pan began, "can't a guy say hello to his family without getting shot around here? Besides, you guys have the guns and someone up in space to jump you out. I'm not a threat to you." He turned to Dok and asked, "What's going on here Cousin?"

"Dad and I were arrested, Pan," Dok said. "The Galliceans and their allies invaded our territory and captured Localus and thousands of our agents. Your dad got so mad that he killed or exiled all of his generals. We were lucky enough to be the emperor's family, or we'd be dead now. Do you remember our dorky nephew Branak?" Pan nodded. "He is now an admiral in charge of the entire fleet! Can you believe that?"

"Enough chatter, you two," Bandamar said. "We need to set up our quarters now."

"Quarters?  You mean you are going to be staying here? Why in heaven's name would you want to stay here?" Pan asked.

Bandamar thought for a moment and shook his head. He put his blaster in its holster and dropped his weapon belt to the floor. He signaled for the other two guards to do the same. "Prince Panoplez, we are stuck here with you now," he whimpered. "We were ordered by the emperor to bring these two here and leave them and these supplies. It's crazy out there. The emperor has ordered all war ships to Palus to mass and take back Localus and then invade Greater Gallia," he continued as he removed the shackles from his prisoners. "With no deterrents, pirates and other societies are starting to attack our frontiers. A Pryrrian cruiser caught up to us two hours ago. They fired at us repeatedly until our shields failed. We barely had time to pull these supplies together and jump ourselves down here before they boarded. I set the self-destruct, but they may have disabled it, I just don't know." He slumped down to the floor and covered his eyes.

"Hey pal," Pan said as he sat next to the other. "Don't sweat it, man. I've been here ten solar cycles. You brought a ton of supplies and I'm sure someone will find us eventually." Pan rose and looked through the pallets. He pulled a box off one and opened it, pulling out a bottle of brandy. He sat next to Bandamar again and opened the bottle, taking a big drink. Then he passed the bottle to the distraught commander. "Here, drink some of this.  It will improve your mood. And just call me Pan. I am certainly not a prince anymore."

Bandamar took a long drink, sat back and sighed. "Thanks, Pan. You can call me Bandy. The other guys on my team are Kanka and Faloo." The others waved weakly at Pan, who smiled back at them. "Somehow I doubt that. Not that many people know about Thuk. It was kept very secret because your father didn't want anyone to find and rescue you. I am only one of four ship captains who know where this place is. Several generals knew it, but they are all now dead or imprisoned. I think this will be our tomb."

Lauren, Mitch and Wally had joined the group, and Lauren sat next to Bandy. "Bandy, always remember while there is life, there is hope," she said as she stroked his head. "There are those who will stop at nothing to find us. Take Zakamar Vondee for example. Then there is my fiancé, Captain Jon Lake and Mitch's sister. They will find us; we just have to be optimistic."

Jake flew over to the pallets and removed a second bottle of brandy. After opening it, he inserted a tendril and drank heavily. "Wow, this is great stuff!" he exclaimed. "There has been little for me to eat since I got here."

Faloo shouted, "What kind of Predaxian is that? He can fly?"

Jake flew over to Faloo, saying, "Sorry Faloo, but I'm not a Predaxian. I am a maklan from the planet No-Makla in the Earth system. We both can trace our ancestry to Ai-Makla and the Great Rebirth, but obviously we have changed a lot since then."

Kanka walked over and poked Jake with one leg, "Wow, this think looks like glass, but it's soft and warm. That's freaky, man! What other tricks can you do?"

"I wouldn't call them tricks, Kanka," Jake frowned, "But I can jump without a portal. I'd jump out of here but there is too much iron and other metals between here and the surface. I can also communicate telepathically with others of my race."

"That's why they picked this place, pal," Bandy said. "Our mind control won't work through this much rock either. Pan here has the strongest mental control ever recorded, isn't that right?"

"I think that was a rumor my dad started to make me seem superior to other Predaxians," Pan said. "Frankly, I gave up those powers long before my father sent me here. I think we are abusing many other civilizations and making them our unwitting slaves."

"I've been hearing many people saying that recently," Kanka replied. "I was in a bar not two weeks ago with a gorgeous woman who kept saying that same thing to whoever would listen.  Come to think about it, she mentioned you, Pan! She said when you became emperor, you would prohibit mind control and free all the other races. Several friends of mine agreed and left with her just before the secret police arrived and started asking questions."

"Zak sure gets around, Cousin," Dok said to Pan. "I told you she was running the rebellion. It's amazing she would have the courage to recruit active duty soldiers on Predax."

"What makes you think it was Zak?" Pan asked.

"Come on, Pan, we both know it had to be her," Dok replied. "She's not afraid of anything."

"That was Zakamar Vondee in that bar?" Kanka asked in disbelief. "You are a lucky man, Pan. She is super smart and beautiful. That's a deadly combination."

"I doubt it could have been Zak," Pan replied. "I mean it could have been her, but how would I know when I'm stuck down here.  I hope it was her, showing my father that the rebels are not afraid of him and his secret police right in his own backyard." Pan took another long drink of the brandy. "Dok, remember what you said the last time you were here to deliver supplies?" Dok shook his head. "That woman is smarter than both of us combined. I'm starting to agree with Captain London over here. With Zak out there looking for us, we will be found, I guarantee it."

"Don't be so sure," Bandy said. "I heard the emperor will have one hundred star cruisers when he attacks Localus. That's a lot more than the Galliceans and rebels can muster in a short time. If the emperor regains Localus and can then take Nom-Kat-La, I think sentiment could turn in his favor."

"Perhaps, Bandy, but when I was imprisoned, almost half of all Predaxians wanted to end our mind control activities," Pan replied. "Now, my father is acting like a mad man, killing his own generals. That has to take a toll on the rest of the military. How long will they accept that? Then there is Zak and the rebels. If they were in a military hang-out bar on Predax, you know they are everywhere convincing others to join their cause. How long can my father hold on when the vast majority of his military and civilians are against him?"

"Bandy," Lauren said, "now do you see what I meant? If the emperor falls, our friends will find us. If the emperor wins, supply ships will return here and rescue you three at least."

"Let's just hope the Pyrrians on the cruiser up there didn't stop the self-destruct, or at least don't know how to use the portal. It would be unpleasant if they reached us first," Bandy sighed, drinking another gulp of brandy.

Four days had passed since the Nightsky and Kong-Fa had resumed their trip to Tak-Makla. Dave and his core team were meeting in his ready room to discuss the findings from the teams who had been investigating the maklan ruins they found in the system near Golden Dawn.

"Dave, so you know, Cara is presenting this same information to De-o-Nu and his team now," Jake began. "Let's start with Planet 3, as those ruins seem to be the oldest. About sixty-five percent of the planet's land surface appears to have been inhabited by maklans similar to those who built Station 801. Most of the structures are extremely old. We estimate that the most current ones are at least six hundred million Earth years old."

Dave sipped his coffee and took a bite of a cookie, "What does that tell us, Jake?"

"Cara and I have a theory that this was the original planet the maklans from Tak-Makla jumped to during the Great Rebirth," Jake replied. "Similar to my own race's situation, we think something occurred around six hundred million years ago that caused them to move to Tak-Makla. It's only speculation, but fortunately we should learn the answers in a few days. There were fragments of ruins much older, but our equipment could not gauge accurately. We feel confident that none are older than the Great Rebirth."

"What about the other planets, Jake?" Darlene asked.

"Let's look at Planet 6 next. The maklans living there grew to enormous dimensions. The antiquities we found ranged from six hundred to two hundred million years old. It also seems the maklans grew larger over time. The oldest building remnants were similar in size to the rooms on Station 801. The twenty-foot maklans could never have lived there. The older ones were also much more developed and modern. It seems they were devolving over time instead of evolving. The elegant structures of the distant past had been replaced by rough huts as time went by. We haven't had time to understand what happened or why it turned out that way. We hope to send more teams to all the planets soon," Jake reported.

"Now we are coming to the meat of this discussion. Tell us about Planet 5 and the apparent Predaxians living there," Dave said.

"This is the most bizarre part of the story," Jake began. "Maklans lived on this planet for about fifty million years, ending about two hundred million years ago. They never built much infrastructure, only a few towns and factories scattered about. The atmosphere was always very thin, and we found evidence of massive domes that covered groups of towns over perhaps a ten mile radius. If we look at the dissipation of the atmosphere, we estimate that it became hazardous about two hundred and twenty million years ago. By two hundred million years ago, we doubt that even the domes would have offered much protection from gamma rays or solar flares."

"So, they burned to death on their planet," Aria shivered. "That's a horrifying thought. But what were Predaxians doing there anyway?"

"That is an excellent question, Aria," Jake replied. "Perhaps further exploration or help from Tak-Makla will help us understand the mystery of the three planets."

Alarms sounded. Dave and Jon rushed back to the bridge. As they entered, Jon shouted, "What's going on, Donna?"

"Something is affecting both ships. We have slowed to dead stop. Engineering reports nothing wrong down below, but Kong-Fa and this ship are not moving," she replied.

Lia said, "Captain, we are being hailed by Tak-Makla."

"From twelve light-years away?" Jon asked. "Never mind, put them on the screen."

A pale blue maklan appeared on the screen smiling. "Greetings, I am Zee Gongaleg, and I am High Consul for Tak-Makla. I am now speaking to both ships approaching our planet and would like to know your intentions."

"Consul Gongaleg," Dave opened, "I am Admiral Dave Brewster of Earth. Our ships are bringing ambassadors from Earth, Greater Gallia, the Kalidean Federation and the planet No-Makla to offer peace and trade agreements with your planet."

"Thank you, Dave," Zee said. "I know you understand we must be cautious when war ships are approaching our planet, even though your two ships are hardly a threat."

"No threat was ever intended, Zee," Dave replied. "Space can be a dangerous place as you know. The ship carrying our ambassador from Kalidus was attacked on his way to join us four days ago."

"I certainly hope the ambassador was not injured, Dave," Zee said.

"He was slightly wounded, but will be completely recovered before we arrive at your planet," Dave responded. "May we have your permission to continue?"

"Not just yet, Dave," Zee said. "It is our custom to invite a few individuals to our world to learn their intentions more clearly before we allow ships to enter orbit. I am certain you understand."

"Not really, Zee, but it is your planet and you can follow your customs," Dave said. "I am certain our ambassadors would be happy to join you there."

Zee frowned slightly, "I understand they are best suited to negotiate, however, we prefer to pick our first visitors based on other methods. If you agree, we will jump four or so from your two ships to my office. You have my guarantee that no harm will come to any of them or your ships. After a few discussions and tours of our world, if further collaboration is deemed worthwhile for both sides, we will invite your ships to come here. If either side decides not to pursue further discussions, we will jump our guests back to their ships and you may return home. Is that agreeable?"

The rest of the team from the ready room had arrived on the bridge. Dave said, "Zee, please give me one moment to talk to our leaders here." The Consul nodded, still smiling.

Dave stepped to the communications console and tapped a button. The Consul's image was replaced with De-o-Nu. "Brother, what do you think?"

"I don't like it, brother," De-o-Nu scowled. "The maklan ambassador says we must accept or go home. I don't think we have much choice, but it is not a good choice."

"Opinions?" Dave asked the rest of his team.

"We have no choice, Dave," Jake said. "This is a great opportunity for all of our civilizations, and all good things require some risk."

"I agree, honey," Darlene said. "I just wish I knew what the Consul meant when he said they select by other methods. I say yes too."

Dave pressed the button on the console again, and Consul Zee was back again, still smiling. "Zee, we agree with your kind offer."

"That is wonderful, Dave," Zee said. "Please don't worry, we can be trusted. If we were evil, we could have already crushed your ships. We have already given you the planets of Beacon Station 801 as a sign of our good intentions. We moved our home world to Tak-Makla long ago for very special reasons, which I will explain to our guests. This place is sacred to us and the entire universe. Once you see its wonders, you will understand."

"Very well, Zee," Dave said. "What do we do now?"

"In a moment, when I find out who has been chosen; those four will disappear from your ships and be here," Zee continued. "Unlike the portals of your time or our relatives the maklans of No-Makla, there will be no flash. They will arrive here, and your crews will be able to see them here with me with their view screens. They will be allowed to communicate with your ships every few hours," Zee said, then paused. "Ah, I have the list of guests, please be prepared and thank you." Zee kept smiling.

"Where's Dave and Charlie?" Darlene shouted. They had disappeared from the bridge. She looked up and saw them both with Zee, along with Jake and De-o-Nu.

De-o-Nu was stunned. He was only slightly taller than Dave now and had no pressure suit, yet he was alive. "I don't understand, Consul," De-o-Nu said. "Why have I become so small and am able to breathe the same air as Dave?"

"I am sorry, De-o-Nu, but we have made some minor adjustments to enable us to work together more closely," Zee said. "When you return to your ship, you will be back to normal. Details like physical size and atmosphere are divisive in the universe. We have temporarily eliminated them."

Charlie laughed, "Brother, I don't think you could carry me right now!  But it is good to look at you eye to eye."

"Zee," Dave started, "I don't understand why you picked the four of us. Could you let us know?"

"Of course, Dave, but please sit down and let's have a drink to celebrate the occasion of our first meeting.  It is another custom, I'm afraid. We tekkans are the product of our customs," Zee answered. He looked at Jake, saying, "Jake, we are maklans to our souls, but with the grand variety that now inhabit our galaxy, we have given ourselves the name tekkan to differentiate ourselves. I hope that does not offend you."

"Not at all, Zee," Jake replied. "We have always called ourselves maklan because we never found any other maklan planets. As far as we know, we were alone."

"Except for the Predaxians, Jake," Charlie reminded him.

Zee shuddered, "Please do not remind me of them. They have been a black mark on all maklan species for a long time. Thankfully, that reign of terror may soon end."

"How do you know that?" Dave asked.

"I do not know, Dave, but The Hive tells me that will likely be the case," Zee replied as he poured large glasses of liquor for each guest and himself. "Please let us toast our future together." They lifted their glasses and drank heavily.

"This is really excellent, Zee," Dave said. "What is The Hive?"

"It is a magical drink, Zee," De-o-Nu said, "but I was wondering the same thing."

"We will discuss The Hive in due course," Zee replied. "Dave asked why we picked the four of you. Let me answer that first. The Hive selected your group. They base their selection on the closeness of your mental bond, what you may call friendship or love. While we could certainly detect love and friendship within each species, such as Dave's love or Darlene, or Charlie's for Aria, when they saw how close the four of you were, and that you represent three different species, they knew they had made the right choice. Such bonding is extremely rare in our galaxy. We have no other species on Tak-Makla, and I must admit I am jealous of you."

Dave smiled, "We are very fortunate, Zee. Circumstances pushed us together and we have become as close as brothers."

"Dave saved our home world," Jake said.

"Well, you saved my life twice, Jake," Dave replied.

"And then Jake and other maklans and humans helped us stop the Predaxian invasion of Greater Gallia," De-o-Nu said.

"It's amazing to see you four together," Zee smiled. "When we made the decision to form The Hive, we feared we would be unable to form real bonds with other planets. The Hive became our obsession, and all of our resources continue to flow into it."

"But what is The Hive, Zee?" Jake asked.

"Very well, we can talk about that now," Zee replied. "Better yet, let us take a shuttle and I will show you my planet. At the end of the tour, we will visit The Hive. Is that acceptable?"

The wall of the Consul's office opened to reveal a dock where a craft was positioned. The group approached the small shuttle, which was virtually transparent. The non-maklans were very apprehensive as it seemed they were stepping into open air, several hundred feet above the planet's surface. Sensing their feelings, the pilot touched a panel and the floor and walls turned metallic. When everyone was secured in their seats, he pushed the panel and the ship became like glass again. On the Consul's order, the ship left its dock and floated noiselessly down toward the surface. The high spire that held the Consul's office appeared to be alone in the center of a massive forest. The craft leveled off twenty feet above the tree tops, which stretched in every direction to the horizon.

"Zee, other than the one spire, there don't seem to be any buildings around here," Charlie asked. "That seems odd. Shouldn't your office be in the capital city?"

"My office is in the capital, Charlie. Please enjoy the voyage and all will be explained soon," he replied. "I have been in contact with my wife and she has asked you all to join us for dinner. I hope that is acceptable to you all." They smiled their approval.  What choice did they have anyway?

After ten minutes of flying, the craft settled down in a large clearing. The walls and floor became solid again and the Consul led them out of the ship. They walked toward the nearest edge of the forest. Soon they could hear the sounds of wildlife nearby. Monkeys jumped through the trees. Hundreds of colorful birds of different sizes and shapes flew among the trees. After another ten minutes of walking, they were deep in the woods. Sunlight dappled the forest floor. Lines of ants moved leaf debris along a path toward their nest. Spiders made giant webs high up in the trees. Dave stopped dead when they entered a small clearing. In the center were twenty large wolf-like creatures like the one that had attacked him on Golden Dawn.

"Zee," Dave said, "those things are very dangerous."

"Nonsense," Zee replied as he walked up to the wolves. One rose to its feet near Zee and rubbed itself against his legs. "There's a pretty boy. How are you today?"

The rest of the group approached the animals. Jake was vigilant to protect anyone the beasts might lunge at. But the wolves sat quietly, enjoying the sun warming their fur.

"I don't understand this at all," Dave said.

"Dave, you may have seen these animals at Beacon Station 801," Zee replied. "Those were wild beasts. This forest is part of a zoological and botanical garden that covers much of the surface of Tak-Makla. You can believe me that nothing is harmful here, although walking long distances can wear ones legs out." He sat down next to the wolf and stroked its ears. It wagged its tail in delight.

After resting for five minutes, the group headed back to the shuttle. It took to the sky and continued the tour. Within twenty minutes, the forest had given way to rolling hills of grain and a large river coursing its way to lower elevations. "This is one of the farming areas of the planet. We have several hundred areas like this. Most of the equipment is automated, although a few tekkans have left The Hive to pursue a more basic life on the land," Zee continued. "We call this river Nanda. We took that name from a nearby planet inhabited by creatures not too different from you, Dave. Their planet is in the same system as our original planet. The Nanda River brings fresh water from the mountain snows to provide fertility to the land in this area. We will follow the Nanda to the ocean now."

Within a couple minutes, the craft flew over a massive cliff, where the Nanda River plunged more than a thousand feet to the lowlands below. The shuttle moved down the face of the cliff following the flow of water. The waterfall ended in a very large lake at the base of the cliff. Water spray shot hundreds of feet in the air in all directions, covering the shuttle. The group winced at the water splashing at them in the clear ship. The area around the lake looked like a rain forest or even jungle. The craft continued following the river down its course. Twenty minutes passed and the forest ended in large grasslands reaching to the ocean's edge. They followed the coast until an expansive beach loomed before them. A number of large dwellings clustered at the edge of the beach. The craft settled down in front of the largest house, and became metallic again. "Welcome to my humble home, gentlemen," Zee said as he led them out into the warm air with the ocean spray in their faces.

Zee led the group to the house which seemed two to three times larger than the mansion where Charlie lived on Earth. It appeared to be made of pure white marble, which glistened in the sun, with large windows covering almost one-half of the walls. The lawn in front was carefully manicured with large areas of blooming flowers unlike any on Earth. Zee said, "This home is reserved for the High Consul. My own home is much more discrete. When my term ends in five solar cycles, my wife and I will return to our work in The Hive, and our personal residence. Val will be happy on that day since we will be much closer to our children. This place can be quite sterile. We entertain various groups most days each week, you know, government business. Please come in."  As he spoke the twenty foot tall glass door slid silently down into the floor.

The semi-circular entry was three stories tall, with a chandelier that seemed to float in the air above them. On the walls were pictures of the previous twenty High Consuls. Since Tak-Makla had been inhabited for four hundred million Earth years, it would not be possible to have images of all the Consuls. Five tekkans were waiting for them at the center of the room. Zee introduced the first as his wife, Val. The others were valets assigned to each guest. Zee pulled a small device from his pocket and showed it to his guests. "This is a communicator device. You will find one of these in each of your guest rooms," Zee said.

De-o-Nu looked concerned. He asked "Guest rooms? Zee, I was not aware that we would be staying here? I thought we would meet you and then return to our ships to either continue here or go back."

"De-o-Nu, my friend," Zee replied, "please do not be concerned. Cementing a bond among our societies is a delicate process that cannot be rushed. You asked about The Hive and many of the workers there will be going home for the night soon. By the luck of timing, you arrived here in our mid-afternoon. Nightfall is only an hour away. Your valets will now take you to your rooms. Your rooms are on the same floor so you can meet with each other if you like. You will find a communicator like the one I showed you in your room. It has only one button. When you press it, you will be connected to your ships. Please speak with them and let them know you are safe. In an hour, your valets will bring you to the patio to have dinner with us. I have invited several ministers to join us. After dinner, according to our custom, we will take a drink and walk along the beach to continue our discussions. Then it will be time to sleep. In the morning, we will finish our tour and go to The Hive. Is that satisfactory?"

Jake spoke first, "Zee, I think your suggestion is perfect. We maklans have waited so long to find another of our species that a good meal and a night's sleep would be appreciated. One night will not make a difference to me."

"Thank you, Jake," Zee smiled. "For all of your information, we have obtained some whisky from Earth and Gallia. I have never tried them, but am looking forward to enjoying some while we walk on the beach. Our Minister of State has told me that both are quite good, although she prefers the punch of the Gallicean whisky."

De-o-Nu laughed, "I have a feeling I will like your Minister of State very much. My brothers from Earth think it is too strong."

The valets led Dave, Charlie, De-o-Nu and Jake up to the third floor. They were walking down a long, brightly lit corridor with doors on both sides. They stopped at the first door on the right. Dave's valet, Ton, pushed a panel and the door slid into a pocket in the wall. They all looked in the opening. It was a large room, at least seven hundred square feet. The far wall was all glass and they could see small waves crashing onto the beach outside. Ton said, "We have studied all of your species, and each room is decorated in a fashion that we hope pleases you. Dave, you will note there is a panel on both sides of the door that opens it. Your friends will be in the next three rooms on the same side further down the hallway. Let us go in while the valets show the rest to their rooms."

Dave and Ton stepped inside. There was a seating area with two armchairs and a couch facing a small marble fireplace. The bed was larger than any Dave had seen, at least double the size of a king bed on Earth. Ton pointed out the bathroom that appeared identical to one on the colony ship Ticonderoga, except larger and all marble. There was a closet with a crisp, white suit, which Ton explained Dave should wear to dinner. A small door in the window opened onto a full-length balcony, furnished with several chairs. Before he excused himself, Ton opened a cabinet to show glasses and three bottles of rare Scotch whisky, an ice machine and several bottles of water. The communicator device was on top of the counter. Ton set a timer on the device to remind Dave when he should be ready for dinner, and left.

Dave opened the whisky bottle, and poured some over ice in one of the glasses. He sipped it carefully. The taste was magnificent and seemed very real, although he wondered how the tekkans had acquired it. He took his glass and the communicator and sat on one of the armchairs. When he pushed the button on the device, a screen descended from the ceiling against the wall. After a few seconds, he could see the bridge of the Nightsky.

"Dave, are you okay?" Captain Jon Lake said. "You just disappeared from the bridge two hours ago. We saw you with the High Consul for a minute or two, then our screen went blank."

"We're all fine Jon," Dave replied. "Apparently, we arrived late in the afternoon. Zee took us on an amazing flight over some of the planet and now we are at the High Consul's residence on a large beach. We are to join a state dinner shortly and then spend the night."

Darlene's image entered the screen. "Dave honey, I don't like the sound of that," she said. "I thought you were going to meet them and they would decide."

"Me too, but these tekkans take their time to make decisions," Dave replied. "I remember all the time you took to try to negotiate with the Galliceans. I'm not worried, yet. I think we just have to keep an open mind and find out what happens next. It's not like we have much choice. You saw what they could do to our ships from twelve light-years away."

"I know you're right, Dave," Darlene said. "The shock of seeing you and Charlie disappear in front of my eyes was too much. I've been talking to the maklan ambassador a lot since you left. Cara let me know how important this occasion is for her people. I'll be fine, but you better take care of yourself."

"Yes, Dear," Dave started when a tone sounded at his door. He walked to the door and pressed the panel to find Charlie there in the brilliant white suit. He waved Charlie in and they sat together on the couch. The screen moved silently to face them on the couch. "Look who just popped in, sweetheart."

"Hi Darlene, I've just been speaking with Aria," Charlie said. While he was talking, Dave poured him a drink and gave him the glass. "Thanks, Dave. We're fine here now, just having a cocktail before dinner. Don't worry."

"Jon, any other news to report," Dave queried.

"No, Dave, it's been very quiet here," Jon replied.

"Jon, I did find out one piece of information already that might help the Kalideans deal with that new race we encountered. Zee gave us the word Nanda, which is either the name of their people or planet or both. Perhaps that can be a first link to their language," Dave said. "I'm going to have to sign off now. As you can see from Charlie's outfit, we have to dress for dinner."

"I love you, Dave," Darlene said.

"I love you too, sweetheart," Dave replied. He pushed the one button on the communicator and the screen went dark and returned to its recess in the ceiling. "Charlie, please keep enjoying your drink while I put on my suit in the restroom." Dave took the outfit from the closet and went to the restroom and closed the door.

The tone sounded again. Charlie went to the door and pressed the panel. De-o-Nu and Jake, both clad in white as well entered the room. While they sat on the couch, Charlie poured them each a whisky and sat with them on one of the armchairs. What do you two think about all of this?" Charlie asked.

"I have never been a diplomat," De-o-Nu said. "I prefer to negotiate the surrender terms with the vanquished. This sit and wait, tour and talk is too much for me. Fa-a-Di told me I would have to learn to listen and work things out, but frankly, it is a difficult transition. At this moment, I would rather be on Planet 5 battling with those birds we saw, or even helping them down one of the giant jellyfish. Those are the kinds of things a soldier does. Seeing those ravenous wolves here got my blood flowing again, but they turned out to be playful puppy dogs instead."

Dave returned to the group and refreshed his drink. The suit seemed perfectly tailored for him. "Are these outfits amazing? I put it on and it was much too large. Two minutes later and it had shrunk to my size," he said.

"Just like me!" De-o-Nu laughed. "I am your size now too!" They all laughed. "Let us sit on the balcony, brothers. Fresh air will do us a world of good."

As they headed to the balcony, the tone sounded again and the door slid open. Ton and the other three valets entered. "Gentlemen, your hosts are ready for you downstairs, please follow me," Ton said and led them down the hallway.

# CHAPTER 31

The valets led the group down to the entrance, through a large living room lined with bookcases and out the back door onto a patio that was several hundred feet wide and reached to within fifty feet of the water's edge. A group of other guests had formed a receiving line to welcome them. Zee led them through the line and introduced them to the VIPs. The group included Fak, Minister of State, Var, Chief Engineer of The Hive, Nar, Minister of Defense, Mak, Minister of Internal Affairs, and Tal, Director of the Zoological Gardens. A long table set with fine china and crystal was reserved for the most important guests. Several dozen tables were filled by the remaining guests.

Ton changed from his role as valet to Maitre 'd. On his sign, dozens of waiters moved among the tables pouring sparkling wine and passing out plates of appetizers. While most of the plates seemed matched to tekkan palates, the plates in front of Dave and Charlie were very familiar, with cheese, salamis, and crisp pickles. Dave recognized De-o-Nu's plate as well. It reminded him of the delicacies Fa-a-Di had presented to Dave after their flight over Jupiter so long ago.

Minister of State Fak sat across from De-o-Nu. She said, "De-o-Nu, Zee has mentioned our mutual fondness for the whisky from your world. I have always loved Gallicean whisky. Frankly, I'm not much of a drinker, but when I want a drink, I go for the best!"

De-o-Nu laughed, "Thank you, Fak. It will be an honor to share a glass or two with you after dinner. I told my brothers here that strong whisky comes from a strong race, which is why our whisky is the best, wouldn't you agree?"

"I think you have a point there," she replied. "My opinion is that the best whisky comes from warrior species, like your own and the Nanda. The Nanda love nothing more than to fight and drink. I think you encountered them a few days ago."

"Yes, but they are a tiny folk," De-o-Nu replied. "As I'm sure you know, in my natural state, I am much larger than this."

"True, but we also have some whisky from Nanda which I would love to share with you later," she replied, almost blushing. "The vegetation on their world is remarkable. Their methods have created something magnificent."

"I look forward to that," De-o-Nu smiled.

"Minister," Jake interrupted. "Zee has told us there are a great variety of maklan cultures which you have found. Unfortunately, the only such culture we have encountered is the Predaxians. If you may, how many have you discovered?"

"Jake, please call me Fak," she smiled. "We have chronicled four hundred and twelve to date. Fifty of those fell into decay and extinction long before we found them. You are quite correct to say knowing the Predaxians is unfortunate. We have tried to isolate ourselves from them. I believe you found our original planet near the planet Nanda."

"Yes, we did," Jake replied. "Why did you leave that world? It seems ideal. Were you trying not to influence the Nanda?"

"No, not at all," Fak said. "Their modern society only developed over the last eight millennia or so. When we moved here, only microorganisms were living in the Nanda oceans. We moved here when we decided to construct The Hive."

Zee interrupted, "Yes, The Hive. That's why we are all here together now. Please let us enjoy the dinner first though. After our other guests have left, my ministers and I will walk with you along the beach and tell you more. Ah, here come the entrees. My wife personally selected these. I'm certain we will all enjoy them."

The group of waiters moved swiftly through the group replacing soiled plates with dinner plates heavy with food and refilling wine glasses. There were large lobster-like tails on Dave and Charlie's dishes, along with a heap of steaming greens and a starch. The waiter set small dishes with a clear green liquid near their plates. Dave looked around and saw that all the plates looked very similar.

Zee spoke, "Dave, this is a crustacean from this ocean. I have been told that it tastes similar to lobster on your home world. The sauce on the side is my wife's personal recipe. It is a blend of several herbs and oils that can only be found on Tak-Makla or our first home world near Nanda. My ministers agree with me it is wonderful. Since they work for me, I can never be certain if they are telling the truth, or just trying to get a pay increase." He laughed.

Dave cut a small piece of the crustacean and gingerly put it in his mouth. It did take like lobster, with a more meaty texture. He cut another piece and dipped it in the sauce. It smelled like wildflowers and the fresh ocean breeze. Dave tasted it. The first sensation was tart and sour, followed quickly by the luxurious mouth feel of butter. Finally, a bit of sweetness and heat ended on the back of his tongue. "Zee, this is truly magnificent," he said. He turned to Val, seated next to her husband and said, "Val, this is the most wonderful thing I have every tasted." She smiled broadly at him.

The dinner continued for several hours. After the main course, a choir from the local elementary school entertained the group. The parents of the children were in the group, so the applause was thunderous. The dessert course followed with a variety of ten small pastries per plate, each completely different. The group was advised to taste from the left to the right. The first was buttery, salty and savory. By the time they tasted the last, it was sweet, rich and full of fresh fruit. Before the coffee arrived, a group performed folk dances that had been performed for over six hundred million Earth-years. The group whirled around the tables and several tekkans were pulled from their tables to join the group.

Zee said, "Dave, I am a trifle concerned about our coffee course. Coffee is something new to us on Tak-Makla. We only discovered it when your ship arrived at Beacon Station 801. I have been told that you and Charlie are coffee lovers and I hope we don't disappoint. We were able to obtain some green coffee from one of your worlds. I don't know if we roasted it correctly, but I personally love it."

A waiter stood behind Dave, who turned to watch. The waiter held a cup in one leg and a small clear pitcher in another. There was a milk-like substance in the bottom of the cup. The waiter began to pour and raised the pitcher until the coffee formed a long arc into the cup. Not a drop was spilled. The waiter set the cup in front Dave and then poured another for Charlie. All of the ministers were staring at Dave as he lifted the cup to his lips. He tasted the drink.

"Zee, this is wonderful," Dave said as the ministers sighed with relief. "Charlie, you have to try this. The cream is so rich with just the right sweetness. Zee, I'm honored that you went to this trouble for us."

"Dave, you are welcome, but it was no trouble," Zee replied. "We first attempted it as a treat for you, but when we found out how wonderful and powerful it was, we became addicted ourselves. If our relationship moves forward, we would be honored if you could provide some coffee plants and some farmers to help us learn to grow it."

The dinner ended and the guests mingled with the High Consul and his ministers for a short time before they returned to their homes. Zee motioned to the group to move to the sand for their walk. Five waiters joined them with a bar that floated three feet above the sand. The bar was stocked with many bottles, ice and glasses. Dave recognized the Scotch and Gallicean whisky bottles. The air was slightly cool and the waves were gently rolling onto the sand. The sky was full of stars since there was little light on the surface to interfere, but there was no moon.

"Our guests would like to know more about The Hive, Var," Zee said to the Minister of The Hive. "Why don't you begin?"

"I will if you like, Zee, however you have run The Hive much longer than me," Var began. "The Hive began as a global university. Our ancestors first began to work with what you call dark matter and dark energy while still on Ai-Makla, our world of origin. That work enabled them to construct the space and temporal portals your worlds use today. It also helped us escape the nova that eventually destroyed Ai-Makla." A waiter rushed over and refilled Var's glass. "Thank you. When our ancestors were deciding who to send on each colony ship, they determined that the top scientists should be together in order to continue this work. They were among the colonists who settled Don-Makla, the planet you found near Nanda."

"Unfortunately, the plan did not work exactly as scheduled," Zee interrupted. "For many generations, the colonists needed to focus on developing their new world. Those great scientists had to forego their studies to build factories and cities. No work on universal power, which we call the combination of dark matter and dark energy, was performed for millions of years. Please continue, Var."

"Ultimately, our ancestors' plan did work," Var started. "The generations that followed those who jumped from Ai-Makla contained the genes of genius from their ancestors. After two hundred million years, the planet became highly advanced and a great center of learning. While a few hundred great scientists had jumped to Don-Makla, now there were millions of their descendants inhabiting the planet. Hundreds of universities joined together to work on the universal power project. Much of the knowledge from Ai-Makla was lost in the dust of time, and it took many generations to relearn. Our government sank more and more resources into the project. The economy stumbled over and again. Over the next hundred million years, the project raced ahead, only to be stopped when commerce crumbled and tekkans rioted in the streets."

"The government and academia had become obsessed with universal power," Zee said. "Yet, the people needed jobs and food. At one point, the situation was so bad that a warlord took power and burned many universities. Universal power was put on hold. We were fortunate that the warlord was also a great merchant. For the next thirty million years, we established relationships with thousands of other societies, including hundreds of maklan worlds. Our economy completely changed from production to trade. We became the richest culture in the galaxy. The last emperor converted the government to a republic, allowing free elections for the first time in hundreds of generations. Trade continued to dominate life. At last, the High Consul of the time, Tok Nokram, restarted the universal power project. With huge economic resources, the tekkans were happy and the project moved forward. That was when the most important discovery of universal power took place."

Var said, "We discovered that universal power formed a net that filled the universe. Its power was focused along grids that reached across the cosmos. Where dark energy was the densest, it formed dark matter. Where dark matter clumped together, galaxies formed. It was revolutionary. In order to understand more, we knew we needed to be in the intersection of those lines to feel their impact and measure them."

Fak said, "Unfortunately, Don-Makla was not near such a node. However, this spot in space was directly at the intersection of several lines."

De-o-Nu drained his glass and said, "That's why you moved to this planet! Now we understand why you abandoned Don-Makla."

"Not quite, De-o-Nu," Zee countered. "There was a planet here, but not this one."

"I don't understand," Dave replied.

"I suppose that planet is still here," Zee corrected himself. "It was a very small planet, less than one-tenth the size of Tak-Makla, and it was amazingly dense, almost like a collapsed nova. Using that planet as a foundation, we built Tak-Makla around it."

Dave looked shocked. He said, "Are you saying this planet is a construction?"

"Yes, Dave, that is exactly correct," Zee replied. "After the great discovery, we decided we needed a suitable planet here.

Since there wasn't one, we had to build it. It took many millions of years and untold generations, but here we are. We had to pull resource materials from hundreds of dead planets in the area, build massive factories and thousands of star ships to move and install what you see around you now."

"But the mountains and oceans, they seem so real," Charlie whimpered. "Are they fake?"

Tal, the Director of the Zoological Garden interrupted, "No, Charlie, nothing is fake. It is my role to take care of the top layers of the planet. When Tak-Makla was under construction, our ancestors knew that our people could not live in a giant building their entire lives. The structures below were arranged to allow for the top surface to be varied. For example, the mountains have structures under the top few hundred feet of rock and soil. Since they jut out of the surface, they make great locations for sensors and weapon systems. After the structures were built, we took rock, soil, fresh and salt water, flora and fauna from hundreds of different worlds. As Tak-Makla became as large as a planet, we started its rotation and imported an atmosphere. Once the oceans were in place, the planet began to function like a natural one."

Zee jumped in, "While much of the surface behaves like a true planet, we have made some adjustments, as you saw in the park earlier with the large wolves. It would be unfortunate if our scientists were eaten by ravenous animals during their afternoon break. We tekkans can jump in space without a portal or implanted device like our friend, Jake. If someone wants to see wild animals, they can travel to Beacon Station 801, for example. We maintain our trading network as well, to provide continued funding to manage the planet and The Hive."

"We still don't know what The Hive is," Jake reminded him.

"For tonight, let us say that The Hive exists at the exact intersection of the lines of universal power. It allows us to see, feel and understand what is happening throughout the universe. After a leisurely breakfast tomorrow, we will head there," Zee replied. He raised his recently refreshed glass. "Dear friends, I must say that today has been a wonderful experience for me. I think we can all agree that we will immediately allow the two ships to join us here. I will advise them when I get inside. Rather than having them travel for several more days, we will jump them into orbit over the planet at sunrise tomorrow. Dave and Charlie, I have arranged little surprises for you in your rooms. Let us toast our new friends from Earth, Gallia, No-Makla and Kalidus!"

They raised their glasses and shared the toast. Afterward, they all said good night and returned to the mansion. Dave walked to his room and touched the panel to open the door. Darlene was sitting on the couch with two glasses of red wine on the table in front of her. She stood and rushed into Dave's arms.

# CHAPTER 32

Dave and Darlene woke early and prepared for their day. A heavy rain was falling outside and the sky was dark and gray. Dave found their uniforms had been cleaned and pressed while they slept. While Darlene was getting ready, Dave sat on the couch talking to Jon Lake on the communicator.

"Dave, it was the strangest thing," Jon said. "The High Consul contacted me and said they would jump Nightsky and Kong-Fa to Tak-Makla at 0700 local time. I can't imagine how they did it, but here we are in orbit. One second we were twelve light-years away, and now we are here. What kind of power do those maklans have?"

"They have harnessed something they call universal power, Jon. It has to do with dark matter and dark energy," Dave began. "Zee and his ministers told us a bit about it last night. I am hoping to learn more today. They also said they were going to form an alliance with us, so that's good news."

Darlene joined Dave on the couch. "Jon, have you had any discussions with Cara or Petrodus?"

"Negative, Darlene," Jon replied. "I was told that the High Consul spoke with them and they too have been jumped down to the planet. I hope you find them."

"Don't fret, Jon. I think this is working out very well," she said. "If they didn't like us, I think they would have jumped our ships all the way to Earth. Meeting and negotiating with a new culture takes time."

"I'm still unclear about the thing they call The Hive," Dave interjected. "I want to know what's going on here to give the tekkans so much power." A tone sounded at the door, which then opened and Ton entered. "We have to go now, Jon. Tak-Makla out."

Ton led them downstairs again and into a small dining room. Val, the High Consul's wife was sitting down, enjoying a cup of coffee and some biscuits. "Good morning, Dave and Darlene. Please sit and I'll get you both some coffee. I'm afraid I can't pour like the waiter last night, but the coffee should be as good." As they sat, De-o-Nu and Jake entered and joined them. Val brought a tray of coffee and biscuits for the group. "Zee has been called to The Hive on urgent business. He asked me to feed you a light breakfast and then make certain you meet him there," she said.

"We hope there isn't any problem, Val," Darlene said as she sipped the coffee.

"There are always problems on Tak-Makla," she replied. "With twenty billion tekkans to care for, including ten billion in The Hive, activity is always frenetic. But nothing serious, I can assure you. Since they rose early, Charlie and Aria went with Zee."

They sat and enjoyed the food for another twenty minutes, learning the life of the High Consul's wife. Val spent most days traveling around Tak-Makla visiting hospitals and schools, opening universities and businesses. Her role was to bring the warmth and compassion of the government to the tekkans. She and Zee had four children. Two were employed in The Hive. One was a merchant traveling to various trading partners to exchange goods. Vee was their oldest. After a distinguished career in The Hive, he had decided to be a farmer. Val told them that Zee tries to take a shuttle home most days so he can fly over Vee's farm.  The flour, spices and nuts in the biscuits they ate had come from his farm. After she sent her guests on their way today, she was scheduled to open a new adjunct to the top university on the planet to train more candidates for the most secret positions in The Hive.

"When will the shuttle come to take us, Val," De-o-Nu asked. "We don't want to keep you from your important duties."

"I am very pleased you are here. Don't worry about my schedule," Val replied. "You won't be taking a shuttle today. That was only so my husband could impress you with the scenery. You will be taking a tube today."

"What is a tube, Val?" Dave asked.

"If you are all finished with your breakfast, I will take you there now," she replied. "Then you will know firsthand how ninety-nine percent of tekkans travel around this planet. I'll be taking a tube to all of my functions today."

The group left the room and walked down another bright marble-clad hallway, which seemed to slope downward. After two hundred yards, they reached a doorway which opened when Val touched it slightly. She told them they could do the same with any door on the planet, except for very few requiring advanced security. There was a small control panel mounted on the left wall. The right wall was covered with a design of the tube networks in this area of the planet, which looked like an incomprehensible maze of intersecting lines. In front of them, just past a short step was a glass-like cylindrical shuttle with ten seats.  The shuttle was closed at both ends with semi-circular clear end caps. Val stepped to the panel and touched the one button.

The panel said, "Destination please."

Val replied, "Hive, Minister's office." The map on the opposite wall changed to dim other lines and highlight the course to the destination.

The panel said, "Ready."

The door on the shuttle opened and Val climbed in. "Come on, I'm going with you. Zee recommended that we not leave you alone on the tubes just yet," she said.

Reluctantly, they climbed in and strapped themselves down. De-o-Nu said, "Now I can see why they had to shrink me down. They'd have to build a new shuttle for the real me."

Val touched a button on her seat and said, "Ready." The glass door slid into place. The wall in front of them opened and they could see a glass tube stretching in front of them that led down into the planet. "I hope you enjoy this," she said.

The shuttle rocketed forward. Dave felt himself plastered into his seat. He could not raise an arm or even a finger. The shuttle moved at incredible speed. They could see hundreds of other tubes around them going in every direction as they shot ahead. Other shuttles could be seen zipping through other tubes around them. The tekkans inside appeared to be chatting or reading with no concern for the speed. Their shuttle lurched and turned into a different tube, flying almost straight downward. Their tube went directly between two walls. Looking up and down, they could see a line of tubes moving in the same direction. Dave imagined that tekkans worked and lived in rooms on the other side of the walls around them. A shuttle shot past them in the tube directly over their heads, going the opposite direction. Dave thought he could hear them talking. Their tube reached the end of the two walls and turned ninety degrees. Above them now was a massive floor as far as they could see. There were lights suspended below them and a large underground garden or farm.

"Hydroponic and mushroom farm," Val said. "No need to waste space on the surface for that." It took their shuttle a couple minutes at breakneck speed to reach the end of the farm. It suddenly twisted and headed straight down again. The mesh of tubes here was so tight that it looked almost like woven fabric, with shuttles moving in all directions. Dave could see another shuttle in their same tube far ahead and they were gaining on it. Another shuttle was coming up on them from behind. When they got to within ten feet of the shuttle ahead, it turned and flew off into a perpendicular tunnel. The shuttle behind them was closing very fast. It seemed only inches away when their shuttle lurched to the left, slowed to a crawl, entered another tube room and stopped.

"Destination, Hive, Minister's office," the shuttle said.

Zee was standing in the room waiting for his guests. "Welcome to The Hive," he said as the glass door slid open. The group climbed out, a bit wobbly at first. Val kissed Zee and went to the panel. After specifying her new destination, she climbed back into the shuttle. The door closed and she zipped back into the maze. Zee led them out of the room and down a short corridor. He touched the door at the end, which opened to reveal the anteroom for the Minister of The Hive. They walked to another door and opened it. Inside was a large glass conference table. At one end, helping themselves to coffee and pastries were Ambassador Petrodus, Ambassador Pakalanalan, Charlie and Aria. Another door slid open, and Var, Minister of The Hive joined them.

The Predaxian battle cruiser, Pondi was high in orbit over Palus. On the emperor's order, enough agents had been moved to the Palian systems to insure that every Palian soldier would be under Predaxian control. Emperor Nokalez Zendo paced back and forth in the ready room that had been converted to his throne room. Captain Anda Borka and Admiral Branak Zendo stood on the opposite side of the room, too frightened to disturb their liege.

Nokalez was mumbling to himself about the upcoming battle to regain Localus and take Nom-Kat-La. Only five ships had yet to arrive at Palus and they were due in the next hour. After a few minutes, the emperor noticed the other two in the room. "My dear Branak and Captain, how good of you to come," he said.

"I'm afraid we have bad news, Great Uncle," Branak said weakly.

"Spit it out, nephew," Nokalez shouted.

"A Pyrrian cruiser has captured the supply ship taking your bother and nephew to the Thuk prison planet," Branak replied. "Our sensors read that the Pyrrian cruiser is still there, but our supply ship has been destroyed."

"That is good news, Branak, my boy," Nokalez smiled. "You should bring me bad news like that all the time. Either the ship was destroyed with my incompetent brother on board or they were jumped to the prison. Both are wonderful answers. Let's have a drink!" The emperor personally poured full glasses of the best Predaxian brandy for himself and the other two.

"Majesty," Branak said, "you have given me the fullest glass. You should have that, Great Uncle."

"You are a good boy, Branak," the emperor smiled as they exchanged glasses. "Your teachers have taught you well." He turned to the captain and asked, "Anda, what is the status of the last five vessels?"

"Majesty, two have jumped here in the last five minutes," Anda replied. "The last three have updated their itineraries and will arrive in the next ten minutes." He sipped the brandy gingerly.

"More good news, Anda," the emperor beamed. "When will all the ships be ready to begin our adventure?"

"On orders from Admiral Zendo, we have been making preparations for the last several hours. I have personally contacted all captains, and we will be ready to leave within five minutes after the last ships arrive," Anda replied.

"Whew," the emperor sighed. "When I saw you two with the hangdog expressions, I thought there was real bad news."

"Majesty, there is some to report," Anda began. "As the admiral mentioned, a number of Pyrrian ships have moved into the dead sector. It appears that they may make a move for several planets within Lozaki space. All of the Lozaki cruisers have come here to join our fleet. We are receiving desperate requests for support from those planets. What should we do, sir?"

"We can only fight one war at a time, Anda. The Lozaki will have to wait. How are our agents controlling the situation on their ships and back home?" the emperor asked.

"The ships are secure. Not well on the planets though, Great Uncle," Branak said. "With only a few thousand agents on twelve worlds, it is becoming difficult to maintain any semblance of order. We have reports of rioting in the streets and plans to negotiate for peace with the Pyrrians."

"The Pyrrians are a scourge on the galaxy. Perhaps after we take Nom-Kat-La, we can send some cruisers back to restore order. The Pyrrian ships are no match for the Pondi and others like her. Captain, please make a plan to do that. Arrange to take as many agents as you need to restore order. You are excused," Nokalez said.  Anda left Branak alone to face the emperor.

"Uncle," Branak said, "I am afraid there is more news."

The emperor downed his drink and refilled his glass. He sat heavily on his throne and glowered at the admiral. "Out with it, Nephew."

"Several of our cruisers on the Kalidean frontier have been compromised by the rebels," he began. "Four cruisers have sworn allegiance to your son and are terrorizing our planets in that region."

"Even from the depths of Thuk, my son continues to disappoint me," Nokalez sighed. "This is your chance to give me all the bad news, nephew, before I send you to join him there."

"Those ships remain near the Kalidean frontier so they should not impact our current mission. At least we have that good news. Also, it is rumored that some Palian agitators who were freed from Localus have gone to various Palian planets to gain support. Some believe those agents have maklans with them to prevent our agents from controlling them," Branak said. "If rumors are to be believed, there may be five or ten Palian cruisers with none of our agents on board flying around inciting riots and revolutions."

"Traitors all!" Nokalez shouted. "If we did not have this urgent appointment on Localus, I would crush them like the bugs they are. Please tell me there is no more, nephew."

"Only one thing, Uncle," he squirmed. "I don't believe this, but some think that a few of the Palian ships in our own fleet are rebel ships."

"That can't be true," the emperor said. "I ordered there to be enough agents on each ship to control every Being on board. Are you saying my orders were disobeyed?"

"No sir," Branak cried. "It is a rumor only. Our agents say they have control, but there are so many ships here now. Perhaps one or two could have slipped through their net."

"If that is true, and any of those ships changes side in the battle, I will have our chief agents sent to Thuk too!" Nokalez screamed. "Your uncle Panoplez will have wall-to-wall cell mates. At least he won't be wanting for company." The emperor laughed hysterically. "No, that rumor must be wrong."

A tone sounded, and Nokalez touched a button on his throne. "Emperor, all ships are in position," Anda said. "We can proceed to Localus on your command, Majesty."

"All ahead full, Captain," the emperor laughed.

Fa-a-Di was pacing around his office on Localus. After he had recovered from his battle wounds, he insisted on joining his friend, Je-e-Bo to defend against the next Predaxian attack. He had commandeered Warden Kogala's office after the invasion. The furniture had been much too small, so new furnishings had been shipped from Nom-Kat-La. He was concerned that Predax had not yet launched an attempt to take back the planet. Fa-a-Di had requested additional ships to support the seventy-three currently orbiting Localus and Nom-Kat-La. Field Marshall Je-e-Bo had sent urgent requests to Kalidus and Earth to get more ships. Earth was still in the process of upgrading the defense and weapons systems on their fleet. High Commissioner Daniels hoped to send three more ships in the coming days.

A tone sounded on his control panel and he touched a glowing button. High Commissioner Noctalus of the Kalidean Federation was smiling broadly. "Fa-a-Di, my brother, it is good to see you again. I am surprised you are not on Gallia," she said.

"Noctalus, it is a pleasure to see you as well, sister. I am here on Localus because I am a soldier first, and politician only second," Fa-a-Di laughed. "My friend Je-e-Bo and I are convinced the Predaxians will attempt to take this planet and Nom-Kat-La very soon. Je-e-Bo is in orbit on his fleet battle cruiser. I am leading the efforts here to glean information from the Predaxian agents we captured. They are a mentally tough group and our progress has been slow."

"There is hope, brother," she replied. "Four Predaxians cruisers in the Tantalus region have turned sides in the last few days. They are harassing the Predaxian planets on their side of the frontier. It is strange they have not engaged any loyal star ships in several days.  What do you make of that?"

"They must be massing an attack force close to here," Fa-a-Di said. "If that force was intent on attacking Tantalus, your rebels would have seen a lot of action. I will have to advise Je-e-Bo. Their attack may be imminent. By the way, sister, will you be able to send any ships to support our fleet here?"

"We will be jumping four battle cruisers today to Nom-Kat-La, brother," she replied. "Unfortunately, we are not completely convinced the rebels are genuine and cannot leave Tantalus unprotected. We have ten cruisers there now."

Fa-a-Di sighed, "I know, Noctalus, it is a difficult decision. When we attacked Localus, we were only fifty percent con-vinced the rebel ships in our fleet would fight on our side. Fortunately, they were very brave in battle and have now earned my respect. Those cruisers in your region could be real rebels or more agents.  Who can know?"

"Exactly, brother," she said. "On another subject, what have you heard about the voyage to Tak-Makla? We lost contact with our ambassador yesterday."

"I spoke with Commander Nan-de-Bo on the Kong-Fa a few hours ago," Fa-a-Di reported. "My brother-in-law had been transported to Tak-Makla from twelve light-years away."

"Twelve light-years?" Noctalus asked. "How is that possible?"

"I believe that is what our team is trying to learn.  Earlier today, the Kong-Fa and Nightsky were transported to Tak-Makla in the same fashion. One second they were in open space, and the next they were in orbit. Amazing! Our ambassadors are now on the planet meeting with the High Consul and some of his ministers. Hopefully we will convince them to join our cause," Fa-a-Di said.

"We definitely need their help, brother," she replied. "The Predaxians may have the ability to outgun us now. From reports similar to Tantalus, it seems that ships are moving away from other parts of their frontier. I assume they will attack you at Localus. If they have a large enough fleet, Localus and Nom-Kat-La could be in jeopardy."

"We will do our best to push them back all the way to Predax, or die trying," Fa-a-Di said. "My family has been military for many generations and we know the cost of war. I am happy to report that No-Makla has continued to send agents to us. We can now see five light-years into Predaxian space from Localus. So far, everything is clear, although I expect to see them coming soon."

"And what of the Predaxian political prisoners you released?" Noctalus asked. "Are they helping or hindering your efforts?"

"Fortunately, one Predaxian cannot control another," the general said. "Many have joined Zakamar Vondee and her rebels. Others remain here with us monitoring the captured agents and working to turn them against the emperor. I worry about what will happen to them if Predax captures this planet again. Their blood will be on our hands if that happens."

"Brother Fa-a-Di, I have the greatest confidence in you and Je-e-Bo," Noctalus smiled. "I remember your actions turning the First Predaxian War around and pushing them back. I know you two will do that again."

"Thank you, Noctalus, for your words of encouragement. I know when the taste of battle is in my mouth, I will do everything possible to end the blight the Predaxians have sown on the galaxy," Fa-a-Di said. "I still remember my father telling me about his friendship with many Palians. It is terrible to see their worlds after a hundred years of Predaxian rule. A proud species has been reduced to slavery. We have several thousand Palians now infiltrating the Palian worlds to undermine Predaxian control. Each has a maklan with them for protection. Many Palian worlds are on the brink of revolution."

"Along that line, I have been contacted by Emperor Valka of Pyrrus. All of the Predaxian ships along their frontier have disappeared. He has lauched several incursions into their space. The ten planets of the Lozaki are close to their frontier. They have also reportedly destroyed one Predaxian supply ship deep in the dead quarter of their space. Five other ships are attacking strongholds on Lozaki planets. The emperor has asked for our help. What do you think, brother?" she asked.

"The Pyrrians are an odd group, sister," Fa-a-Di responded. "We have no contact with them since they are so far from our space. "They seem barbaric to me. I would caution against providing them with too much support."

"I agree, brother," Noctalus said. "At this point in time, neither of us has any free resources. We are totally committed to the Predaxian frontier. Perhaps after you defeat the Predaxian fleet, we will reconsider."

"Agreed," Fa-a-Di said. "Sister, I am getting a priority call. I will call you back later. Localus out." The connection was cut and the image of Field Marshall Je-e-Bo filled his screen. "What is happening, my friend?"

Je-e-Bo sat back in his chair and sipped a glass of whisky. "Fa-a-Di, my dear brother, the enemy has launched its fleet from Palus. We are reading one hundred star cruisers headed our way."

"Ah, the war has begun in earnest, my brother," Fa-a-Di smiled. "When will they arrive?"

"They are traveling at near full speed. It appears they have some older ships slowing them down. We estimate their arrival in two days. Have you had any luck obtaining more assets for the battle?" Je-e-Bo asked.

"Some luck, brother," Fa-a-Di replied. "Besides the three Earth ships, High Commissioner Noctalus is jumping four more to Nom-Kat-La today. That will give us eighty ships to their one hundred."

"Pretty difficult odds, brother," Je-e-Bo sneared. "This will not be like our great victory at Nok-lak-a, friend. We are in their space and there are hundreds of thousands of their agents deep inside Localus. If they take the planet, they will unleash that horde on Nom-Kat-La. I still shudder when I think how easily the Predaxians controlled me. I have been talking with High Commissioner Pakalanalan about a plan."

"Please tell me the details, brother," Fa-a-Di said as he filled his glass with captured Predaxian brandy. He sipped it and sat back.

"We know that only ten or twenty of the Predaxian fleet will be manned exclusively by Predaxians. The rest will have enslaved crews and probably half of those will be Palian," Je-e-Bo began. "Arroflenides has agreed to increase the number of maklan agents here by eight hundred thousand. That group will lie in wait on Localus. When the enemy fleet is in range, they will jump to each of the non-Predaxian ships. Our hope is that the maklans will disrupt the mind control of the Predaxian agents. If we can get any of those vessels to change sides, it could turn the battle in our favor."

"That's brilliant, Je-e-Bo," Fa-a-Di smiled as he drained his glass. "Perhaps we will live to fight another day. I do have some additional news. Our Palian agents claim to have taken over four of the Palian ships in the fleet.  With the overall size of their fleet, the Predaxian agents haven't been able to maintain absolute control. Kogala has told me those ships will turn to our side when we need them most. They will also make certain they do not hit any of our ships."

"Wonderful, Fa-a-Di. That is great news," Je-e-Bo laughed. "Those two tactics may be enough to win the day. I only hope we hear from De-o-Nu and Dave soon with good news. Time is very short and diplomacy is slow and complex. Tak-Makla seems to have the ability to do miraculous things. Let us hope they come to our aid."

"God willing, they will, Je-e-Bo," Fa-a-Di said. "I will take a shuttle up to your flagship later today so we can begin the battle plan. Localus out."

"First, I want to thank you for journeying to meet with us," Zee said. "We had a wonderful evening yesterday and I trust our guests enjoyed the dinner we held in your honor?"

"It was fabulous, High Consul," Darlene began, "and we are grateful that you have allowed our ships to visit your world. As you know, we are looking to establish relationships with new civilizations. Your culture is clearly one of the most advanced in the galaxy, and it would be an honor to work and trade with you."

"I agree," Ambassador Petrodus said. "Kalidus is very interested in our mutual trade. We believe your vast network of trading partners will bring many new cultures into our circle of friends."

Nar Benadar, Minister of Defense entered the room. He apologized for his tardiness and sat next to the High Consul.

"Thank you ambassadors," Zee said. "Now that Nar has arrived, there have been some issues related to our meeting that trouble us. Nar, please continue."

"Thank you Consul," Nar said. "We are aware of the continuing struggles of your worlds against Predax. I understand that completely. We had friendly relations with Predax several million years ago, but when they perfected their mind control techniques and began to expand their empire, we cut all ties. For your information, The Hive advises us that one hundred ships controlled by Predax are currently traveling toward the frontier with Greater Gallia. There are more than seventy ships from your fleet there already. We fear that hostilities may begin in a day or two."

"I was not aware of that, Consul," Dave said. "Does the possibility of war with the Predaxians bother you?"

"Not at all," Nar answered.  The other tekkans smiled. "We are happy to see the end of their slavery in that sector of space. We are quite concerned that your ships are outnumbered though. But that is a matter for your leaders, not us."

Zee said, "Let us cut to the chase. What are your intentions with our home world?"

De-o-Nu asked, "I don't think we understand the question, Consul. We want trade and peace with Tak-Makla, nothing else."

"Not this planet!" Zee exclaimed. "We are talking about Ai-Makla, the original world of the maklans. Why are there agents from Earth, No-Makla and Predax there? I understand the sanctity of that world to those maklan species, but why are humans there?"

"Consul," Ambassador Carakala Pakalanalan interjected, "we do not know where Ai-Makla is. I can't imagine there are any maklan agents there. Can you provide any additional information about this? How many maklans and humans are involved on Ai-Makla?  Where is this planet?"

"Zee, The Hive does not report any anomalies here," Var Kandalan, Minister of The Hive reported. "Our guests appear to be telling the truth."

"Perhaps Var," Zee replied. "I can understand how many maklan cultures could have lost track of the home world. Our original settlers included many great astrophysicists who enabled us to keep its location. The nova that destroyed Ai-Makla burned off the atmosphere and much of the crust of the planet. What exists there now is a solid rock and iron core circling a white dwarf star. That site is sacred to us, and we have been monitoring Ai-Makla since the Predaxians began to modify it. The Hive has seen structures inside the planet now. Predaxian ships have been visiting it for more than ten solar revolutions."

Var continued, "Recently, more Predaxian vessels have been stopping there. Currently, The Hive has seen six Predaxians, two humans and one maklan in the structures within the planet. Our ability to see there is very limited due to the vast amounts of rock and iron between space and the chambers within. There are those in The Hive who imagine the worst. We have found that Ai-Makla is one of the few spots in the galaxy with more lines of universal power than Tak-Makla. If your species could build a world there such as this one, a Hive there could be far more powerful than ours."

De-o-Nu said, "Gentlemen, I know that none of the species present there could possibly compete with your culture. Humanity is just beginning to explore space. Their technology is far behind that of Greater Gallia, so you can imagine how far below you they are. Also, Dave and Charlie are my brothers. I trust them with my life. They will never be your enemy. The Predaxians are too vile and warlike to spend time and resources on such an adventure or to form an alliance with Earth or No-Makla. While the maklans of No-Makla are an amazing race, I cannot see how one could make any difference."

"It's a prison planet," Petrodus interrupted. "The Predaxians are notorious for installing prisons for their political enemies deep inside planets. It is documented that their mind control cannot penetrate thousands of miles of rock and iron. It is the perfect place to imprison their most dangerous opponents."

"It must be the cell for Panoplez Zendo," De-o-Nu said. "He is the son of their emperor. He had a falling out with his father and began to recruit Predaxians to overthrow him. It was rumored that the emperor built a special prison just for him. Deep in a dead planet in their dead quadrant would be an ideal spot. Are Predaxian ships still going there?"

"The Hive reported a Predaxian ship there two days ago. A Pyrrian cruiser was attacking the ship, which jumped five Predaxians into the planet. The ship was then either destroyed or self-destructed," Nar said. "The cruiser left the area and proceeded to a Lozaki planet."

"Dave, my brother-in-law reported that two humans and one maklan had been imprisoned on Localus," De-o-Nu said. "They had been moved to an unknown prison within Predaxian space long before our invasion."

Dave stood and said, "Zee, I need to get to that planet and rescue our prisoners. Can you help us?"

"Of course, Dave, it would be an honor," Zee replied. "To insure your intentions, I would like to entertain the Kong-Fa and the ambassadors until the mission is complete. Perhaps Charlie and Aria could remain as well. I will send one hundred tekkan soldiers with you for support. We do not know what may be encountered there. Nar, perhaps you can lead your team. We will jump the Nightsky to that area after lunch. Hopefully, you will all return in time for dinner. We have planned another feast for the full crews of both ships this evening. I'd hate for you to miss it."

"I think that would be perfect Zee," Dave smiled. "Our ambassadors are much better than me for negotiations. Perhaps all of our differences will be resolved and new treaties can be signed soon."

"I think you are a bit optimistic, Dave," Zee laughed. "Diplomacy is not a quick exercise. Once Ai-Makla is free again, I can assure you that we will work as quickly as we can to complete the process."

"Thank you, Zee," Dave said. "I think I can make a commitment on behalf of all of our civilizations. Once the Predaxian horde is defeated, we will grant your planet control for the entire quadrant where Ai-Makla is located. If any civilization can build a new planet to rival this one, it will be the tekkans."

Zee laughed out loud, stood and hugged Dave. "Brother Dave, if I may call you that, I want to thank you for easing my mind on this issue. We still have a few hours before your ship will leave us. I have promised to show you The Hive. Our engineers have been working diligently since you were jumped here. Rather than show you The Hive, we would like you to join The Hive for a couple of hours. This is an honor that has never been given to any non-tekkan. Hopefully, in our new future of sharing and trading, we will do this for our other brothers and sisters as well. Let us go now."

# CHAPTER 36

Zee and Dave left the conference room and returned to the tube room where they had arrived from the Consul's residence. Zee tapped the panel and it asked for a destination. Zee said, "Hive, level six-eight-four-four-two, ring one." Zee put his face up to the panel. A soft green light illuminated him.

"Security scan confirmed. Welcome, High Consul. Ready," the panel said. The shuttle door opened and they stepped in and strapped themselves to the seats.

Zee touched a panel and said, "Ready." The shuttle zipped out of the room and barreled straight down for several moments. There were few tubes in the area and more of them veered off while they continued to plummet downward, until they were in the only tube visible. The shuttle slowed and turned into another tube room and stopped. "Okay, Dave, this is your stop," Zee said. "This is Engineer Nok," he said pointing to the female tekkan waiting in the room. "I'm returning to the meeting. Nok will take care of you and see that you get to your ship on time. I hope you enjoy your visit." Dave shook hands with the Consul and exited the shuttle. The door closed and it zipped out of the room.

"Welcome to The Hive, Dave," Nok smiled. "Please follow me." They left the tube room and entered a curving hall that seemed to go on indefinitely. "We are on level six-eight-four-four-two, which is the lowest section of The Hive where top secret clearance is not required. I was assigned to study your anatomy and develop an entry point into The Hive that would be compatible with your body and brain. Please, if you experience any discomfort, let me know. We only had a few hours to study you and we may have missed something." They continued walking past circular doors on the inside to the curve.

"What is The Hive, Nok?" Dave asked. "We've tried to ask that question over and again, but the answers are confusing."

"The Hive is a tool we use to explore the universe Dave," Nok said. "When we are part of it, our minds join together with universal power and we can explore any part of the universe."

"So, it's for science," Dave said.

"Only partially Dave," she replied as they stopped at one of the circular doors. She pressed a panel and the door opened like a camera shutter. "Let's go in, Dave." After they were inside, the door closed behind them. The room was around ten feet square with two chambers sitting side by side. The far wall was opaque black glass. "The Hive is also critical to our trade. With it, we can find new cultures to trade with and new resources we never imagined before."

Nok walked to the black glass and touched it, causing it to become transparent. Dave was stunned as he walked to join her at the glass wall. There was a large empty central cavity that seemed to reach forever up and down. There were hundreds, if not thousands of similar windows all around on this same level and too many levels to imagine. Colorful filaments of light shot up and down the opening, illuminating the other rooms in The Hive.

"Each window represents a cell like this one. Most have two chambers like this one," Nok said as she pointed to the fixtures in the room. "Below here, in the secret area, there is only one chamber per room." She put her hand on one chamber, saying, "This is a standard chamber, which I will use. The chamber connects us to the minds of the other billions of tekkans working here. We created this helmet to enable you to connect with us." She picked up the helmet and handed it to Dave. "Please try it on."

"It fits perfectly," Dave said. "What do I do now?"

"Just lie down in the chamber and relax. Once I am in my chamber, both will close and we will be part of The Hive. I will explain more once we are inside," Nok replied.

Dave lay on the pad in the chamber and it adjusted itself around him. "Do I close my eyes or what?" he asked.

"Yes," she replied. "The sensation of The Hive would confuse your eyes. In a way, you might feel like you are dreaming, but I'll be there the entire time so you know it's real. The High Consul said I needed to make sure you get to lunch in his office in two hours, so let's begin. Just relax and try to enjoy the experience. And remember to let me know if you are experiencing any discomfort, okay?"

"Yes, Nok, I'll let you know," Dave said. Nok climbed into her chamber. When she was in position, both chambers closed.

Dave felt a bit dizzy and thought about saying something, but before he could say a word, he felt his mind separating from his body. He thought he could see his body lying below him on the table with a slight smile. A strong force pulled his mind out of the chamber and into the center opening. He felt himself being absorbed into the filaments of light that filled the open center of The Hive. He was totally disconnected from his body and wondered if he had died. Millions of other strings of light surrounded him and they carried him upward. More and more strings joined the group as they shot out of The Hive and flew into space. The billions of lights streamed outward in every direction. Dave could see them flowing out along a faint pattern, which he guessed must be universal power. As his light-string flew around the planet, he could see the Kong-Fa and Nightsky in orbit. He thought about Jon Lake. His string turned to the ship and dived into the bridge. He could see and hear Jon talking with Fleet Admiral Adamsen about the coming battle for Localus.

"Wow, Dave, you got the hang of this right away," Nok said as her silver filament of light wrapped around his blue filament. "I thought I lost you for a minute but then figured you'd be looking for your ship."

"Are you telling me that I really am aboard the Nightsky, Nok?" he asked. "I can see and hear the crew talking. Can they see or hear me?"

"No, Dave, they cannot," Nok replied. "If they focused their instruments, they might notice a slight power surge, but that's it. You are still in the chamber next to me in The Hive. We have joined the collective mind of The Hive now. Our thoughts are able to go anywhere and see anything. That includes traveling through time. Since we are only mental energy, we can't affect the course of time, so there is little risk. What do you want to see?"

"How about the Nanda?" Dave asked. "We were not able to decipher their language and are trying hard to learn it now. If we went to Nanda would we understand them?"

"Of course," Nok said, "as mental energy, we can understand any language because we are not hearing their voices; we are touching their mental images, which we have found to be universal. Just follow me?" Nok's silver light shot away. Dave thought about her and his light followed.

"Nok, when we first left Tak-Makla, I thought I saw a dim pattern the other lights were following. Is that universal power?" Dave asked.

"Not exactly, Dave," she replied. "The pattern shows the lines that universal power uses to glue the space and time together. Universal power tends to be the greatest where the number of converging lines is highest, such as at Tak-Makla and Ai-Makla."

They were rapidly approaching a small planet with large oceans and small continents. Dave could see Kalidean research vessels and one Gallicean cruiser in orbit. Nok led Dave straight down into the atmosphere and toward a large city on the edge of an ocean. They moved through buildings and trees and stopped inside a large space craft hangar. A group of Nanda stood inspecting a recently completed small star cruiser. Nok stopped directly in the middle of the group.

"Admiral Kleeg, I hope you know what you're doing," shouted one Nanda to an elderly female. "Finishing this ship has cost us a fortune."

"Don't worry, Commissioner Valkor," Kleeg replied. "I can't stand by and allow those hideous creatures to orbit our world. I know they are planning an invasion. They have killed or captured my daughter and I demand that we rescue her."

Valkor said, "We know that we lost ten pilots that day. What makes you think we stand any chance of defeating them with this ship?"

Nok's filament wrapped around Dave's again. "Dave, if you look closely in their eyes, you can see their own filament of light." Dave looked and was astonished to see the lights behind their eyes. "All living Beings have the light within them. For most Beings, the light will only be free when their body dies. We believe they join with the stream of universal power and become the source that manages the universe."

"On my home world, we believe we can learn much about another by looking in their eyes, Nok," Dave replied. "Perhaps unconsciously our light is seeing theirs."

"I believe that is true, Dave," Nok said. "There are those in The Hive who believe that universal power is or contains universal consciousness. Those tekkans are generally housed in the top secret areas of The Hive. At the levels between four-seven-two-five-zero and six-eight-four-two-two, we are focused on exploration. We find new planets and civilizations in all the galaxies of the universe. The top levels search of new resources and keep and eye on existing civilizations and our trading partners. The lower levels are very secretive. We believe they are traveling in time and trying to unravel the mysteries of the universe. They may also be keeping an eye on each of us."

"It fascinates me that I feel like I am standing here in this room on Nanda and these Beings are including me in their conversation," Dave said.

"They can sense our presence, Dave," she replied. "We have found that after a few minutes, any Beings around us start to be uncomfortable. Their inner light is probably recognizing ours. They don't see anything, but somehow they know they are being watched. We should probably leave here. Where else would you like to go?"

"Can we go to Ai-Makla? I'm supposed to go there later and rescue some prisoners," Dave said. "If I could see them and their condition, we might be better prepared."

"Follow me, Dave," Nok said as her light shot away. He thought of her and his light once again followed.  Stars and planets were zipping by almost too fast to recognize. Nok slowed as they approached Localus. Dave could see the mass of ships in orbit, waiting for the Predaxian attack. A few seconds later, they reached the Predaxian fleet which was speeding to battle. Nok flew directly into a room on the Pondi and stopped. In front of them was Emperor Nokalez Zendo, pacing back and forth. Two empty brandy bottles were on the floor. Another Predaxian was passed out on the floor. They zipped back into space.

They passed hundreds of stars and thousands of planets. After a minute, the number of stars declined and space became even more dark and foreboding. Dave looked back and saw his string of light reaching out to infinity. "Nok, where does my string of light end?" he asked.

"In the chamber with your body, Dave," she replied. "It will only separate from you when you die." They slowed rapidly as they approached a black rock floating in space. Nok's light stopped on the surface. The black rock was a large dead planet. Dave stopped next to her. "This is Ai-Makla, Dave."

"Do you think our lights can penetrate to the chambers inside?" Dave asked.

"I don't know," she replied.  "We have had many others visit here and they have only seen glimpses of what is inside. We can try. I'll wrap my light around yours, and you imagine yourself inside the chamber below.  We'll see what happens."

Dave imagined a dark cell buried in the center of the planet. He thought about the human and other prisoners there hoping for freedom. He tried to imagine the emperor's son, imprisoned by his own father.

"Pan, do you think we'll ever get out of here?" Lauren London asked.

"That's pretty somber thinking for one who believes there is hope as long as we live," Pan replied.

"I know, but I feel helpless, Pan. I am a soldier and I should be in space fighting to defeat the emperor," she said.

Mitch walked toward them, then stopped suddenly, turned and looked at the spot where Dave and Nok's lights were floating. He seemed to stare directly at Dave's light-string for a moment, then turned and joined the others. "You know, I think I am more optimistic now than I've been in a very long time, although I have no idea why," he said as he sat next to the other two.

"Why the sudden optimism, maklan?" Dok asked from across the room as he fumbled to open a box of food.

"I don't know," Mitch continued. "It's just a feeling that others know where we are and the cavalry is on the way."

Lauren put her arm around Mitch and said, "Mitch, your optimism is helping my mood greatly." She turned to Dok and shouted, "Hey Dok, save some food for the rest of us. You look like you've gained five pounds since you arrived here." The rest laughed.

Dave Brewster popped out of thin air onto the bridge of the Nightsky. Jon Lake had been lost in thought when Dave appeared. "Yikes!" Jon shouted. "You practically scared me to death, Dave."

"Sorry Jon," he apologized, "that's just the way the tekkans do things. Prepare the ship to leave orbit as quickly as possible. We have found some prisoners-of-war deep inside a dead planet in Predaxian space. The tekkans are going to jump our ship directly there from here."

"Where are Darlene, Aria and Charlie?" Jon asked.

Dave replied, "Everyone else is staying here, Jon. The High Consul asked me to leave them here while we do this mission as a sign of our good faith. It will also give our ambassadors an opportunity to negotiate the alliance and trade agreements."

"I'm not sure I like the sound of that," Jon said. "How is kidnapping a sign of their good faith?"

"Jon, please. Just follow the orders for now. There is too much going on to sit here and quibble about the details," Dave replied. "There is more, Jon. I can't tell you how I know this, but I'm fairly certain that Lauren is one of those prisoners."

Jon's eyes filled with tears. "Dave, how can you know that?"

"Jon, please get the crew ready. A group of tekkan soldiers will be joining us. Nightsky will jump to the planet. We will jump inside the cell and jump back with the prisoners. Then the ship will jump back here," Dave explained. "You have seen what the tekkans can do, Jon. They could have crushed our ships when we were twelve light-years away. What need do they have for hostages?"

"Aye-aye, Admiral," Jon said. He barked orders at the bridge crew and stations lit up as preparations were made. "Donna, make sure offensive and defensive systems are at peak. We may be arriving in a war zone."

"Aye-aye, Captain," she replied. "All systems show green. I'm powering up the defensive array now."

Minister Nar and five bodyguards appeared on the bridge. The group was in full battle gear. "Ah, Dave, I see you have returned from The Hive," Nar said softly. "I trust you enjoyed the experience."

"Yes Nar," Dave replied. "It was amazing. I could never imagine something like that could exist."

"I have been told it is a wonderful thing. As a soldier, I have never had the opportunity to enter The Hive. I suppose I am a bit jealous of you, Dave," Nar smiled. He turned to face Jon. "Captain, my squad has jumped to your shuttle bay. I trust you can find somewhere for them to be comfortable."

"Yes sir," Jon replied. "Donna, please see that the tekkan troops are moved to our armory and introduced to our ground commanders."

"Aye-aye, Captain," she said. "I've signaled Major Masterson to escort them."

"Thanks to all of you," Nar replied. "I have signaled Zee that we are ready to jump, is that okay?"

"Aye-aye Minister," Jon confirmed. "All stations report ready."

"Just relax everyone," Nar said softly. "It should only be a few moments." The bridge crew sat rigidly, not knowing what to prepare for.

The bridge lights fluttered for a split second. "Captain, Tak-Makla is gone," Lia said. The vast green planet was no longer in the view screen. In its place was a black scar of a planet, dimly visible in the weak light of its dying sun. It seemed roughly the size of Earth but was clearly lifeless. The entire surface was scared and blistered as though a giant blow-torch had been applied to the surface.

"It seems we have arrived at Ai-Makla," Nar said calmly. "We should prepare our landing party. Dave, can your crew scan the interior of the planet for the cells inside?"

"Captain, we have trouble. I am reading a Pyrrian cruiser closing fast on these coordinates," Donna shouted. "Defensive array is at maximum."

Laser blasts hit the Nightsky near the engine nacelles. The ship rocked and Nar fell to the floor.

"Damage report, Donna," Jon shouted.

"No damage, Captain. Defenses are at eighty-seven percent. Shall we return fire?" she replied.

"Negative. Hail that ship and tell them we are not Predaxian," Jon said. "We are only here to rescue our prisoners."

The narrow insect-like face of the Pyrrian captain appeared on their view screen. Other Pyrrians could be seen scurrying around behind him. "We have no interest in your mission," squawked the Pyrrian captain. "You have invaded Pyrrian space and are now subject to extermination. Surrender your ship or die!"

Nar had been picked up by his bodyguards. "Dave, please let us handle this," he said. "We are quite used to dealing with the Pyrrians."

The Pyrrian disappeared from the view screen, replaced by the external view. The bridge crew could see the cruiser began another attack run. As it closed in on Nightsky, they could see the Pyrrian's weapons glow white as its laser array was recharged. Just as it neared attack range, the ship veered away and dived toward the planet. They watched it plummet downward for several seconds until it crashed onto Ai-Makla in a thunderous explosion.

"You killed them all?" Jon said to Nar in disbelief over what he had just seen.

"Not at all, Captain," Nar smiled. "The cruiser was the problem here. We jumped the crew back to Pyrrus and turned the ship away from us. The Hive doesn't see another such vessel within ten light-years, so we have more than ample time to complete our mission.  Shall we go, Dave?"

"I want to go too," Jon said.

Dave replied, "Nar, when I was in The Hive, I visited the cell. None of the Predaxians are a threat there. I believe they are prisoners as well. Please don't send them back to Predax."

"We would never deliberately endanger anyone, Dave. My entire group will jump with you, Jon and me," Nar said. "We may need their energy to be certain the group can jump back here. The last thing we want is more prisoners buried in that rock. Are we ready?"

As Dave and Jon stood up, they found themselves in the dark cell. There was no light and no sound. "Lauren!" Jon shouted.

Pan pressed the panel to turn on the lights. The prisoners had all been sleeping. Lauren jumped to her feet and ran into Jon's arms. "How did you find us, Jon?" she cried.

"With a little help from our friends, Sweetheart," Jon said as he kissed her again. "We don't want any of you stuck here even a minute longer. Get everyone together near Minister Nar and his troops."

The others rushed to join the group, leaving Panoplez Zendo sitting on the floor. "Pan, it's time to go," Mitch said.

"That's okay, guys," Pan replied. "I guess I'm getting used to this place."

Dave walked over to Pan and sat on the floor with him. He touched Pan's head and said, "Pan, it is an honor to meet you. My name is Dave Brewster and we have come a long way to get all of you out of this place. At this moment, one hundred Predaxian controlled ships are heading to Localus to attack around eighty ships who are trying to free the galaxy of the tyranny of your father."

"Dave, I hope they are successful," Pan smiled. "But what does that have to do with me?  I'm just one person."

"That is definitely not true, Pan," Dave replied. He pulled an envelope from his pocket and set it next to the Predaxian. "Almost half of the ships trying to stop your father are from the Free Predax movement. They have been flying all around Predaxian space making trouble for the emperor and recruiting more rebels. That is the movement you started long ago, Pan. This letter is from the current head of Free Predax. She gave this letter to General Fa-a-Di of Greater Gallia. He had copies made for all command level officers in Greater Gallia, the Kalidean Federation and the Human Community. She hoped one of us might find you one day and bring you back. I'm sure you know who I am talking about."

"Zak," Pan said softly. "She's alive?"

"Alive and leading her fleet into battle in a couple days," Dave replied. "She wants you to join her. With you in charge of the Free Predax movement, we know they will win. Let's go, Pan." They rose and joined the rest of the group. In a flash, they were gone.

# CHAPTER 38

Captain Vandamar Narka was reviewing the battle plan sent to him by Field Marshall Je-e-Bo while he sat in his command chair on the star cruiser Parax. The Free Predax fleet was in position for the battle which would commence in less than twenty-four hours. He had sent requests to the remaining rebel ships in Alliance territory to get to Localus as soon as possible to improve the odds against the larger Alliance fleet. As he glanced around the bridge, six Predaxians and twelve armed tekkans appeared on the bridge in front of him. "Pan, is that you?" Van asked.

"Van, you old dog," Pan smiled, "it's good to see you again!" Pan hugged Van. "Is your ship ready for the fun?"

Van was in shock. Pan had disappeared long ago amid rumors that the emperor had killed or imprisoned him. No one had heard anything about the emperor's son since that day. "Pan, how did you get here? Who are these other people?" he asked.

"Good day Captain, my name is Nar Benadar. I am Minister of Defense for the planet Tak-Makla. My troops and I have just released some prisoners from a cell deep within the maklan home world of Ai-Makla," Nar said in his typical calm and measured tone. "At Pan's request, we are releasing the Predaxians to you."

"What is Ai-Makla?" Van said.

"It's a long story Van, and I'll tell you later," Pan interrupted. He turned to Nar and said, "Minister, thank you for your help in saving my friends and me. Please thank Dave Brewster and Jon Lake as well. I know you have to return to the Nightsky."

"You are quite welcome Pan," Nar replied. He turned to Van. "Captain, I am afraid my team must take our leave of you now. Please know all the tekkans on Tak-Makla are wishing you great success in the upcoming battle. The mind control of the Predaxians must end if they are to be accepted into the galactic community as equals." Without a word or a sound, the tekkans were gone.

"What the heck is going on Pan?" Van asked.

"Not now, Van!  Is Zak on board?" Pan asked. Before Van could answer, the ready room door opened and Zakamar Vondee walked onto the bridge with maklan Ambassador Konomalocus Nolobitamore. When she saw Pan, she broke down crying and ran to embrace him.  Pan kissed her softly and held her tightly.

"Pan, how did you get here?" Zak cried. "This isn't possible. Am I dreaming or hallucinating?"

"I'm here Zak," Pan said as he held her. "I'm back to help you. Admiral Dave Brewster gave me a copy of the letter you gave to Fa-a-Di. I can't believe what you've done with the resistance! This is marvelous. Finally my father will pay for what he has done to so many other civilizations. And it's all because of you!"

"I did it for you Pan. I did it all for you, my darling," she cried.

Van interrupted, "Zak, you should have seen it. Two minutes ago, Pan and these others popped out of nowhere onto the bridge with twenty heavily armed troops. Nar, the leader of the troops says he just rescued Pan and the others from a prison planet. The troops then disappeared. It was so weird. I'm still in shock."

Zak was finally able to let go of Pan and looked around at the others. "Dok, is that you?" she asked.

"Hi, Zak. You remember my dad," he said as he pointed to Altamar Zendo.

"Aren't you the head of the secret police?" she asked. "Van, keep an eye on that one."

"It's good to see you, Zakamar," Altamar said. "What you are saying is true, but when Nokalez arrested me and most of the family, I knew I'd made a big mistake supporting him."

"If it's all the same to you Pan, I think we'll keep these guys in the brig until after the battle," Zak said.

"We can't do that Zak," Pan implored. "If they are captured, they will be executed along with us. We need Altamar's tactical skills. He can help us. I'll keep an eye on him. If he turns on us, I'll kill him myself."

"Okay, I guess so Pan. I think you and I should introduce him to Fa-a-Di and Je-e-Bo and let them decide if his knowledge is any use to us," Pan said.

"I can prove my worth right now," Altamar said. He closed his eyes tightly. All the bridge crew stood and formed a circle around them. They joined hands and began to sing an old Predaxian folk song. Then the circle of Predaxians started to dance around the group in the middle. After a few minutes, they stopped and returned to their seats.

"We were all raised to believe one Predaxian could not control the mind of another," Altamar said. "I hope I have just proven that not to be true."

Van shouted at the helmsman, "What's going on?"

"All systems show green, Captain," he replied.

"What was the singing and dancing about?" Van shouted.

"What are you talking about, Captain? Are you well sir?" he replied.

Altamar continued, "Only about one Predaxian in a hundred million can do that. That is why Nokalez selected Thuk as the prison for Panoplez. Even the emperor doesn't know who has this power. He buried Pan there to be certain he couldn't use it if he had the power. But I know every Predaxian who has this ability! When I discovered this genetic anomaly, I searched the database of our agents for it. Almost none had the anomaly. Then I searched the general population and found a few hundred. I personally recruited them to be my secret security detail. While they serve in the emperor's army, they remain loyal to me. I need to reconnect to them and insure they are still alive and loyal. They would be a significant force to combat my brother."

"Excuse me Pan" the maklan ambassador said, "I am very happy that you have been rescued. I apologize if my presence is a problem now."

"I'm so sorry, Kono," Zak apologized. "In all of the excitement, I forgot you were here."

"No apology needed Zak. I am very happy for you," Kono replied. "Pan, can you tell me if there were any maklans like me in that prison?"

"Yes, Ambassador," Pan said, "there was one. He's a great guy and really helped us all through our stay down there. His name is Michamanades Nolobitamore."

Tears welled in Kono's eyes. She said, "Thank you, Pan. He is my brother and our family has been distraught since he was captured. Where is he?"

"Mitch stayed with the human crew on the Nightsky," he answered. "They were jumping back to Tak-Makla. Don't worry, Mitch is fine now."

"Thank you all for such wonderful news. I will return to the Texas now. We will meet again in battle soon," Kono smiled. She glowed bright white and disappeared.

"Pan, I agree with Zak," Altamar said. "I think we should contact Fa-a-Di in private to discuss what you have just seen. This could make the difference in battle."

"Does Pan have the power, Altamar?" Zak asked.

"No dear, he does not. There are two others in this room who do though," Altamar replied.

"Who would that be, Uncle?" Pan questioned.

"Zakamar should have power equivalent to mine, if she was trained to use it," Altamar replied. "But the Predaxian with the highest potentially ever recorded is my own dear son, Dokalak."

Pan was laughing. "Dok has the power? You've got to be kidding me, Altamar. He's never done much of anything."

"He's right, Dad," Dok agreed. "You know me better than anyone. Just give me a few drinks and some pretty girls and I'm done for the day."

"Son, I said you have the potential. You and Zakamar need intense training to be able to utilize this tool," Altamar explained. "After we meet with Fa-a-Di, I want to work with you both to unleash this force. The three of us could turn this battle around."

"Come on Dad, you know I'm not smart enough to do this," Dok laughed.

"Son, we have to try," Altamar replied. "There are billions of lives at stake. We may win or we may lose. But we are not going to give up by not trying. Have faith in me, Dok. I have faith in you, Son."

The crews of Kong-Fa and Nightsky had been transported to Zee's residence on the surface of Tak-Makla. A major festival was planned for the evening to celebrate the liberation of Ai-Makla and the new friendship with Kalidus, Gallia, No-Makla and Earth. The patio of the residence was covered with hundreds of tables decorated with fine china and crystal glassware. A receiving line of tekkan ministers and the ambassadors of the representative worlds greeted all the guests for the party. Dozens of waiters circulated through the throng with large trays of appetizers and all types of drinks.

After the reception was completed, all present began to mingle and share a laugh or story with new friends. Minister of State Fak Mondoka moved through the crowd looking for Ambassador De-o-Nu. She carried two bottles of whisky. Fak found him at the edge of the patio with Dave Brewster, looking at the waves crashing onto the beach. "My dear friends, I have found you," she said, waving the bottles in front of her.

"Fak, it is a pleasure to see you again. And we can see you are bearing gifts!" De-o-Nu laughed as he held out his empty glass.

"De-o-Nu, these bottles contain two of the best whiskies I have ever had," she smiled. "Excluding Gallicean, of course! This one is from Nanda. We spoke of this last evening. The other is from another civilization that is in a different galaxy. It is my personal favorite."

"By all means, Fak!" De-o-Nu beamed. "I love to try new things and whisky is my favorite thing to try"

She poured the dark green liquid into their glasses and smiled. De-o-Nu sniffed its bouquet and his head shot back. "Wow," he said, "this is very strong stuff." He sipped it gingerly. "Amazingly good. Dave, you have to taste this."

"It is very good," Dave replied after sipping the drink. "I'm afraid it is too strong for me." He coughed. "Where did you say this was from? I've never seen a green whisky."

"It is from a culture called the Draniks. Their worlds are in a nearby galaxy. I believe humans call it the Andromeda Galaxy," Fak explained. "The chemical makeup of their environment is quite different from the worlds we have found in this part of our galaxy. When they char their barrels, the surface becomes very dark green."

"How can you do business in another galaxy, Fak?" Dave asked. "Andromeda is more than two million light-years away, isn't it?"

"Dave, I know it sounds unbelievable, but since you have been in The Hive, you realize that many things are possible that most Beings cannot imagine," Fak replied. "Today, we jumped your ship more than one thousand light-years in the blink of an eye. Would you have ever thought that was possible?"

Zee had joined the group and put an arm on Dave's shoulder. "Fak, you are confusing our friends," he began. "Dave, the things we do everyday must seen unreal to a human from the twenty-first century. Please remember that our culture is billions of years old, while humans have only existed for a few million. We learn about new places and cultures with The Hive. When we feel a direct meeting is appropriate, we can access universal power through The Hive to move our ships incomprehensible distances. In order to provide resources to our people, we need a very large trading base."

"You are right about me being confused, Zee," Dave replied. "Tak-Makla is an incredible place. Even the life I led before coming here was so radically different from my twenty-first century existence that I was living in a state of constant disbelief. Being with the tekkans has made even that life seem mundane."

"Fak and De-o-Nu," Zee said, "I need to talk with Dave in private, so I will leave you to your whisky. Could you please join me on the beach, Dave?"

As they went down the steps to the sand, Dave glanced back and saw Fak opening the other whisky bottle. De-o-Nu was laughing loudly. They walked almost to the water's edge and turned to walk further away from the gathering.

"Dave, I hadn't had the chance to ask you about your experience in The Hive," Zee said. "Engineer Nok seemed to think you enjoyed it immensely."

"Yes, Zee, it was an amazing experience," Dave replied. "I could never have imagined my life energy traveling through space while my body stayed here."

"Frankly, I'm surprised it worked at all, Dave. Nok and her team are brilliant, but with only a few hours to develop the interface, it shocked me when it worked," Zee said. "Minister Var told me there was only a ten percent chance it would work, and I thought that was optimistic."

"I'm glad it did work out, Zee," Dave responded. "It would have been a shame to have missed it."

Zee stopped walking and looked out to sea. After a moment, he continued, "There is more to tell, Dave. After you returned, Nok met with Var and others to review the system. Apparently, the helmet was not functional."

"How did I join The Hive then, Zee?" Dave asked. "I thought only a tekkan mind could access The Hive without an interface device."

Zee said, "That is what we believed as well, Dave. While you were on your mission, we invited Darlene, Charlie and Aria to visit The Hive. We put them in their chambers without any helmet, and all three entered The Hive with no issue. I have asked a team of physicians to study human DNA and anatomy to see if they can find anything. I expect their report in the morning. I do have one theory though."

"I'm no scientist, Zee, but it would seem there must be strong similarities between human and tekkan neurology and DNA," Dave said.

"That is my theory exactly," Zee said. "But I have no idea how it could have happened. We have had no contact with Earth. I told you last evening we acquired green coffee from Earth some time ago. That came from a trading partner of the Kalideans who also trades with us.  Kalidus would have no knowledge of the indirect connection to Tak-Makla."

"Zee, when I first met Jake, he told me that his maklan society had lived on Earth millions of years before life left the oceans and moved onto land," Dave replied. "Could their DNA have been left behind and impacted human development?"

"Var thought about that too, Dave," Zee continued. "He asked Jake to enter The Hive this afternoon. It didn't work. Jake felt great pain when we connected him, so we immediately broke the connection."

"This is indeed a quandary, Zee," Dave said as he sat on the sand. "Somehow, tekkans must have traveled to Earth and inadvertently altered our DNA."

"While that seems the simplest solution, it is quite unlikely," Zee replied, joining Dave sitting on the sand. "We appear to have an open society here, Dave, but really we are quite regimented. Half of our people work in The Hive. One quarter travel the universe trading with our millions of partners. The rest live here, working in government or businesses supporting the work of the rest. Each of us knows our role in society. The Hive was not so named just due to the shape. Our society runs a bit like a bee hive on your home world. Rather than one queen, we have a group of ministers. Everyone else understands their roles and works diligently to improve life for all. It would be unimaginable for a tekkan to defy the rules and travel to an unapproved planet."

"Perhaps one of your trading partners inadvertently took tekkan DNA and left it on Earth long ago," Dave guessed. "Similar to your purchase of green coffee, you may have traded with Kalidus, for example, and their crews visited Earth, leaving the contamination behind them."

"I hope you are right, Dave Brewster," Zee said somberly. "I must tell you that my ministers have a different idea that is very disturbing. You and your friends from Gallia and Kalidus live in this small area of our galaxy with us. As Minister Fak mentioned at last night's dinner, we have found more than three hundred and fifty living cultures that are descendants of the settlers from Ai-Makla. You already know the Predaxians who are cruel and barbaric."

"Our troops will face them in battle very soon, Zee," Dave replied.

"Yes, I know," Zee acknowledged. "Unfortunately for the memory of our ancestors, the Predaxians are not the only barbarian maklan civilization. Not long after The Hive became operational, our scouts discovered a large, friendly maklan culture on the other side of the galactic center. They were called the Maklakar. They inhabited ten thousand systems and had a population of five hundred billion souls. We established trading arrangements with them that were very beneficial for both of us. That relationship lasted for millions of years."

"Did they change and become warlike?" Dave asked.

"Unfortunately, the truth is worse than that!" Zee exclaimed. "Gradually, our trade with them lessened, which is quite common. Our mutual needs changed over time. Eventually, we lost track of them. Many millennia later, we found new resources we thought might interest the Maklakar. We sent scouts through The Hive to see how they were. All of their colonies had either been destroyed or taken over by a different maklan race, called the Paxran. We checked every planet and could find no evidence that any Maklakar were still in existence."

"The Paxran killed an entire civilization?" Dave said.

"Yes, Dave, that is correct," Zee confirmed. "We managed to obtain some of their DNA when one of their ships entered our space. They are genetically almost identical to tekkans, which is exceedingly unlikely. That may mean that Paxran traveled to Earth and contaminated the DNA. We do not know what else they may have done there. While they were living, the Maklakar told us they were trying to develop a technology similar to our

Hive. If the Paxran stole that technology and built a Hive of their own, they might take over the entire galaxy. Their rule would make the Predaxians seem like harmless pets."

Dave stood and said, "That's why you were so irate about the people inside Ai-Makla. If we controlled that planet and gave it to the Paxran, it would be a disaster."

Zee rose and put an arm on Dave's shoulder. "Exactly Dave. That was why we were concerned. We have several million secret agents in the lower levels of The Hive who check on the Paxran continually. We are looking for other planets in their region suitable for Hives and looking for any of their activity in this part of the galaxy. The Paxran occupy six thousand systems. We have found no such planets in their space. There are a few within a thousand light-years of their region which we monitor daily. Any activity on a planet hot with universal power gets our immediate attention."

Dave smiled, "Your advice is to stay away from their part of the galaxy then."

Zee laughed. "Not exactly, but it is a safe idea. I believe the Paxran will inevitably move into our region. Our cultures need to be tightly connected so we can stop any such incursion. We can help our friends understand the technologies where the Paxran are stronger, thereby improving your ships and weapons. We can help you contact thousands of new civilizations that want peace and trade. That will grow our alliance. When we are strong enough, the Paxran will not dare invade us."

"You are very generous, Zee," Dave said as they began to walk back to the party which was now in full swing. "What can we do for our part?"

"I'm glad you asked that, Dave," Zee smiled. "We desire trade, peace and defense. We are not an aggressive race like the Nanda or Galliceans. We will not be able to go into battle against the Paxran. It is not in our DNA. We can provide information through The Hive to help your forces. I believe any incursion by them is millennia in the future, so that should not color our agreements yet. However, building a stronger defense is a great option. Dave, Charlie told me that you would be known as Dave, Founder of a Thousand Worlds."

Dave laughed, "Yes, that's what I heard too. Just so you know, I've only fixed two colonies and just established two more. I haven't earned that title yet."

They stopped at the bottom of the steps to the patio. Dave could sense many at the party staring at them. "Dave, we now know humans can enter The Hive. You are just beginning to know its power. There is much more to tell you about that, but not tonight. I think our guests are feeling our absence. When you do build those colonies, please let us help locate ten or twenty at strong intersection points of universal power. Then we will build ten or twenty more Hives within our space. They can be manned with tekkans or humans or both. Other races that have the ability to join a Hive can be invited too. As we all learn more about universal power, the presence of twenty Hives would be an awesome force that would not only block the Paxran, but would also enable all of our civilizations to travel to the edges of the universe and beyond."

"Brother Zee," Dave laughed, "having been in The Hive and seen the power if only for an hour or two, I have to agree with you completely. Let's have dinner and break the news to your guests!"

At the top of the stairs, Dave and Zee could see everyone in the crowd looking at them anxiously. Zee grabbed Dave's arm and they thrust their arms into the air. The crowd cheered loudly and applause filled the air.

General Fa-a-Di paced angrily about the bridge of Je-e-Bo's flagship, the No-De-Ka. Je-e-Bo was barking orders to the bridge crew. A number of war ships were not maintaining their ordered formation. Several Free Predax ships were not accustomed to Galliceans protocols and kept breaking formation and moving around the fleet.

"Captain Narka, this is Je-e-Bo," he shouted into the com-link, "get your ships in formation now! Your ships are getting into the firing lines of the fleet. We will not be able to fire on the enemy with them in the way."

"Acknowledged, Field Marshall," Van replied. "I don't know what's going on either, sir. All my captains have their orders. We are hailing them, but they don't seem to want to fall into position."

"Je-e-Bo, this is Altamar Zendo. I think I know what is happening," he said. "I believe the bridge crews of those ships are compromised by Predaxians with the power I mentioned yesterday. I need three maklans to jump us to the ships in question. I will take care of this mutiny!"

"I will go there now with two others, Fleet Admiral," Kondi replied. "If Altamar turns, I will jump him into open space and leave him there." She flashed off the bridge.

"Well, there goes your bodyguard, Fa-a-Di," Je-e-Bo laughed.

"I believe she will do more for our cause there than here, brother," Fa-a-Di replied.

Captain Valamaz Kalmar was frantic. His ship was out of formation and he demanded to know the reason. The helmsman did not respond so he jumped up and rushed to the station. The helmsman pulled a blaster and pressed it into the captain's chest. Two other crew members grabbed Valamaz and dragged him back to his command chair and held him down. The helmsman put the blaster on his console and kept pressing buttons frantically. The ship's weapon system began to energize as the ship veered off course further and turned toward the No-De-Ka.

"Valamaz, what are you doing?" Van's voice screamed over the com-link. "Have you all gone insane?"

Altamar and Kondi flashed onto the bridge. The helmsman raised his blaster and Altamar shot him square in the chest. He glanced around the bridge until he recognized the science officer, who had been part of his special team. "So, Nark, we meet again."

"Altamar, you old fool," Nark said as he aimed his blaster at his mentor. "Prepare to die." Before he could pull the trigger, Kondi jumped on him and flashed out into open space. A second later, Kondi returned alone. Altamar took over the helm and pulled the ship back into formation and ordered the weapons to stand down. The stunned helmsmen stood and looked bewildered.

"Valamaz, your bridge crew had been under control by a secret agent of the emperor. That agent, your former science officer is now dead, floating in space. Please don't hold your crew responsible for this. It was out of their control. We give you your ship back. Kondi, let's go to the next one," Altamar said. He and Kondi flashed off the bridge.

"What is God's name is going on over there, Valamaz!" Van shouted again.

"I'm not sure, but I think we're okay now, Van. I don't believe it, but I just saw Altamar Zendo on my bridge," Valamaz replied.

Thirty minutes after she had left, Kondi flashed back onto the bridge of the No-De-Ka. "Field Marshall, I think we have corrected the issue," she said. "We found ten special agents hidden among the bridge crews of seven ships. They have all been eliminated."

"Excellent work, Kondi," Fa-a-Di laughed. "If we survive this day, you will certainly get a medal."

The weapons officer, Zu-No-Pa interrupted, "I'm sorry, sirs, but the enemy fleet is less than one hour from us now. I have advised all ships to energize their defenses and weapon systems."

"Thank you, Zu-No-Pa," Je-e-Bo replied. "When will we be in range for the maklans on Localus?"

"We are in range now, Je-e-Bo," Kondi replied. "However, our troops won't flash over to the enemy ships until we are ten minutes from contact. If we go too early, the enemy may have enough time to react to our actions. We need to create confusion and disarray in their fleet."

"Kondi, when should we launch our fighters?" Fa-a-Di asked.

"I'm still not certain I like the idea of you in a fighter, brother," Je-e-Bo said. "There won't be much steel between you and the vacuum."

"We've discussed this too much, brother," Fa-a-Di replied. "We have a disadvantage in the number of capital ships. When we launch a thousand fighters from Localus, it will intensify the disarray within the enemy fleet. We will pick at their defenses while they try to maneuver to attack your cruisers. Besides, these are our most advanced fighters. Their shields and weapons systems are not much less than yours. Plus we have a few surprises for them."

"Fa-a-Di, we have been through so much," Je-e-Bo sighed. "I have the feeling that we may never drink whisky or fly through a Dar-Fa again."

"Brother, our fates are in God's Hands," Fa-a-Di said. "You and I are simple warriors, Je-e-Bo. Our duty is to fight to protect our planets and our children. If it is my fate to die today, so be it. I personally think you and I have many more adventures ahead of us. By the way, I have twenty bottles of the best whisky in my quarters. When I return, we shall share a couple of them, my friend."

"Yes, my brother," Je-e-Bo confirmed. "God willing, we will take many Predaxians with us, and especially that dog, Emperor Zendo!" The two Galliceans hugged and saluted one another. Then, Fa-a-Di and Kondi flashed off the bridge down to Localus and their waiting star fighter.

"Field Marshall," the communications officer reported, "the Kong-Fa and Nightsky have just appeared in our formation. I did not see them a second ago, and then there they were."

"Thank you for the wonderful news," Je-e-Bo smiled. "Our odds have just improved. Make certain their captains know our plans."

# CHAPTER 41

The Predaxian fleet broke into two groups of fifty ships. In the center of one cloud of cruisers were eight troop transport ships. That group fell slightly behind the first group which was led by the imperial flagship. Pondi's group focused their fire on the center of the defensive line of cruisers, which had left orbit to confront the attackers ten thousand miles from Localus. Two Gallicean cruisers took the brunt of the attack. Their defenses failed and laser blasts cut great tears in their hulls.

The attackers aimed to slip through the defensive line as the two heavily damaged ships crept away from the scene of battle. Five Kalidean cruisers flew through the opening and blasted the Pondi with their weapons. One of the Pondi's engines exploded in a ball of fire and the ship swerved to escape further contact. The rest of the Predaxian ships returned fire, damaging two Kalidean ships and re-opening the path through the defending fleet. Dozens of ships twisted and tumbled as they battled for firing positions. As the opening in the defensive line grew, the second group of Predaxian ships flew through the gap and approached Localus.

Zakamar Vondee flashed onto the bridge of the Palian cruiser Daplago with her maklan bodyguard. The Daplago was leading the group of transport carriers. She shot the helmsmen with the blaster in her left hand which was set to stun and ducked behind that console. The bridge crew returned fire which glanced off the console. Zak concentrated as Altamar had taught her and glanced around the room. She saw one of Altamar's protégés clinging to the chest of the captain. She drew her other blaster from the right holster and shot the Predaxian at full force, which fell to the floor dead. More blasts hit the console, which was about to crumple when they flashed back to the Parax.

"Pan, there were too many of them," Zak panted. "There must have been ten Predaxians controlling the Palians on the bridge alone. There was one special agent that I killed."

"Damn it," Pan shouted, "where are the maklans? They were supposed to handle that for us." He turned to the captain, "Van, blast the bridge of that ship now!"

"Belay that order!" came a voice over the com-link. "This is Jake Benomafolays. My team and I are on the bridge of the Daplago and we have the situation under control. The captain was a personal friend of Fa-a-Di and he has turned his ship to return to Palus." As they watched on the view screen, the Daplago changed course and headed back into space. The Parax bridge crew cheered as Jake and his agents flashed onto the bridge.

The Parax shuddered as enemy fire tested its defenses. Van turned his squadron of ships and reengaged the enemy. After a moment, the maklan team flashed off the bridge again.

The transport ships arrived in orbit over Localus and hundreds of shuttles began to ferry troops to the surface. All but ten of the cruisers in the second group left orbit to join the battle, which was beginning to turn in favor of the Predaxians. Their numerical advantage was proving difficult to overcome. As the first shuttles entered the atmosphere, hundreds of fighters flew at them from the planet. The ten remaining cruisers moved to intercept the fighters, but not before many shuttles were either destroyed or retreated toward the relative safety of the transport ships.

Fa-a-Di's swarm of fighters headed toward the transport ships which were aiming fire in their direction. The weak weapons on the transports were no match for the upgraded defenses of the new generation of star fighters. On his orders, the fighters broke formation and fired at the shuttles and transports. They zipped between ships, taking easy shots when possible. Fa-a-Di kept his ship between the transports and their protecting cruisers, hoping an errant blast from a cruiser would hit their own ships instead. One transport was opening its shuttle bay to receive returning shuttles. Fa-a-Di slipped around the transport and flew in formation among the shuttles. As the bay doors opened to maximum, he accelerated to pass the shuttles and blasted the unprotected interior of the shuttle bay. The transport shuddered with explosions and began to lose altitude. Fa-a-Di had to accelerate again to avoid being hit by the large ship as it fell toward the atmosphere. It broke up as it dropped toward the planet and exploded again upon impact.

Emperor Nokalez Zendo moved his flag to the cruiser Bankalo when the Pondi was heavily damaged. He sat despondently in the command chair next to Captain Fondaya Benkomar. His great nephew, Branak had died when the blasts from the Kalidean ships had ruptured the hull of the Predaxian ship. He had been told that his own brother and son were leading the Free Predax ships that were attacking him now. Several Palian cruisers had deserted and were returning to Palus, where more enemy agents were systematically eliminating Predaxian mind control agents. While the battle continued outside, he thought only of how hard he had tried to maintain the great Predaxian Empire his ancestors had built for him. His ships were not losing the battle in space, but they were not winning either. A stalemate in this battle would end his reign, he was certain of that. The populace had grown tired of mind control and imperial rule. They had grown soft with the comforts their hated empire provided for them.

"Majesty, our troops are approaching the prison gate on Localus," Captain Benkomar said. "They are awaiting your orders."

Those few words shook Nokalez out of his mood. "That is unexpectedly good news, Fondaya," he replied. "Tell them to attack! We've got to free our agents in the deepest parts of the prison. With another half million loyal agents, we may yet win this war."

"By your command, Majesty," Fondaya said, as he sent the orders to the soldiers on the planet's surface.

"Fa-a-Di, this is Dave Brewster, please come in," said the voice in Fa-a-Di's headset. "The ground troops are assaulting the prison gates. I'm not certain how long we can hold them off."

"Dave, what in God's name are you doing on Localus?" the general demanded.

"Brother, you know I am not an able soldier," Dave replied. "Jon Lake is commanding the Nightsky and Charlie and I are here managing things on the ground."

"Okay, my fighters and I will head that way to slow them down," Fa-a-Di said. "I strongly recommend you abandon the planet if they penetrate the gates. They will likely execute any non-Predaxians they find there."

"I know, brother. We have enough maklans here to jump us up to the fleet. How is the battle in space going?" Dave asked.

"Unfortunately, it is looking like a stalemate, brother," Fa-a-Di responded. "Neither side has adequate force to overcome the other. We may need to negotiate before too many more lives are lost. My fighters will be in range for a strafing run in three minutes."

"Thank you, Fa-a-Di. Localus out," Dave said as he cut the line. A tone sounded on his ear-piece. He touched the contact, "What's going on Charlie?"

"Dave, the enemy has breached the prison gates," Charlie replied. "We are taking some casualties, and I've ordered our people to retreat to the security level."

"Okay, Charlie, please keep your head down," Dave said. "I hope Fa-a-Di can come to the rescue soon." Dave knew there were many thousands of maklans on the planet managing the mind control activities of the agents held deep in the planet. A few thousand Galliceans served as guards. There was little chance they could all escape if the invaders accessed the security level of the prison.

Dave could feel the hair on the back of his neck stand straight up. He spun around in his chair, but there was no one else in the room. He checked the settings on his pressure suit. Perhaps lack of oxygen was affecting his mind. The gauges read normal. He heard a buzzing in his ears and looked around again. Still nothing. Gradually, the buzzing resolved into a soft voice, "Dave, it's Engineer Nok. Can you hear me?"

"Nok, where are you?" Dave thought to her.

"Standing right in front of you, Dave," she said. "Well, to be more accurate, my inner light is floating in front of you."

He squinted, but there was nothing there. "I must be going crazy," he said aloud. "Too much time in this pressure suit is wearing me down."

"Dave, the hours we spent together in The Hive have linked our minds," she continued. "I didn't think it would work with non-tekkans, but Zee insisted I try."

"Why are you here, Nok? What does Zee want? You can see we're pretty busy fighting an invasion now," he said.

"Dave, Zee is frightened that you may die today," she continued. "You remember that you agreed to build more Hives to protect all of us from the Paxran Empire. You can't do that if you don't survive this battle."

"Nok, no one here yearns for death, but what can we do? I must protect this planet from the invaders who now have the advantage. They will probably take this position in twenty minutes. I am not going to abandon my soldiers," Dave replied.

"Dave, Zee has a plan that will protect you and may end the scourge of the Predaxians. But you must trust him," Nok pleaded. "Zee believes no more lives need to be lost on this planet. We still believe the only way to stop the space battle is with the death of Emperor Zendo. We cannot be involved in that, but we have a solution for the situation on Localus."

"I trust you, Nok," Dave said. "I'm not convinced about Zee, but you are a great friend. What do we do now?"

A loud commotion startled Dave Brewster. He drew his blaster and ran from the room. The security door opened and Charlie and his Gallicean team rushed in. Laser blasts shot around them as the door slammed shut again. Several Galliceans were wounded. Charlie's pressure suit was splattered with blood, but his suit seemed to be intact. "Dave, I guess you can tell the enemy is on the other side of the door. I might take ten minutes to breach it." He sat heavily on the floor. "Maybe we both should have stayed in the twenty-first after all."

"Charlie, the tekkans have a plan," Dave said. "I don't know what it is, but hopefully it will work before that door opens again."

"There are ten thousand Palian soldiers on the other side of the security door, so I hope you are right!" Charlie panted.

All of the view screens in the room came to life with the face of a Palian general demanding their immediate surrender. The door was buckling and weakening by the moment. It wouldn't be long now. Dave imagined his string of light traveling across the universe, detached from his dead body. He looked at Charlie as the door flew open.

Dave and Charlie were sitting on the deck of bridge on Nightsky. The bridge crew aimed their blasters at them until they realized there were humans in the suits. Lia Lawson ran from her communications station to depressurize her father's suit and removed the helmet. Then she did the same for Dave.

"What is going on here, Admiral?" Jon asked.

"I don't know either, Jon," Dave replied. "A second ago the Palians breached the security door and were storming in and now we're here. What's the situation on the planet?"

"I read no life on Localus," Ali announced. "Every living thing has disappeared from the planet. How is that even possible?"

As they watched the view of Localus on the main view screen, the planet began to collapse and break into massive chunks. Those pieces crumbled into ever smaller rocks. Waves of gravity shook the nearby ships as the planet became smaller and smaller. After a few seconds, Localus had completely disappeared.

The image of Zee Gongaleg, High Consul of Tak-Makla appeared on the view screens of every ship and fighter on both sides of the battle. "Dear friends, we have decided that this battle must end. We have taken all the Beings from the planet and returned them to their home worlds or their ships in space. Since Localus was at the core of your ambitions, we have eliminated it. Be advised that although we abhor violence, we could have just as easily eliminated your ships and their crews. I now direct my words to Emperor Nokalaz Zendo of the

Predaxian Empire. We kindly request you to cease hostilities and return to your home world. We also want you to stop using mind control on the helpless civilizations that you control. All of our planets have wonderful roles in the future of the galaxy. We must come together as friends. I leave it to your good judgment." The image faded out.

Captain Fondaya Benkomar turned to the emperor, saying, "Majesty, what are your orders?"

Nokalez was seething with anger at the words of the tekkan High Consul. He thought for a moment and said, "Fondaya, order the fleet to attack Nom-Kat-La. Zee has won the day for us on Localus. Where are the agents who were on Localus?"

"Apparently, all of them arrived safely on Predax, Majesty," he replied.

"Too bad, we could have used them to control the Galliceans on Nom-Kat-La," Nokalez said. "After we take the planet, send five cruisers back for them. Full speed ahead!" The Alliance fleet broke contact and headed toward Nom-Kat-La.

Most of the defending fleet followed behind the Alliance ships, trying to take shots at them as they moved away. Five Gallicean ships held back to retrieve the star fighters which did not have sufficient range to reach the planet. Fa-a-Di climbed out of his damaged craft and hurried to the bridge where he was met by Jake and Mitch.

The maklans reported great confusion and anger on the Alliance ships. Almost all of the Lozaki ships had retreated to their home worlds to defend against the Pyrrians. Several Palian cruisers had also abandoned the fight to return home when they were freed from the mind control agents. Concern was very high on the Predaxian ships as well. Many had seen Altamar, Dokalez or Zakamar jump onto their ships. They had been receiving transmissions from Panoplez himself, trying to convince them to support him as emperor. The troops were clinging to their life-long devotion to the empire in desperate hopes that all would return to normal soon, although few truly believed that. Now was the time to strike at the emperor himself.

The ten fastest Gallicean battle cruisers caught the Alliance fleet easily and began to attack in an attempt to slow them and break up the fleet. The Bankalo swerved to avoid separation from her protecting cluster of ships. The Kong-Fa, the fastest ship in the Gallicean fleet dived between the protectors and blasted the Bankalo's engine room. The defenses were weakened but held. Bankalo fired back, but it was a clean miss. No-De-Ka, Je-e-Bo's flagship followed closely behind Kong-Fa and targeted the same spot on the Bankalo. The engine exploded and the Bankalo began to tumble out of control. After several rolls, Bankalo hit the cruiser Zolonow and the two exploded in a massive ball of fire. In the midst of the turmoil, the emperor moved to a Palian cruiser, the Bologo which was now leading the fleet toward Nom-Kat-La. Withering return fire forced the two Galliceans to retreat to the safety of their fleet.

Emperor Zendo entered the massive bridge of the Palian ship. The Palians were around ten feet tall, and the Predaxians were like dolls to them. "Captain, what is your report?" he demanded.

"Majesty, I am Captain Nokeke of the Bologo, and it is an honor to have you on our ship," she began. "We will arrive at Nom-Kat-La in thirty minutes. All transport ships report ready to send troops to the surface when we arrive."

"Majesty, I am Panakar Valonez, and I am your lead agent on this ship," said the Predaxian on the chest of the captain. "The

Palian crew is fully under our control. We will protect you with our lives, liege. You should know there is great turmoil among our agents on this ship and others. We have seen several Predaxians jump onto ships and break our control." The Palians continued their duty, oblivious to the mind control agents.

"Who is behind this treachery?" the emperor shouted.

"Me, father," Pan said as three Galliceans and two Predaxians flashed onto the bridge. The Galliceans pulled their war daggers from their scabbards and attacked the crew, aiming first to disable the agents connected to them. Pandemonium filled the room. Pan pulled a large Predaxian war blade from his belt and approached his father. "Dad, the time for mind control is over. Let's go home now."

Nokalez drew his blaster and shot his son in the chest. Pan flew across the room and fell in a heap. "You were always a fool, Pan," Nokalez laughed. "I had great hopes for you, son. Now you will die a traitor." He approached his son and withdrew his own war blade. He stood over him and placed the blade between Pan's eyes. "Sorry son."

Zakamar Vondee plunged her blade into the emperor's back. He reached back and hit her across the room with his hand. He pulled the blade from his back and walked to Zak with both knives in his hands. "Treacherous hag," shouted Nokalez as he spat out blood. "You turn my son against me and now you threaten me! Now I will have the pleasure to kill you too."

As he approached the unconscious Predaxian, a loud laugh filled the room. He spun around to see a massive Gallicean standing in front of him. "This is the end of your tyranny, little bug!" Fa-a-Di shouted as he plunged two of his war daggers into the emperor, who fell to the ground dead.

Pan went to the communications station and hailed the Alliance fleet. "To all ships of the fleet, I am Emperor Panoplez Zendo of Predax. My father is dead. You owe your allegiance to me now. You are ordered to disengage and return to your home planets. All agents are ordered to discontinue mind control activities now and forever." He allowed the Palian officer to resume his station, and ran to Zak who was now conscious and sitting up. "Zak, we won," he cried, "The war is over and we can go home now."

"Yes, your majesty," she smiled. "I am so happy for you, Pan."

"Sweetheart, you know I'm going to abolish the empire and hold free elections," he replied.

"That's what we both want, isn't it?" Zak said.

"Yes, but maybe before I do, we can have an imperial wedding. What do you think?" he said. "You deserve to be Empress for at least a week before we give it all up." They hugged.

Dave and Charlie sat near the beach. Small waves rolled onto the sand a few feet from their small table. Kally approached the table and refilled their coffee cups. "Anything else, gentlemen," he said.

"Do we have any chocolate croissants, Kally?" Dave asked.

"I have some coming out of the oven soon, Dave. I'll bring them out shortly," Kally smiled as he returned to the house.

They could see High Consul Zee approaching them from his residence next door. Fa-a-Di and De-o-Nu were with him. Charlie and Dave rose to greet their guests, who then joined them at the table. Charlie went to tell Kally about their guests, but saw him already approaching with a tray and more drinks.

"My friends, it is great to be with you today," Zee began. "I am told that two freighters will arrive today with green coffee and a few expert roasters. Our relationship continues to prosper." He looked at his communicator. "I only have time for one cup of coffee before I have to meet with Ambassador Brewster and High Commissioner Fa-a-Di in the city. Where is Darlene, Dave?"

"She left early today, Zee," Dave replied. "She wanted to review the treaty one more time before the signing ceremony. Darlene felt there was still some questionable wording around the treaty with Predax and Palus."

Zee sighed. "We have tried to help the Palians deal with the loss of Localus, but it is difficult. I feel they will use that against us in negotiations."

"The Palians are a cantankerous people," Fa-a-Di laughed. "I remember my father telling me about his relationship with their traders before the First Predaxian War. Two weeks ago, their entire race was enslaved by Predax, and now they want to turn our rescue to their advantage."

"Yes, negotiations are always rife with such tactics," Zee acknowledged. He sipped the coffee and bit a piece of croissant. "My, this is wonderful coffee Dave. I hope the roasting experts coming here will help us duplicate it."

"I believe they will surpass this," Charlie jumped in. "If not, we'll send more experts until they get it right, Zee."

Zee laughed, "Thank you Charlie. Your words are very comforting. I must take my leave of you now. I too wish to review the treaty before Field Marshall Fongula Nokka connects to our meeting. Do any of you wish to take a tube with me now?"

"Most gracious, Zee," Fa-a-Di said. "I think we would like to enjoy each other's company a while longer. We Galliceans have only a minor role in this negotiation. My brother-in-law and I will join you soon."

"Very well then," Zee said. "I will see you two in my office soon. Dave and Charlie, I hope you will join me there later today. I have arranged a shuttle home and would love to show you more sites on our world."

"We will be there by 1600, Zee. I hope we can stop at your son's farm and be introduced as well," Dave said.

"Of course, that would be wonderful. To save time, may I use your tube station?  I am already late," Zee said. They nodded and he walked toward the house.

"It is another wonderful day on this manufactured world," De-o-Nu began.  "I only wish we were full sized so my brother-in-law and I could fly you around ourselves." He pulled a flask of Gallicean whisky from his belt and filled the four coffee cups to the brim. "We want you to know that you both fought with honor at Localus. When we found you were on the planet, we both feared the worst."

"And when the tekkans crushed the planet into dust," Fa-a-Di interrupted, "you can imagine the panic we felt. I could never imagine that I would see you eye to eye without a pressure suit or glass wall separating us. Now, here we are." He pulled two small boxes from a compartment on his belt. "These two medals are the Order of Gallia. Our High Council has commanded us to give these to you for your exceptional bravery in battle and for saving Nom-Kat-La and all of Greater Gallia from the Predaxian hordes. There were four thousand Gallicean guards on Localus who would have died if not for Dave's connection with the tekkans."

The four stood and embraced one another. "My dear brothers, I don't know what to say," Dave replied.

"Well, that's a first," Charlie jumped in. All laughed loudly.

Fa-a-Di raised his glass, and the others followed and touched them together. They drank and sat back down. "I have it on good authority that there will be many more medals for all of us," Fa-a-Di said. "Pan and Zak want us to go to Predax for a celebration of freedom with their former colonies. Several high commissioners want us to join similar celebrations on at least a dozen planets. That might keep us busy for a while.”

“Where is our little friend, Jake?” De-o-Nu asked.

“He accompanied Mitch Nolobitamore back to No-Makla. Their families have been worried sick about them,” Dave replied. “I am told that Mitch is going to be made ambassador to Predax.”

“And what role will Jake fulfill?” Fa-a-Di asked.

“He is the lead on the human DNA project on Earth,” Charlie said. “We all knew that would happen one of these days.”

“After today’s meeting, I must return to Gallia,” Fa-a-Di said. “Now that the war is over, the business of government calls to me. Perhaps we can have a few days here though. These surroundings are so unfamiliar to creatures like my brother-in-law and me. It is interesting to see how terrestrial Beings live. De-o-Nu tells me that Fak has an excellent selection of whiskies that I must try. De-o-Nu is lucky to spend much more time here.”

“Brother, perhaps I can go with you and we can stop at Planet 5 in the Golden Dawn system?” De-o-Nu asked. “The wildlife on that planet is amazing.”

“I think Charlie and I might be convinced to join you there for a flyover,” Dave smiled. “Just don’t drop me like you almost dropped my wife!”

“That is a perfect plan,” Fa-a-Di beamed. “We’ll stay here five or more days and then head for Planet 5. It continues to be an honor for me to call all of you my dear brothers.” He filled the glasses with more whisky. He stood and said, "To brotherhood! May we always fly and fight together!"

# ABOUT THE AUTHOR

Karl J. Morgan

Karl Morgan grew up fascinated by science fiction, beginning with Victor Appleton's Tom Swift novels that he read as a young boy. Later, he became enthralled with the works of his favorite author, Isaac Asimov, especially his Foundation series.

Those early experiences inspired his life-long love of science fiction and interest in hard science, focusing first on astronomy and later cosmology and quantum mechanics. Karl had the great honor to take his first astronomy course at the University of Iowa from the legendary scientist, Dr. James Van Allen. More recently, the brilliant works of Drs. Stephen Hawking, Brian Greene, and Michio Kaku helped him understand that our physical universe is still a magical and mysterious place.

It is that sense of magic and mystery that brings Karl to write about his alter ego, Dave Brewster, an unemployed accountant who finds himself a thousand years in the future with new friends and adventures far beyond anything he could have imagined. There, he can find answers to questions that befuddle mankind today. The truth he finds is no different from what we know today. Life is always about loving and caring for our family and friends.

Karl lives in San Diego with his wife, Aida and their beloved puppies. Their two grown children have fled the nest and started their own adventures in life.

# *Other Books by Karl J. Morgan*

*Remembrances: Choose to Be Happy and Embrace the Possibilities*
ISBN: 978-0-9826461-9-9


## *The Dave Brewster Series*

*The Dave Brewster Series: Showdown Over Neptune*
(Book 1)
ISBN: 978-0-9860270-0-0


*The Dave Brewster Series: The Hive*
(Book 3)
ISBN: 978-0-9860270-2-4
Available for purchase early 2013


*The Dave Brewster Series: Tears of Gallia*
(Book 4)
ISBN: 978-0-9860270-4-8
Available for purchase early Spring 2013


## *Heartstone*

*Heartstone: Sentinels of Far Sun*
ISBN: 978-0-9860270-3-1
Available for purchase early Spring 2013